DREAM HOUSE ON GOLAN DRIVE

DREAM HOUSE ON GOLAN DRIVE

David G. Pace

Signature Books | 2015 | Salt Lake City

To my wife, Cheryl, who has become that place
for me where empty armor comes to rest

Cover design by Ron Stucki. Book design by Jason Francis
© 2015 Signature Books | www.signaturebooks.com

Signature Books is a registered trademark of Signature Books
Publishing, LLC. All rights reserved. *Dream House on Golan
Drive* was printed on acid-free paper. It was composed, printed,
and bound in the United States of America.

20   19   18   17   16   15   6   5   4   3   2   1

LIBRARY OF CONGRESS CATALOGING-IN-PUBLICATION DATA

Pace, David G., author.
Dream House on Golan Drive / David G. Pace.
pages cm

Summary: "It is the year 1972, and Riley Hartley finds that he,
his family, community, and his faith are entirely indistinguish-
able from each other. He is eleven. A young woman named
Lucy claims God has revealed to her that she is to live with
Riley's family. Her quirks are strangely disarming, her relentless
questioning of their life incendiary and sometimes comical. Her
way of taking religious practice to its logical conclusion leaves a
strong impact on her hosts and propels Riley outside his observable universe toward a trajectory of self-discovery. Set in Provo
and New York City during the seventies and eighties, the story
encapsulates the normal expectations of a Mormon experience
and turns them on their head."—Text from publisher.

ISBN 978-1-56085-241-4
1. Mormons—Fiction. 2. Provo (Utah), setting.
3. New York (N.Y.), setting. I. Title.
PS3616.A324D74 2015   813'.6—dc23   2015031404

ACKNOWLEDGMENTS

Heartfelt thanks to those who encouraged me and critiqued my work, especially in the Emerging Writers Group of Brooklyn: Derek Bacharach (founder and facilitator), Henry Alpert, Philip Carter, Viviane Casimir, Adam Falik, Joshua Kennedy, Carol Mason, Jonathan (Jack) Rapp, Mary Sauers, D. Mark Speer, and Mimi Yamazaki. Thanks also to my missionary buddy Marcus Ruefenacht for suggesting that I write about my missionary experiences, and to long-time friends Gail Weinflash and Mark Weeks for looking at an early version of the manuscript, as well as to my brother-in-law Kim for insisting that I submit it for publication. Thanks to fellow writing and drinking buddies Maximilian Werner, Larry Menlove, and Ben Shaberman, and to Julia Coopersmith for her advice and help in locating an agent. A big thank you to the Utah Original Writing Competition for awarding the manuscript its top fiction prize.

There are a few other people I need to acknowledge: the poet/journalist Carolyn Campbell, who coined the phrase "latter-day sometimes saint"; Cheryl Pace for her unpublished poem "Redemption," from which I borrowed the line "where empty armor comes to rest"; the late Ogden Kraut, a practicing Mormon polygamist whose writings shed light on the current practice; historian D. Michael Quinn for his research on Utah polygamy; and former *Journal of Mormon History* editor Lavina Fielding Anderson for her details about the Utah Territory. *Dialogue* published my short story "The Postum Table," which was an early version of chapter 2. Thank you, finally, to my publisher, Signature Books, and especially to editors John Hatch and Ron Priddis.

This is a work of fiction. Except for names of actual places and persons, such as certain political figures and LDS Church authorities or celebrities, all characters are my creation.

CONTENTS

1 | AS FOR ME AND MY HOUSE

Riley was ten when his father, Gus, told him that they would be moving into the new house. He said it was the work of the Lord, as the name of the street address indicated. It sounded like the beginning of one of Gus's clearing-the-throat lectures. "Golan Drive," he said, "like in Israel." Riley's father was well-known on the church speaking circuit, a featured lecturer at firesides in Utah and adjacent states. Everyone assumed he was on his way to becoming one of the top "Brethren" in Salt Lake City, which is how they all referred to the highest officers of the church.

It wasn't that you could actually apply for the job of a "general authority," all of whom were called directly by God through the prophet who sat at the top of the church administration. In the meantime Gus sold life insurance and made the rounds to firesides, mostly in California. It was on one of those tours that he had met an enraptured college-age student who suggested to her parents that they sell Gus their second home in Utah for next to nothing. According to Gus, who wept at the Lord's goodness to his sprawling family, the young woman had said she wanted to lift Gus up like he had lifted her up spiritually.

The new house in "the heights" would suit the Hartleys, being in the foothills overlooking Utah Valley, she said. The family would be more visible there. They would like the way the high-desert sunshine warmed the house in what Gus called "a suburb set on a hill," to paraphrase the biblical term. The houses were so conspicuous, it was as if they had been sculpted out of the mountains by a mining company. A few older homes were tastefully modest, but the new ones showed off their vaulted ceilings, floor-to-ceiling windows, and wooden decks launched precipitously over the mountainside, looking like the prows of ships.

Brother Hartley was educated but not in a profession like the doctors and lawyers who made up the neighborhood and drove Lincolns and Mercedes Benzes. Gus drove a Ford Falcon and didn't notice the difference. Other people had boats, and their kids had braces on their teeth. The Hartleys would have to do without some things.

The day they moved in, a next-door neighbor arrived at the door bearing in her plump hands a casserole topped with potato chips. "Marba Pratt," she said introducing herself, "like Abram in the Bible but backwards. Everyone here calls the heights Snob Hill," she added, rolling her eyes in mock disapproval, her face shiny from exertion.

"Snob Hill?" said Joan. Riley's mother placed the dish carefully in the fridge and calculated that it would serve only six. She glanced at her reflection in the plate-glass window and adjusted her moving-day hair before returning to her guest. All of the kids, nine at the time, gathered around to stare at their new neighbor as if she were part of the local fauna.

"Most of the homes have valley views," Mrs. Pratt continued, looking around at the piles of boxes in the front hall, "but we've had to be content with a view of your beautiful home!" she said and laughed so hard her bosom, a virtual shelf, leapt up and down under her floral dress. Mrs. Pratt could not stay long, she said, but paused long enough for Riley's mother to reveal what Mrs. Pratt and the other neighbors were hoping to confirm.

"We're LDS," said Joan directly, opting for the official acronym of the church.

"Oh, I know you are," said their new neighbor. "We thought we recognized your husband's name. Welcome to the ward!" Once this commonality was established, it was like the July sun had suddenly appeared in the room and everything was good with the world. Soon the two women were touching one another's hands and arms as they talked and hugging each other goodbye, demonstrating that, like the refrain in the pioneer hymn, "all is well!"

The family had been on Golan Drive for about three months when they gathered one evening for Family Night. There was a box of Sees chocolates wrapped in glossy white paper on the Postum table, or what everyone else in America called the coffee table. Because of the church's injunction against coffee, Mormons felt uncomfortable calling the table by its common name and came up with all sorts of suitable euphemisms. The chocolates were from one of Gus's admirers who regularly sent them via mail. At the end of a Family Night when chocolates had materialized, the family had a tradition of passing the box around from youngest to oldest and letting each person take one of the tempting morsels from its accordion wrap, beginning with two-year-old Jessica and ending with Gus, who always complained that someone had chosen the dark caramel-filled square he particularly liked, although no one ever seemed to pay attention to him.

Riley looked at his sister Muriel, the oldest. She did not want to be there and was making sure everyone knew it. She was a junior in high school and had better things to do. Settling back into the flowered couch with pink cushions, her arms crossed on her chest, she closed her eyes while they waited for Jody, number two. Gus leaned over the wrought-iron railing that guarded the stairwell to the lower floor. "Jody!" he hollered, his voice betraying an emotion-laden staccato that spelled trouble. He waited, leaning over further so that his foot lifted out of his house flip flops and showed a pink underside.

Muriel's eyes flashed in annoyance. Their mother was annoyed too. Joan told Jessica to stop coloring in her book. Jody appeared, muttering something about a phone call, and the rest of the kids stared at her like she was delaying the Second Coming.

"Honey," said Gus, "your friend Debbie knows it's Monday night."

"Not everyone has Family Night," said Jody. She pushed her octagonal wire-rims up the bridge of her nose. Muriel thought Jody's glasses looked like cells from a honeycomb.

"Now listen, kids," Gus said. Muriel opened her eyes. "I don't want you planning anything on Monday nights, understand?" He looked around at the four oldest, a line-up that would shift down as college approached. Right behind Riley in age and height was his only brother, number five, Cade, who was nine. He sat next to Muriel. On his other side sat Winnie and Chums, numbers six and seven. The four of them looked like they were waiting to see a doctor.

Candace, two years Riley's senior, was on the floor next to him, flipping through a health text Riley had looked at and found the most explicit description of the sex act he had ever read. Perched on a bar stool next to her was Jody, named after her cousin Jo, who had choked on a wad of gum and died, and her father, Uncle Dee. It was because of Jo that the Hartley children were not allowed to bring chewing gum into the house, even though Candace had a hidden stash of Juicy Fruit in her room.

Gus glanced at Joan in the rocking chair with the baby in her arms, its dark hair matted against her blouse. "Jeepers!" he said. Joan smiled and batted her eyes the way she did to humor him. "Well, now that everyone's here, we can start," he said.

"I need to put you-know-who to bed," she said. The You-Know-Who, Jessica, got the hint and looked up from her crayons to say "No bed!"

They were a family of eleven. When you said all the children's names together without stopping, with the right stresses like Jody did, it sounded musical: Muriel-Jody-Candace-Riley-CADE-Winnie-Chums-Jessie-Agnes TOO." It seemed like there were enough of them to start their own country. As Family Night began, the chocolates seemed a millennium away. Gus had set up a chalk board and drawn stick figures on it representing Adam and Eve.

As Gus suggested they sing a verse of *O How Lovely Was the Morning*, Riley could sense his father's irritation over having not been taken seriously. When they sang about the rapture-filled bosom, Cade glanced at Riley and snickered out loud. After the hymn, he was asked to give the invocation for being disrespectful.

Obediently, Cade stood like he would if he had been at church, folded his arms, and bowed his head. He looked different than his father and brother, with fair skin and galaxy of freckles on his head and neck. "Dear Heavenly Father," he mumbled into his chest. "We thank you for our many blessings."

"We thank *thee*," his father corrected. Cade had his arms wrapped tightly around himself, squinting in concentration.

"We thank thee for our many blessings, for our family. We pray for the prophet. We ask thee …" Cade opened an eye and looked at Gus "… to help us to get our year's supply of food, and we ask thee to get us out of debt. In-the-name-of-Jesus-Christ-amen." Simultaneously, with the prescribed ending, he fell back down onto the couch with a bounce and everyone said "amen." Gus said amen the loudest.

Family business was always first on the agenda, and Gus always turned it over to his wife, like he would do if he were the ward bishop conducting a worship service. Mom always had a list of family problems. "I don't know what happened Saturday," she said. She had a precision in her speech that carried over from her training as Miss Utah, when she traveled to the Miss America Pageant in Atlantic City. "When my visiting teachers came by, not a single thing had been done in the kitchen or living room, and it was three o'clock!"

Jody objected that she had to wait for Candace to dust before she could vacuum.

Candace smacked her sister's leg. "I did dust, you stupid idiot."

"Girls!" Gus sputtered.

"Well, I did, Dad!" cried Candace. Jody started back in. "Muriel says you dust like a cheerleader."

"I did *not* say that!" Muriel said with a guilty grin.

"All right, all right," said Mom. "I don't know what the problem was, but when Sister Walker and Sister Slaughter walked in and saw … two bowls of cereal from breakfast and Riley's dirty socks under the piano bench!"—she looked at him when she said that—"I was embarrassed to tears."

Riley knew when his mom was angry or hurt because she said things like "embarrassed to tears." Once when he was eight and they still lived in the river bottoms, he was jumping up and down on the couch and finishing his mother's sentences and she was telling someone on the phone that a woman they were talking about "had several cute little girls already," before "the next daughter … "

" … who was the ugly sister," Riley said, laughing gaily as he continued jumping. She glared over the receiver, her lips tightening to a white line. That meant he was in trouble. When she got off the phone, she said she'd been talking to the bishop's wife about her cousin Sally, who had muscular dystrophy. "I could have crawled in a hole and pulled it in after me," she said. She left the room, went to the bathroom, shut the door, and didn't come out for a long time. Riley never knew if his mother actually shed tears from embarrassment, but he admired her colorful range of sayings.

Even though Riley had only seen Sally, a girl who was easily twenty years older, a few times, he felt guilty about having unknowingly ridiculed her disability. He went to his room and tried to feel the appropriate emotion for the occasion but nothing came to him, so eventually he gave up and went looking for bra ads in the Sears catalogue.

Joan continued by detailing what the Saturday chores would be, reminding them once again the procedures for washing windows so they wouldn't streak and of the importance of sorting the utensils into their plastic-molded compartments.

"You heard your mother," said Gus with finality. "Now let's do it!" After a slight pause, Gus added, "I have something as well." Watching his father speak, it seemed to Riley that Gus had a spring in his jaw, activated by lifting an eyebrow like the way Colonel Klink on *Hogan's Heroes* talked.

"When I came home from work today," Gus said, "every single light was on downstairs. So was the curling iron!" Everyone looked at Muriel, the most likely candidate.

Muriel shrugged and sighed, "Okay, I know."

They had been at Family Night for twenty minutes and still hadn't begun the lesson. Unlike other people who had fun and played a board game or watched re-runs of *Flipper* on Family Nights, Gus was a stickler for following the church curriculum outlined in the manual. By the time he had pulled the chalkboard out front and center, Winnie and Chums were poking at each other.

"Stop touching me!" screamed Winnie.

"Keep your hands to yourself," Joan said, directing her remark to Chelsea, the younger child, whose feet barely hung over the edge of the couch. A wisp of a girl, the name Chums suited her better than Chelsea, her real name. "There's plenty of room there for both of you," Joan said.

The little girl's wounded eyes shaded into defiance, and once Gus started talking again she placed the pinkie of her right hand ever-so-lightly against Winnie's pant leg.

"Stop *touching* me!" Winnie screamed again, louder, pushing the hand away.

"She's hogging all the room!" Chums gasped, a defensive sob rising in her five-year-old throat.

When Winnie slugged her, Chums grabbed her sister's hair with a power that rivaled a vacuum cleaner, eliciting an even more powerful sweep of Gus's arm, the girl transported like a wriggling spider to her room.

"I can't believe this," Muriel said with disgust. "I've got so much homework to do."

"You do not," said Jody, taking advantage of the fact that Gus was out of earshot. "Which boy will you be studying?"

"Shut up, you spaz," Muriel said, glancing sideways at her mother.

"Mommy, Muriel said a bathroom word," Winnie said, rubbing her scalp.

Joan took the bait. "Muriel," she said, "I don't care what kind of language they use at that high school, but at home you'll watch what you say."

Riley thought what a strange expression that was, "watch what you say," as if the words were floating in space and observable. Maybe they turned red when they hit oxygen, like blood.

Gus's brow was furrowed, his chest heaving as he returned to the living room. They could hear Chums screaming through the nursery door she was kicking against with mighty thuds. One had to hand it to her, she fought like Samson.

"This has been disappointing," Gus said, referring to the family pow-wow. He seemed to be trying to form an appropriate expression of gravity in his face flushed with exasperation. "This is like a circus. Now, let's sit up and study the gospel."

They did. By *gospel* he meant the restored gospel of Jesus Christ as revealed in its fullness to Joseph Smith and fused to the sermons of the current prophet, a short octogenarian with a funny voice who, along with his twelve apostles, wore a suit and tie and lived fifty miles away in Salt Lake City. Gus had a reputation for teaching the gospel with an electrifying fervor, even if his congregation consisted of young people, whom he entertained with the same zeal he demonstrated in adult Sunday school lessons at church and on the road. On this particular Monday, even

Muriel seemed to have finally realized that the only way out of Family Night was through it.

Gus held the chalkboard in one of his meaty hands, and in the other he sketched with surprising dexterity the entire PLAN OF SALVATION, starting with the creation of the world and moving from there to the Garden of Eden where Adam and Eve fell from grace. At this point Gus re-drew the stick figures upside down to show how they tumbled into the lone and dreary world. Even the younger girls laughed at that, which was okay since that's what Gus was going for.

Suddenly Chums's head appeared around the corner, peering into the living room, drawn by the laughter when Gus gave Eve long hair that was flapping in the wind. Chums kept shyly to the doorway, a finger in her mouth, her eyes red with tears. She had a bad case of post-cry hiccups.

"Are you ready to come back in?" Gus asked with a reproving look. She nodded soggily and returned to her rightful place in the family order next to Gus, who was down on one knee. She placed her small dimpled hand on his calf, and when he rubbed her back she hiccupped.

From Adam and Eve, Gus took them through the stories of Noah and the flood, the Tower of Babel, and God's command for Abraham to sacrifice his son. "Now then," he said, then stopped. "I was going to say 'brothers and sisters'," he admitted, smiling broadly. He always forgot where he was when he got into the spirit of it. "Sorry, kids." He actually blushed, and the children moaned with an irritation that was only mild considering their new absorption in the illustrated PLAN OF SALVATION.

He continued. "The story of Abraham and Isaac foreshadowed

Heavenly Father sacrificing his own son, the Christ," he said, emphasizing the last part to invoke awe. "Let's say for the moment that I'm Abraham. Riley here is Isaac. Riley, stand up for a minute."

"What?" Riley asked.

"Just stand here for a minute, will you?" said Gus, moving the box of chocolates off the Postum table and handing it to Cade, who seemed galvanized by this duty like one of the magi, bearing frankincense in the annual Christmas pageant. "I need your help," said Gus.

Sometimes being one of only two boys in the family had advantages. There weren't as many hand-me-downs to wear. But being the only choice for an object lesson on human sacrifice did not sound promising. That kind of thing happened all too often, that his father needed a boy for his object lesson. Riley would rather sit on the sidelines and comment under his breath about his sisters' bad acting.

Gus helped Riley lie down on his back on the Postum table. Winnie and Chums giggled. Gus cleared his throat like he did when he lectured. "Just for illustrative purposes," he said, "let's say I've taken Riley to the mountains."

"Like Y Mountain?" said Chums, her eyes now wide with interest. She was referring to the mountain behind them, a pile of flinty rock topped with pine, with a whitewashed block-letter Y that tagged the nearby presence of Brigham Young University.

"Let's say Y Mountain, yes. I've taken him up there because the Lord told me it's necessary to sacrifice Riley to show my obedience."

From where Riley lay, legs and feet cantilevered off the end of the table, he could see his father's torso and head, the intent eyes behind his father's black-rimmed glasses. He could feel the heat from his body and smell the warm, beach-like odor of his skin. His father cleared his throat, and Riley saw that Gus was wearing his Moses face, flushed with righteous indignation. It was the face he wore when he gave talks in church or at firesides, his stocky legs spread apart. Emphatic in teaching a principle, Gus would ever-so-slightly caress his chest with a finger, gaze intently into space, and lift one eyebrow as if he were in pain. He'd add even more drama by talking with a high-pitched voice that drained the blood from his face. This sort of thing made Riley uncomfortable. Wouldn't people think his dad was angry? Or delirious? But the effect was predictably profound—the people in the congregation always responded with teary-eyed awe at the spectacle.

Gus had grabbed a hairbrush and held it up, his other hand on his son's chest. "Now kids, try to visualize Abraham explaining to his son that the offering was not going to be a ram or a sheep." He paused. "It was going to be his son, Isaac." The baby started to fuss. In the ceiling Riley saw for the first time a thin crack in the plaster toward the wall behind the couch.

"I like to think," continued Gus, "that Isaac was about eighteen or so and that he had as much faith as Abraham did." Riley wondered what it would be like to be eighteen. "That's why Isaac lay down on the stone altar without having to be tied down."

Cade asked why someone would have to be tied down. Riley felt his back start to throb, but Gus kept him in place when he tried to shift his weight. The rolling handle of the hairbrush turned in Gus's hand.

"Can you imagine Abraham's anguish?" he said as he held the imaginary knife above Riley's head. Riley could see a few strands of his mother's blond hair hanging from the brush and floating blurrily above him. There was another pause. Everyone was quiet, and Riley wondered how much longer he was going to have to lie there, especially since he had a homework assignment due the following day. Finally, he looked up at Gus, the brush still raised above his head, his face turned upward. Tears were streaming down his face. No one said anything.

"Can I get up now, Dad?" Riley said. "This is hurting my back."

As he sat up and straightened his T-shirt, Joan handed her husband a tissue for his eyes. Riley looked at Muriel, then at the box of chocolates forgotten in his brother's lap, Cade's eyes wide with a new appreciation of something. Cade had narked on Riley the week before when Riley had eaten half a bag of chocolate chips. Even so, it was too bad Cade hadn't been chosen for the drama. He would have liked that, including being chosen ahead of Riley.

Gus blew his nose and bore testimony about how God the Father sacrificed his son for us and that we would all be asked to sacrifice in some way. We wouldn't have to sacrifice a child, but we would all have to give up something special because that was how God worked. It was how he purified and perfected his children. They knelt in prayer.

Afterward, Jody carefully removed the quilted paper that covered the chocolates and placed the Sees box into the upside-down cover, handing it to Jessica, who froze in its presence, arrested by so many choices. As always, she touched each chocolate as she pondered which one to choose. The others waited in agony.

After Jessica decided on the one in gold foil, the box was passed up the line like the bread and water at church on Sundays.

They were all silent as they savored the creams, the liquid cherries and nuts, nibbling at the corners of the angular confections to make the flavors last, eating one half and then the other, then finally breaking the spell of their pleasure to bargain for the better half of someone else's sweet, held aloft by one of their munching siblings. On the Postum table lay, forgotten, Mom's hairbrush—the weapon which had worked its way into several hearts.

3 | OUR DAILY BREAD

Gus received his Abrahamic test after his book was published and one of the apostles in Salt Lake, Elder Gray, came to Provo and castigated him for its content. People thought Gus passed the test with flying colors, that the experience vaulted him nearer to what Jesus prescribed when he said, "Be ye therefore perfect, even as I or your father who is in heaven is perfect."

The shock waves from Gus's public humiliation reached me, one of the few people on earth who actually *is* perfect, although not in the way people usually mean when they quote the scripture. Another profound misreading of a text if you ask me. And I should know. As one of the three immortals from the time of the Nephites, I've been here not only as long the other two but as long as the wandering Jew, Ahasverus, as well. When you're one of us, you have to witness a whole lot of sacred writing over time getting twisted up, co-opted to justify less-than-admirable needs. Whenever I run into him, Ahasverus shrugs at these observations of mine.

"It's inevitable, get over it," he says. "It's the way of the world. What does it matter to you, Zed? How does it change your predicament?"

"But the text … "

"And stop calling it a text," he says. "They're just stories. They're not set in stone."

"Just stories?"

"Exactly."

That is where Verus and I part company. Despite having a similar condition, we don't agree on much. My immortality is a calling, whereas his is a curse, more like a mistake that condemned him to become a thirty-year-old all over again every hundred years. He grows older while I stay eternally middle-aged.

Right now I'm supposed to be keeping an eye on Riley, my current charge, named after his great-great grandfather, Riley Reid, who had three wives and an adventurous spirit. The original Riley didn't mind crossing the Great Plains with his family in a covered wagon when he was sixteen, along with about 100 other Mormons. In fact, after they arrived in Great Salt Lake City, Riley wanted to push on to California because of the gold rush.

Brigham Young didn't like it. "Brother Reid," the barrel-chested man said, jutting out his chin, "I prophesy that if you abandon your family and chase after filthy lucre, you'll lose every material possession you have."

"I don't have any material possessions," said great-great-grandfather.

"Nor will you have when you return. Just go and be damned!" Brigham thundered.

Riley promised that when he returned, he would bring a cast-iron frying pan for his mother filled with gold. In fact, he did secure a cast-iron frying pan filled with gold, but on his return he was robbed of everything but his pony, a pathetic animal that was so small Riley's feet nearly touched the ground as it clopped back into Great Salt Lake. Brother Brigham's prophecy had come to pass.

At least that's how the story gets told. How the Hartley family tells it now again and again. In fact, Great-great-grandpa Riley's family was overjoyed to see him, penniless though he was. Brigham took a different view and told him to get the hell out of his Zion. Poor Riley, crawling back wearing a battered miner's cap and no crown. Undaunted, the young man married a girl he met on the trail in California, whom he thereafter referred to as his "frying pan of gold," and stayed put. He became a ward bishop with three wives and the father of twenty-four children.

The Hartleys descended from the second wife, Ann, who followed Riley to Mexico when he moved there to escape arrest for polygamy and died with him in Colonia Juárez. In the solitary surviving photo, taken from an old tintype, he has the typical Reid forehead, broad as the business end of a shovel, and a wiry beard with salt-and-pepper bristles. His eyes look exactly like the dark and deeply set visage, with thick brows, that his great-great-grandson inherited. Looking into his ancestor's piercing eyes, the modern Riley wondered if his pioneering forebear was able to foresee the scraggly livestock and hard-earned orchards he would end up with in Chihuahua.

Riley spent hours pawing through the myriad books of family history one of his unmarried aunts had patched together. How could any of these grandparents have imagined where their off-spring would end up, living comfortably on the Provo bench? Other than the eyes, Riley was not anything like his spirited namesake. The most outdoor adventure the young man could hope for was with the Boy Scouts. "You're a pioneer too," his mother reassured him, but he recognized it as empty encouragement.

"We all are," she said one day while kneading dough. Riley couldn't see how. It was his mother's habit to make eight loaves of bread each week to help make the food budget stretch. She didn't enjoy baking, evidenced by how hard she threw the dough onto the counter to get rid of air bubbles.

Riley thought that to be a pioneer you had to wear buckskin or gingham, a cowboy hat or a bonnet, and carry a rifle. Great-great-grandpa Riley's baby brother was trampled to death by oxen during a thunderstorm on their way to Utah. His mother had wanted to butcher the oxen just like the oxen had butchered her boy, but on the trail draft animals could not be spared. "All they had to wrap that dead boy in was a burlap bag," Joan said, "and stones to mark the grave."

"We're pioneering modern life," she repeated, her nose powdered with fingerprints of flour. Riley knew his mother's blond features from the Swedish side of the family were considered attractive, at one time earning her the epithet of the "Mormon Grace Kelly" when she competed in pageants. She handed Riley a bread pan to smear in shortening. Based on the family's new surroundings in their dream house, they were a far cry from being pioneers, he thought. He gingerly stuck his fingers into a square of wax paper and then into the can of shortening.

"When we lived in L.A.," she said, warming a little to the subject, "your father was called to be a counselor to the bishop. There were a lot of college students in the ward and some of them were getting caught up in the hippie things. Our non-Mormon neighbors didn't think much of religion."

"Why not?" Riley asked, diligently finger-painting the bread pan.

Joan stopped talking for a few seconds to watch him. "Make sure you get the corners, Riley. Last time I tried to dump the bread onto the rack and the corners stuck." Her crabbiness at having to bake bread was manifesting itself. She monitored his progress for a while and then continued. "UCLA was a nest of radicals, all of them getting caught up in that … you know, all the stuff that was going on back then."

"What stuff?" Riley asked.

"There were students who were taking pills to see pink elephants and things. You've heard of the flower children, I'm sure, and … I don't know, the Beatles, rebellious kids." His mother's ideas of danger in music and fashion were hopelessly dated. At that moment, Riley could have retreated to the older girls' room and listened to their hidden stash of LPs, including the *Suitable for Framing* album from *Three Dog Night* and *Jesus Christ Superstar*, which the church had expressly forbidden its members to attend.

"Even some of the married members of the church got involved," she said, buttering the loaves with a pat of margarine on top. "Remember the Sanders family?" she asked quietly. He did. On more than one occasion, Nicole Sanders and he had retreated to her parents' bedroom to pull down each other's pants and have a look. Her father was at UCLA getting his doctorate.

Joan shook her head. "Clyde wanted the church to give the priesthood to Negroes," she said, resting her veined, greased hands lightly on top of a cantaloupe-sized ball of dough. Riley could tell his mother was registering one of her rare moments of confessional reminiscence, like the time she admitted she didn't care if Elizabeth

Taylor was vilified in the *Love vs. Lust* tract, she still thought she was the definition of beauty. Riley nearly held his breath while his mother stared off into the distance. He was afraid that if he moved, he would remind her that he was still in the room.

There was emotion in the silence, like bubbles rising in Muriel's lava lamp, until his mother suddenly remembered her bread duty. "The Lord is testing us, Riley," she said in her regular voice. "We don't know why Negroes aren't allowed to hold the priesthood. We're pioneers of faith. We have to believe that this is how the Lord wants it for now." What she meant was that the Lord would speak only to the prophet in Salt Lake City about such things.

"What about Brother Sanders?" he asked, twirling his finger in the bottom of the pan.

"Clyde was getting the kids involved in marches and writing letters to the newspaper." She looked at him circumspectly. "He thought your dad was wrong for just accepting what the Brethren were saying." She paused for a moment, as if remembering something. "It was hard on your dad," she said. Then she threw the dough ball down so hard, Riley instinctively turned to see if any of the dishes behind him in the hutch had broken.

None had. He turned back around. A tiny puff of flour sat innocently on each of Grace Kelly's breasts as a cloud filled the air in front of him, then settled onto the newly greased pan like lint.

4 | LEAD US NOT INTO TEMPTATION

When Riley was nearly twelve, Lucy came to live with them. She had been the kind of person Brother Sanders would have led in marches. Bertha Barclay was her real name. If Riley had a name as antique as Bertha, he would have called himself something like Bud. Or so he thought at the time. The only Bertha he had heard of was the one in the "Bertha Butt Boogie" they played on the radio. Happily, by the time she came to live with them in 1973, she was Lucy, borrowed from a performance of "In-A-Gadda-Da-Vida" at an Iron Butterfly concert.

Lucy was born and raised near San Jose as a Presbyterian. Her story about ending up in Utah was filled with *Sturm und Drang*: the kind of high moralism and paranormal phenomena that any Latter-day Saint would honor. It had to do with nearly dying from a heroin overdose, a penitent prayer when she returned home from the hospital, a vision of Satan himself, followed by the sudden miraculous appearance of the missionaries at her door.

This wasn't the first time one of Gus's disciples had found their way to the Hartley home. As part of the church's lay priesthood, Gus had been called to be bishop of a BYU student ward and thereby ended up bringing home to dinner many a walking testimony of how the gospel finds worthy latter-day repositories.

His acolytes would step reverently into the front hall, the family portrait at one end positioned like a lighted crucifix in a Catholic church, and humbly share their stories over meat pies and green salad.

Lucy was different. Despite her conversion and removal to the colorless but safer city of Provo, she still had, at twenty-one, the breezy candor that made her the most exciting person in Gus's ever-growing coterie of followers. She moved in because, she explained in a trembling voice one night, she had had a revelation and the SPIRIT had told her that, for some reason, she was to live with Bishop Hartley, the man who was fast gaining a reputation as a spiritual giant among the Latter-day Saints. She did not know why she had the revelation, but her parents, upon finding out their daughter had embraced Mormonism, had cut off her college funding. They helped her through her heroin addiction, but the fact that she had become a Latter-day Saint was a bridge too far.

In the weeks after she moved in, Lucy launched into a dizzying array of questions unlike Riley had ever heard. Why do we keep our temple ceremonies secret when the Book of Mormon specifically condemns secrets? she asked. Why did the Lord revoke polygamy when the early prophets taught it was *the Principle* with a capital *P*? If the church follows the Word of Wisdom, how could the family justify meat pies during the summer when fruits and vegetables were abundant?

Riley noticed how appealing Lucy was when she made a forceful point, the corners of her mouth turning up in a half smile and conveying some mystery. How small her ears were compared to her large angular face, and how her skin seemed so delicate next to her coarse black hair. She was not exactly pretty, but when she talked he could not stop looking at her.

Joan would remain tight-lipped during Lucy's volleys, on the assumption that silence was the best response to the irreverent vixen with frizzy hair. It unnerved Joan that the young woman called her husband Nelson, Gus's real first name, instead of Brother Hartley. Gus seemed to like competing in these ad hoc college bowls and would valiantly rise to the occasion like a warrior, square-jawed, fearless, full of rectitude. During the meat-pie controversy that evening, he cleared his throat loudly in preamble to a sort of practiced indignation.

"Lucy," he said, leaning over his plate, his signature piece of bread in one hand, dripping honey onto his plate, "the Word of Wisdom is just that, a suggestion. It's not a commandment."

"I understand that, Nelson." She slid her knife through the tines of her fork and leaned back in her chair. She wore little make-up and had a hearty masculine laugh. "We practice it as if it *were* a commandment. You don't think my bishop would let me drink coffee, do you?" In fact, Lucy was always badgering her bishop for special allowances.

"I like the way coffee smells," Riley announced, thinking this was an appropriate way to introduce himself into the conversation. "Aunt Sylvia let me smell hers last time we were in Arizona."

"Riley, I have half a meat pie left in the oven," interrupted his mother, pushing back her chair with purpose. She stood up, placing her crumpled paper napkin gingerly next to her plate, and went to the kitchen. The Word of Wisdom was the most distinguishing feature of the Latter-day Saint faith, and the Hartley Family, like others in the neighborhood, would never think of violating its prohibitions on tobacco and coffee. Riley had come close once to breaking the taboo when he had found half a pack of cigarettes in the street. He took them into the bushes and smelled them for about five minutes, then the Holy Ghost whispered in his ear that if he were to take a puff, he would be addicted forever and would have to smoke through a stoma in his neck. He noticed his father begin to squirm and blush.

"The Lord has directed us to abstain," Gus said, his voice lowered in patience. "That's where he draws the line, at smoking and drinking. Things can change, but that's the policy for now, and it's the beauty of having a living prophet who receives revelation about these things."

"It just seems a little inconsistent, Nelson," Lucy countered. She bumped down on all four legs of her chair and flipped her hair so that it shot out from the sides at a hard angle. "I mean, if coffee and tea are so bad—the caffeine I mean—then why doesn't the prophet tell us not to drink Coca Cola?" All of the kids looked at Gus, whose nervous laugh was turning more pronounced. Before Gus could respond, Joan was at Riley's side, holding the small pie tin in a mitted hand.

"It's the difference between the spirit of the law," Joan said, "and the letter of the law. Everybody's free to embrace the larger meaning and decline soft drinks."

"What about hot chocolate?" interrupted Lucy.

"Think moderation," Mom said while she flipped the pie over onto Riley's plate and removed the mitt. Gus was silent. "It all comes down to your testimony," Joan said. She clutched her napkin and looked directly at Riley. "If you have a testimony of the gospel, these questions aren't important, now are they?" Silence. "That is, in the eternal perspective. Enjoy the pie."

That was how discussions were likely to go. Gus would flail about until he started to look like a rhetorical wimp, and Joan would put it all back where they had started, in whomever's lap— in this case Lucy's—and then talk about less important things.

Even during the summer, meat pies were not as egregious a violation of the Word of Wisdom as Lucy thought. There was more yellow gravy and pie crust than chicken, in any case.

5 | IN THE BEGINNING WAS THE WORD

That summer Lucy secured a full-time job as a research assistant for her sociology professor, so that Riley didn't see her beyond dinner and sometimes on weekends. The previous school year, she had helped him with book reports. Joan was too busy with the little girls. Lucy showed him a special vocabulary notebook she had started on a road trip before her conversion, and asked him to start one and promise to jot down any new words he picked up over the summer. She told him to look up their definitions in a blue-backed composition notebook she presented to him as a gift. On the front cover, she had carefully stenciled, "In the beginning was the word."

But summertime never was designed for building one's vocabulary. That first full summer on Snob Hill, Riley connected with another twelve-year-old, Eric Whitworth, and they built a fort in the attic of the dream house. They nailed scraps of plywood over the rafters above the kitchen ceiling, and on top of that they tacked down carpet fragments and brought an old stereo and other fixtures into the space for sleepovers. The exposed beams served as backdrops for cartoon portraits of Alfred E. Neuman, with other tiny marginalia from *M.A.D.* magazine. The fort was a retreat from the public side of boyhood, a place where they felt autonomous and could listen to Billy Joel and load salt crystals from the water softener into Eric's BB gun. The real social currency at that age was sports, not forts built in attics, and Riley and Eric were considered about as low as flightless birds, consigned to the dirt with underdeveloped wings.

Gus had played high school football and did something called tumbling. Based on photos from Arizona yearbooks, tumbling looked like a cross between shirtless cheerleading and gymnastics. Riley found the pictures of the chesty young men inspiring. Sports had seemed natural for Gus. His advantage was in being built close to the ground and having thick sinewy limbs. "What's it like having a dad with a body like Steve Reeves?" Gus would say to his boys as he stood shirtless in front of the mirror and flexed his chest. The difference between Gus and Hercules was how much thickly matted body hair Gus had, spreading from the front to the back of his torso.

Every morning before scripture reading and prayer, their father did deep-breathing exercises and sit-ups. He did his calisthenics in his church-issued, one-piece undergarments that he rolled down to his waist. There was no place for Riley to pose, it seemed, no way to test his strength. When his father wrestled with him or his brother, the former high school star would pin them helplessly to the ground and laugh as they cried, saying they were poor sports. Riley was left with scant alternatives for those who could not convincingly throw off an opponent: Tactics, indifference, other interests, … which gradually came to include sex.

Once during a sleepover in their attic fort, Eric was extolling his powers of hypnotism when Riley decided to indulge his friend and pretend to be hypnotized—half closing his eyes, moving slowly like he was underwater. As the boys lay next to each other in sleeping bags, Eric suggested that Riley was on his honeymoon and that Eric was his wife, that Riley should do what couples do on their wedding night.

Riley wasn't sure how he was supposed to act under hypnosis or what married people did in bed, so he chose to do nothing. That only motivated Eric to see if his friend was really under hypnosis. He had Riley shoot himself in the toe with a salt crystal. Somehow Riley managed to stay calm and not flinch. With his toe still stinging, he followed Eric's command to get onto his knees. Eric reached over and pulled his friend's boxer shorts down. He rubbed Riley's penis. Strangely, this produced in Riley the impulse to hug his friend. Then everything got hot, tingly, and Riley thought he was going to maybe die but somehow did not care if he did. He almost doubled over, then he started to shudder. A wave of hot oil seemed to move through him like a thundershower, unimpeded and inevitable until, with a start, he seemed to open like a ripe flower in time lapse. It was over. And he had left a curious mess on the floor. He felt oddly powerful.

He couldn't resist sharing this secret with Paris Carter, the gifted pianist who had grown similarly weary of his lack of athletic prowess and the critical comments of his peers. Riley remembered first seeing Paris at the new ward as a blushing boy who rocked back and forth when playing the piano and who adored his mother, who led the congregational singing with a white plastic baton. Once when she was rhapsodizing about how many miles Johann Sebastian Bach had to walk for music lessons, she openly wept.

By the time Paris was in junior high, he was studying under

a BYU professor. Music was the only thing Paris took seriously. He cracked stupid jokes, leaking laughter through his humongous teeth. "Question: What did one *fly* say to the other?" As he waited for the answer, he held his mouth askew like a puppet on *Sesame Street*. "Answer. Your *man* is open!"

He was tall. By the time he hit puberty, everyone else his age was a foot shorter and still unable to match their socks. One afternoon Riley confided the strange thing that had happened between him and Eric and took Paris into the fort for a live demonstration, proceeding mechanically as if showing him how to strop his Sunday shoes with a high-shine rag. When the moment came for Paris, his eyes rolled into his head and he did a sort of half back flip off the plywood platform and stepped through the rafters and kitchen ceiling. Barely had they gotten his foot free and his pants pulled up before Gus came crashing up the attic ladder to check on them.

The fort was declared off-limits after that, and it slowly returned to its natural state of blown-in insulation, the portrait of Alfred E. Neuman tacked to one of the beams turning brown and gathering dust, left to ask no one in particular, "What, me worry?"

Riley and Paris didn't know what to call their new after-school activity that Eric had so generously provided through his hypnotism, so after a few more tries they came to call it "rubbing the genie lamp." Riley would make a wish and summon an imaginary genie, and in his mind ask it to keep them from being discovered, especially by Lucy since she was a new convert and was supposed to learn from his good example for her.

The night before school started, Riley stumbled on the notebook Lucy had given him. It was under the bed next to his long-lost, four-color Bic pen. He opened and stared at its green, rule-lined pages. In red ink he wrote, "Genie: A spirit of Arabian folklore, traditionally depicted inhabiting an oil lamp, which appears when the lamp is rubbed three times."

6 | DELIVER US FROM EVIL

"When I snap my fingers," Eric had told Riley the night of the hypnosis, "you won't remember anything that happened here." Eric had failed at snapping his fingers—an acquired skill—and did a hand clap instead. Either way, Riley was glad to have a reason to feign amnesia in the presence of the perpetrator of their crime and to be able to maintain his reputation for righteousness. With Paris, of course, it was another matter, and Riley chose not to think about what effect he was having on him.

Was the hidden deed written in his face? Riley couldn't stop thinking about it. Wasn't this related somehow to the intensity of feeling Gus talked about when he spoke of the SPIRIT overcoming him when he bore testimony of the gospel?

Other words accumulated along with *genie* in Riley's note-book—*mendacity, suffragan, oleaginous, copulation.* The pages were tissue-like after a while as he repeatedly returned to review the signifiers of his life, carbon dating the impulses that had no public space and no connection to his other activities. The righteous side of him might later seem like a mere performance for outsiders and even for his family. Even so, it had to be protected. Mostly what had to be protected was the performance he enacted for himself, shaded with all the codes and resonance of a perfect family in the perfect neighborhood and the perfect faith.

Lucy had been with them long enough that it seemed she had always been there, but it had only been two years. They all loved her. Even when Muriel moved into the large alcove off the family room, closed off by a panel-fold door, Lucy still shared a room in the basement with Candace and Jody. It was there that the five older kids would assemble after family prayer, and Lucy would light candles to cast shadows across the walls and ceiling. She would sit cross-legged on her tiny, second-hand bed that Gus had procured at Deseret Industries and brush her hair with such thorough strokes, static sparks would sometimes fly.

Pretty much anything could happen when Lucy was in the room. One time she stage-directed a short version of what she remembered from the musical *Godspell*. She punctuated her irritation at life's vagaries with, "WHAT a drag! That's SUCH a drag! Don't be such a DRAG!" When the subject of sex came up, she used the correct terms like *vagina* and *sexual intercourse* with the kind of off-handedness Riley remembered from Candace's health text. If the kids acted shocked around Lucy, she would stop and say, "WHAAAT?" Surely she knew that sexual sin was next in seriousness to murder, something Riley had forgotten for some reason when it came to waking up the genie in the attic.

Of course, whenever one of the kids did or said something gross—when Cade flipped Riley the bird or when Candace told a booger joke—Lucy was quick to chastise them. "And YOU, the child of Nelson Hartley!" she would say. Figuring out Lucy's territory of sacred opinion was difficult. She had an impulse to re-cast the gospel through her own unique lens, which produced a foreign image. There were always her questions—at times maddening.

"Why not let Jimmy fondle you under your bra?" Lucy said one evening before bedtime. Several strands of her hair lazily rose from the brush's electrical charge. She was talking to Muriel, who had just explained how hard it had been to keep Jimmy's hands to himself during the recent homecoming dance at Provo High. "I mean, if you let him kiss you, what's the difference? You've already become pretty intimate with him."

"I'm just sure!" said Muriel. She was considerably cooler toward Lucy ever since a week earlier when the two had gotten in a fight while they were doing the dishes, ending with Lucy forcing a dirty dishcloth into Muriel's mouth. There had been *those* kind of words.

"You're talking about petting, not just a peck on the lips," said Muriel, forgetting that her brothers were in the room.

"A peck?" said Jody from behind her honeycombs, "on the lips?" She was seated at the desk, trying to write an essay on *Macbeth*.

Candace, who was sitting next to Cade and Riley on the floor, was quick on the uptake. "You always said you weren't going to kiss anyone until you got married," she said. Candace's new polka dot pajamas barely covered her midriff, and she was much more sultry than her two older sisters.

Muriel looked at Candace with contempt. "I never said that," she snapped. "I said I wouldn't *French* kiss anyone until after the wedding."

"That means you want to do it!" said Cade, suddenly glad to be a part of it. "Riley said that, that you really want to do it!" He appeared thrilled with his derring-do.

"Riley!" said Jody, turning around in her chair. "What have you been telling Cade?"

Riley had said lots of things. He'd told Cade what VD stood for, that when girls cried a lot it was because they were bleeding between their legs. He said the rock singer Alice Cooper was Mormon. He let Cade read the passage about sex in *The Blue of Capricorn*, saying a lava-lava was a jock strap even though he wasn't sure. It was like Cade to blab something he had said, to tell everyone that he, the oldest son of Nelson Hartley, trafficked in salacious thoughts. Everyone was looking at Riley with a "how-dare-you!" expression on their faces, so he felt he had to say something.

"That's a buncombe," he said confidently.

"What?" asked Muriel.

"What Cade said about … you know, what he said I said. It's just buncombe."

"You're so weird, Riley," said Candace. "Why can't you just collect baseball cards like everyone else does?"

"Nobody around here collects baseball cards," he said. "*You're* the weird one."

"I'll bet you don't even know what that word means," said Candace, lifting her chin.

Riley took a quick breath. "It's something you say just for show," he said with a pretentious air. "It's empty talk." For the first time in his life, Riley thought he had found a use for words. In this case to silence someone.

Candace rolled her eyes. "Words are stupid if no one understands you."

Lucy stopped brushing her hair. "Words aren't stupid," she

said. "Riley knows words are important. Bright is the ring of words when the right man rings them," she quoted "Robert Louis Stevenson, and don't you forget it." Without missing a beat, she turned to Muriel. "The point is …" She put down the brush and smoothed her hair into a pony tail the size of a large duster. "… there are levels of intimacy. It's not what you do, it's what it means."

"We learned that," Candace agreed. "It's the difference between love and lust," she repeated from the church tract. "Spencer W. Kimball, and don't you forget it." She was indirectly accusing Muriel of something, but Riley didn't comprehend it. Even in the dim light, he could see that Muriel's face had reddened. She pulled her flannel robe across her chest.

"Well, it's not like you should be talking," Muriel said to Lucy, Muriel's pink nostrils flaring slightly while she feigned an interest in Jody's homework on the desk. "You know that's due tomorrow?" she said, trying to change the subject.

"What do you mean by that, Muriel?" Lucy demanded.

"What I mean is that you said you went on a trip with that guy, Monk, all the way to Philadelphia on a motorcycle."

"That was before I met Brother Hartley and your mom," said Lucy, showing her own signs of embarrassment. "That was before I joined the church and came here."

"I wish I could have gone on a road trip before I joined the church," said Candace.

"You were eight when you got baptized," said Muriel. "What would you have done? You didn't even know what Tampax were."

"Muriel!" said Jody, turning around with a start. "The boys are here." Riley and Cade looked at each other as if they had forgotten they were male.

From time to time, Lucy allowed the youngsters a glimpse into her previous life, but all Riley could remember was that Monk had left her back east and that Lucy's father had had to wire money for her bus fare. It was not until that night, sitting on the floor of the older girls' bedroom, that Riley realized a trip across the country on a motorcycle with someone probably meant you were sleeping with them. He wondered what other code words and phrases there were that he had missed out on. He felt a certain envy toward his sisters, even Candace who was just two years older but seemed to be more in the know.

"I did things I'm not proud of," Lucy said, rising. She picked up the candle and took it to her bed, her shadow growing taller as she walked to her corner of the room.

"You mean stuff with Monk?" asked Candace, sitting up on her knees.

"That's what baptism is for," Lucy said firmly. She pulled down the covers to her bed. "That's what my patriarchal blessing says." Riley was still too young to have had the blessing from the local church patriarch that was a sort of map for your life. Lucy had shared hers, where it said she would be the mother of many and would defend the gospel in these latter days.

"That's why they talk about repentance at church. It's what you do before baptism. Anyway, I don't think Brother and Sister Hartley would want me to dredge that up, not to their kids." She blew out the candle. The dim yellow lamp at Jody's desk was the only remaining light. They heard the box springs squeak as Lucy got into bed.

"Time for sleep," she said, sounding far away, the darkness

plundering her voice. Candace headed for the bathroom. The others stood up to go.

"Dredging up all of that wouldn't do anyone any good," Lucy continued from her corner, her words starting to slur. "It's a real DRAG living in the past. Be happy you don't have to. You just have to endure to the end and you'll be fine."

Riley was sweating when he woke up from a dream that night in which his sisters had died and he was wondering whether he should cry or if it would mean he didn't believe in the resurrection. It was still dark outside. Getting up for a drink of water, he saw a light on in the family room where Lucy was turned around at the couch and on her knees praying, but in a kind of fallen-over position as if she might be asleep. Behind a closet door with a metal scrim, a click announced that the furnace had been activated, followed by a whooshing of air. Riley felt he should turn away, but the vision of Lucy in her nightgown, crumpled on the couch in the middle of the night, her fingers loosely interlocked, enticed him. He remembered what her breasts looked like through her nightgown without a bra. What could she be doing? Maybe she was praying out loud like Gus told people they should do. Or had she actually fallen asleep?

He walked up, thankful for the white noise from the furnace in-take, and heard a sniffle, then saw Lucy's head move slightly. As he stopped behind her, the furnace shut off and he heard a delirious voice say, "my baby … Dear Father, please …"

7 | THE SPIRIT OF THE LAW

When Joan announced that she was pregnant with number ten, Gus started in on the usual routine, telling everyone that Lovey, as he called her, was expecting their "third son." He had said that for the past four pregnancies, none of which had produced boys. "I have nine children," he would sometimes tell adoring fans, "all of them sons except seven."

Because of the church's encouragement to have as many children as possible to provide bodies for pre-mortal spirits in the pre-existence, Riley's little sisters and brother had collectively reached a critical mass of domestic pandemonium. Living with them had turned into a kind of comic opera, a Disney version of *Lord of the Flies*. There was constant drama—laughs and pokes alongside shoves and teases, hair pulling, and icy glares, a crying child coming from stage right to collapse into the lap of Gus, while Joan exited stage left to comfort another fussing child. One day after school while Riley was trying to carry on a conversation with his mother, three-year-old Jessica, number eight, stood in front of them modulating her screeches like the siren on a fire truck.

"It's like her mouth is separate from her body," he said with as much astonishment as bitterness. "I think she was born with a mouth, and at some point her body became attached to it."

Riley pitied any additional child in the family. It was already nearly impossible to find bathroom time. The older girls perpetually occupied the bathroom downstairs. Assuming you could get into the girls' inner sanctum, you had to navigate the unavoidable eyelash curlers, bras dripping off the shower rail, a riot of multi-colored panties thrown into the corner like afterthoughts, tampons, and other evidence of their domain. "Go outside," they would say on weekday mornings when Riley pounded on the door, pleading with them to let him relieve himself. "Go outside! You're a boy!" One morning Muriel consented to his showering while she finished doing her hair. Gus had outlined the hot water routine during one of their Family Nights. After moistening his skin, Riley was to turn the water off during the lather-up stage, then stand shivering until the person upstairs turned the water off as the signal that he could rinse. Suddenly he heard Muriel screaming when she realized the steam from his rinse cycle was taking the curl out of her hair.

Where would the crib for the new baby go? everyone wondered. The six bedrooms were full to overflowing, with only one exception where Muriel occupied the makeshift room alone. Then came Susan, ready or not, born in January before Gus could get out of his office to his wife's side. Joan was accustomed to this sort of thing, having waited until her contractions became apocalyptic before acting on them. She finally asked Sister Pratt to drive her to the hospital. By the time Gus rushed in, his wife was already sitting up in bed reading a magazine, the baby sleeping next to her. Joan seemed to relish her time away from the family even though she had to share the room with another mother.

Before Joan left for the hospital, she commissioned Lucy to take care of the house, and Lucy became a drill sergeant about turning off the lights and keeping everyone from watching television or even listening to the radio on Sunday.

"We listen to the radio when it's general conference," Riley retorted, angrily.

"Oh, Riley," she said, taking her hair band off to reveal a giant Brillo Pad of frizzy hair, "that's not showing the spirit of the law, is it?" Riley suddenly hated her. She wanted to be his Mom, and what did she know?

Lucy also soon developed a fanatical view of what constituted a clean house. One Friday after school while Riley and Cade were watching *Gilligan's Island* and she was sorting utensils, she complained that someone—probably Candace—had just dumped the silverware into the drawer haphazardly. Nor had Riley vacuumed the living room. She abruptly marched over and stood between the boys and the TV, waving a bunch of mismatched spoons in her hand. Riley yelled for her to move, at which she walked behind the set and pulled the plug. "Cunt," he said. Cade gasped.

Riley didn't know exactly what *cunt* implied—it was not the sort of thing he could find in the dictionary—but he had heard Jody use the word during an argument with Muriel that summer when the two of them were tending the younger kids. Muriel had wanted to watch a re-run of *Love, American Style*, which Jody reminded her was on their parents' blacklist. If his older sisters thought it was appropriate to call each other cunts, he thought at the time, he figured he might as well enjoy watching an immoral show, which he did. Lucy, on the other hand, laughed at this new-found imagery and told Riley he was going to have to come up with something more innovative to offend her since she had gone to rock concerts and had heard much worse epithets than that.

"Why did you have to come live with us anyway?" Riley said, pulling out the stops. "Mom says we don't have enough money to feed you since you're such a pig!" Of course, Joan had never said anything of the sort, but it had an effect on Lucy. She retreated to the kitchen to finish sorting the utensils in silence. Riley plugged the TV back in.

Joan came home from the hospital in the middle of a snow-storm, greeted by hugs from all her children in the front hall. Jody's glasses fogged up from tears when she saw the baby. Gus took the bundle from Joan and held it for everyone to take a look. The miniature creature was wrapped in a now inappropriately themed blanket covered in baseballs. When he pulled back the blanket so they could see the baby, all that greeted them were tiny stockinged feet. "Oh, for heck sake!" he said. "She's upside down!" Shocked, everyone screamed DAAAD! Then Joan started laughing. Always grateful for any kind of audience, Gus beamed at his own ineptitude. Joan kept laughing so hard, she had to sit down and put her head between her knees. It wasn't *that* funny, Gus said.

That evening he dragged the kids out coatless into the drifts and started throwing snowballs at them. Jody had sewn mittens for everyone from scraps scavenged from stray socks, and the kids repaid her by always taking them off first chance they got. It was easier to carry books and pack snowballs without sock mittens on. Gus was breathless, with two kids hanging from him and another wrapped around his ankles. On impulse, he started cramming everyone into the station wagon, saying he was going to spin donuts at the church parking lot down the street. Mom looked out the window and saw what was happening. The car doors were slamming and Gus was shushing the giggling girls. She flew to the door in protest.

"Nelson, we talked about this last time! Absolutely not, for crying out loud. Are you mad?"

"The kids love it!" Gus protested.

"You're willing to risk their lives so *you* can get a little thrill?" she shouted from the front porch. Back and forth they went in the frigid air until she relented on condition that she go with them. "That way, if we die, we die as a family," she said. Lucy said she'd watch the baby.

"Lock the doors!" Joan yelled. "Nelson, if you kill us, I'll never forgive you!" Gus backed the car out into the street and tested the ice by briefly hitting the brakes.

"This works better if you have a standard shift," he explained. "More control that way." Riley felt like he was an accomplice in his father's determination to be reckless. Jessica, who had sensed her mother's concern, began to cry, so Riley put his arm around her and told her everything would be okay, they were going to have fun. Riley could feel her shoulders rapidly rise and fall in sync with this strange new order of family recreation.

"I don't like the snow!" Jessica said and made them all laugh. Cade was bouncing up and down on the seat as if he had to pee. He looked at Riley, hardly able to contain himself, and even though Riley's heart was pounding he thought his brother's enthusiasm was childish. Riley concealed his anxiousness for Jessica's sake.

In the first three attempts, the car only spun a hundred and eighty degrees, to the girls' squeals. On the fourth try, Gus revved the engine at the far end of the lot and shifted into drive with a lurch and the car tore through the blue evening, tires spinning, snow blowing up over the side windows like the spray of a water skier. "Now Nelson. NELSON! NELLSON!" Joan said in steps of increasing volume. She clutched at Agnes for herself as much as for the toddler planted against the dash board. Then in a flash, Gus turned the wheel and hit the brakes and they went spinning around in a giant arc, the headlight beams bouncing wildly across the tops of trees and snowflakes funneling at them so that it looked like space travel.

"Whoa, whoa, whooooa!" screamed everyone, and Riley heard his father laugh mightily. Riley's heart was so determinedly in his throat, he figured it would stay there, and he thought this was the way it would always be, his huge family together spinning out of control for the thrill of it, his father laughing as freely as if he were Cade's age.

It was eight weeks after Joan and Susan got home before they could have a family portrait taken. With such a large family, timing was everything. Muriel was attending church college in Idaho, and Uncle Ralph from Flagstaff had offered to wall-paper the living room. Buckets of opaque sticky paste sat waiting for an order of Regalia-patterned wall paper to arrive. Meanwhile, Joan had been on a diet for a month.

Candace woke up on portrait day with a blemish in the middle of her forehead, symbolic of her life. She had begun spending afternoons under an ultra-violet tanning lamp and was hanging out with boys who smoked. A week after she received a learner's permit, she totaled the Falcon.

Lucy moved out, and Candace, who had taken over Muriel's bedroom, moved back in with Jody. The downstairs would become Joan's new ballet school to supplement Gus's patchy income. Roommates once again, Candace and Jody were having trouble getting along, like Candace and Muriel had before. Clearly, Candace was the problem.

"It's not going to happen today," she said to Gus, her zit pulsing. "We can't have the picture taken today!" Gus had come home from the men's early-morning priesthood meeting to help

Joan get everyone ready for Sunday school. The portrait would be taken in the afternoon. "I scrub my face every night. I use Clearasil. Why does Heavenly Father do this to me?"

Joan was monitoring the crisis while trying to dress herself and several children. With ten minutes to go before they would have to walk out the door, she was still in her slip and on her hands and knees looking under a bed for Jessica's dress shoes, which naturally no one could remember having seen since last Sunday. Riley was passing by to the hall mirror to clip on his bow tie and could feel the emotional temperature rise as it did whenever his mother and Candace were in the same room. "You're not going to mess this up," Joan said to Candace with an alarming edge. "Muriel has to go back to school tomorrow. Stop whining and use some make-up to hide it."

Riley edged toward the door of the bedroom. He could see his mother, clench-jawed, having to deal once again with Candace's bad attitude, after Candace's debauchery the week before when her boyfriend's buddies got him soused and dropped him off on the lawn of the dream house. Joan had brought Henry inside and handed him a large sauce pan to heave into while he slouched woozily below Grandma's "Christ is the Head of this House" needlepoint. Riley had come in to look at him in his drunken state, and it seemed to Riley to be the most resplendently wicked thing he had ever seen. The young man seemed to be weak, his head moving on an imaginary line between his neck and his knees, and he had a devil-may-care grin on his face like it was a rubber mask.

"I don't know why we have to have a family picture anyway. It's stupid," Candace said, her own jaw set in defiance. Suddenly

Joan was backing out from under the bed like a spider, grasping a hand-held egg beater and holding it up for emphasis in front of Candace. Dust balls floated down from the wire whisks.

"You know, Candace, you're not the only one in this family. You come and go like a princess, sleeping in and having your own little feasts any time of day or night. You wear shorts we've asked you not to wear, and you're mean to your brothers and sisters." She was referring to the morning when Riley was practicing piano with rare determination and Candace stormed out of her bedroom in her pajamas to complain that he kept making the same mistakes. She grabbed the sheet music and said she never wanted to hear "Für Elise" again until he could play it perfectly. She tore it in half.

"The least you could do, young lady," continued Joan, "is show some concern for our family. Show us that you give a hoot." She whirled around, opened the closet door, and began tearing through a cascading pile of little girls' clothes.

By now Gus was trying to ferry Candace into the hall. Riley was trying to get the stubborn tie clip to close but was distracted by the scene. "At least I'm not the one with a million babies," Candace said. "Henry says people with ten kids are sex maniacs." The word *sex* was never used in the Hartley house, so when Candace insinuated that her parents were sexual, Riley knew some kind of rupture had occurred in the household membrane that might not be reparable. The tie clip suddenly closed with a snap.

Joan crashed through the doorway with a little shoe in one hand, the other hand at her mouth in shock. She leaned against the wall before stumbling toward her room. They heard a sob. Gus followed Candace, who was now retreating to her own corner of the hallway, near the stairwell. Her father was saying

47

something about daring to criticize the woman who had "entered the valley of death for you children," to which Candace said, "Yeah, right." At that, Gus grabbed Candace by the arm and pulled her to the top of the stairs.

"Dad! Leave me alone!" she screamed. "What are you doing?"

"You're going down to your room and staying there until I tell you to come out," he shouted.

"Oh, right. I'm just sure I'm doing that. I'm sixteen," she retorted, breaking loose. With that, Gus threw his arm across Candace's chest and dragged her backward down the stairs. She screamed, her bare legs twisting and pumping as she tried to stand upright.

Brother Fournier, the fussy French convert with a red face, knew nothing of this when he arrived that afternoon and arranged the family in front of the fireplace. Lucy was there to adjust the lights. After a few false starts and half a dozen *Zut alors*, Brother Fournier stood behind his tripod and, as if conducting an orchestra, uttered the magical word: *Fromage*! He clicked the camera.

"*Fromage*?" the younger girls all asked at the same time.

"*Zut*," Brother Fournier said again, winding the camera.

When they got the proofs back, Joan held them carefully at arm's length between flat vertical hands and looked at them one-by-one. When she put down the last one, her hands were trembling, she was so overwhelmed by how beautiful her children were and how many there were. Brother Fournier, despite his fastidiousness, turned out to be less of a professional than he had presented himself to be. He didn't have the right lens, so the shots were distorted. Riley, though only thirteen, looks bigger than Gus.

There they all are, twelve of them, standing in the corner of the newly remodeled living room next to the white stone fireplace. Joan is seated in the center, Susan on her lap, the baby's plumage the shade of Gus's black hair. She is wearing the long lace dress each of the kids was blessed in. Joan has a black turtleneck blouse and a black skirt, with a black-and-white checkered jacket with six-inch lapels. Her hair is coiffed, piled high on her head with a flip of a curl sculpted over a dark left eyebrow.

Behind Joan is Gus, standing there with his affable good looks, thinning hair slicked back and dolloped to the right, one hand on the back of his wife's chair and the other on the shoulder of seven-year-old Chums. In front of everyone is two-year-old Agnes, her eyes partially gummed even though they'd been swabbed all day to stave off infection.

Lined up to one side is Jessica in a wildly flowered dress with poufy sleeves, cobbled in her older sister's shoes for the day and boasting a knowingly pert look. Behind her, to her side, Riley stands ramrod in blue plaid slacks, a sweater vest, and matching butterfly bow tie. To his left is Jody, now a senior at Provo High, who has Gus's dark hair and square jaw. In her high-collared red dress, she looks like Ali McGraw in *Love Story*.

At the other side of the portrait is Cade in a two-inch-wide, faux-leather belt. His bow tie, made of velvet, is the size of a shoe. He shares the same kind of exuberant grin as Winnie, to his right, the same height and equally interested in musical theater. Next to Cade, Muriel is radiant, filled with the afterglow of a year in college, her hands held behind her back and her hair displaying her surrender to the new feathered look.

Directly behind Mom's Matterhorn of a hairdo, Candace sports a scooped neckline and attractive gold chain around her tanned neck. She wears a smile like the rest of them, poised, marinated in the heady infusion of stage adrenalin. She is the best looking of them all, even with the slight red mark on her forehead. She looks like she has seen more in her days than Joan has at forty.

9 | LOT'S WIFE

As far as the family portrait went, I was there too. If you look closely in the mirror to the right of Cade, you can see a blurry red-haired figure standing by, looking more surprised than posed. Unlike the mythology of the undead, you can see my reflection in the mirror. And as with the mere suggestion of my image in the Hartley family portrait, humanity as a whole is not very far at all from the smell and taste of God, a pre-cognitive blip away in the brain's synapses. What separates us is that thin porous membrane between this world and our former existence as a spirit. As God's spirit children, we are destined to return to that former sphere of existence after death. Sometimes spirits transit through the old earth life itself to a different time and place, which is as simple as slipping through a celestial drape for those who do so. But God blocked my passage, even though I can see the veil and know where the transit is. My assignment is to prevent Riley from approaching the veil prematurely, which isn't that bad a task. The kid reminds me of myself at that age, although I was born two millennia earlier.

Gus decided to run an experiment the next evening, prompted by the miracle of a new little one in the family who had so recently

been in the presence of Heavenly Father. It was assumed that
Agnes, number nine, could serve as a medium. She had astonished
all of them with surprising feats of syntax for a two-year-old, and
like the new baby, she was, according to Gus, also young enough
to sense the undulations of the VEIL to which everyone else, world
weary, had grown callous.

Riley was not sure what *callous* meant but wrote it down when
his father said it, sure that Candace, who was sitting on the floor
painting her toenails, was the epitome of it. Since the blow-up over
calling her parents "sex maniacs," no one had mentioned a word
about the incident, and Riley was sure that Candace was unre-
pentant. The day before Joan had caught her dancing in her clogs
on top of the Postum table for the entertainment of her friends,
leaving a dozen nicks in the hardwood surface.

Agnes was busy flipping through *Goodnight Moon* for the
third time when Gus explained that he would casually ask her
about where she had come from before she was born and who
might be visiting them unseen in the room. "Let me do the
talking," Gus said. All of them, except for Candace, absorbed
by her toenails, were hushed and watching with anticipation,
fully expecting a running account of everything from the color
of Heavenly Father's eyes to what kind of breakfast cereal people in the pre-mortal state consumed. Lucy, who visited them
on Family Nights, sat cross-legged on the floor, unable herself
to resist examining the ends of her hair. At dinner she had been
in rare form in discussing Watergate. A Republican, she said,
was someone who was born on third base and thought he had
hit a triple.

"But Nelson," she said, looking up from her split ends, "don't you think this is like necromancy—or let's say looking for a sign for the fun of it instead of believing without seeing?"

Joan rolled her eyes. She was sitting in the rocking chair and nursing the baby, fiddling with the blanket that shielded them from a view of her breast.

"I mean, we have a veil over our minds for a reason, don't we?" Lucy continued.

She could be such a killjoy sometimes. Riley had yet to understand, at thirteen, that he had contributed to her decision to move out of the house. Whenever she came by, she asked how Riley's words were coming. By then he had twenty pages of them, including *smegma* and *bibulous*.

"You could construe this that way," said Gus, "but prayer might be considered sign-seeking too. I assume prayer's okay, don't you agree?" Lucy mumbled something like "I guess so."

Having dealt with the objection, Gus cleared his throat and directed his attention to his daughter. "Agnes, honey, what are you doing over there?"

Agnes looked up from her book and smiled at Gus. "*Goodnight Moon*!" she announced, pointing to the open pages. Gus followed with more small talk, and Agnes stared into space while she answered yes and no to his questions.

Finally Gus asked, "Where did you live before you came to our house?" There was no response. "Did you live with Heavenly Father?" Still no response. Gus decided to take another tack. "Who's in the room today, Agnes. Is Mommy in the room?"

"Yes."

"Is Daddy in the room?"

"Yes."

Gus went through the entire family, including Lucy. "That's good, honey. You have such a good memory. You're a good girl. Now is there anyone else in the room here with us?"

"Yes," said Agnes.

Lucy looked up, and Riley saw his father's eyes widen as he leaned forward in his chair.

"Is Grandpa Swenson in the room?" said Chums, excited by the prospects.

"Shhh!" said Gus. Grandpa Swenson had died of a heart attack at fifty, before Riley was born. It left Gram with two sons at home and nearly destitute, but with something to feel some pride over, at how the family had faced adversity and survived it.

Agnes looked at Jessica, then to Gus. Jessica had fallen asleep on the couch. She stirred, her head lolling from one side to the other. The entire family's attention had fallen on Agnes and her Pooh-like world of Little Yellow readers and a stuffed chimpanzee with a missing eye. She became coy, protective, her chin pressed into her pink hands, her elbows resting on the Postum table.

"Agnes," said Gus slowly, "is Grandpa Swenson in the room with us?"

She seemed to be thinking. She looked around. "Yes," she said.

"Who else is in the room with us? Can you see anyone else?" said Gus.

"Yes!" said Agnes. She looked at Riley, then stood with one foot on top of the other. "Grandpa likes Riley!" she said cheerfully. She started singing a Primary song she had heard her sisters rehearse about how pioneer children crossed the Great Plains and "sang as they walked and walked and walked and walked."

"Grandpa likes Riley!" she said again, throwing her arms into the air and giggling. Gus looked at Joan warmly.

"Agnes," he said, leaving his chair and sitting on the floor. He put his arm around her tiny shoulders. "Do you know who Grandpa Riley is?"

"Yes!" said Agnes impatiently, as if her father had just asked her her name. She wriggled free of Gus and began swinging her stuffed chimp by both its arms. "Pioneer children sang as they walked and walked and walked and walked," she sang, then threw the chimp across the room. Gus returned to his seat.

"Well, I think this has been rather fruitful. I think our grandparents and great-grandparents could very well be present with us."

"Grandpa Swenson!" someone said. Gus paused for dramatic effect while Cade sniffed the air and Lucy forgot to close her mouth. Jody seemed spellbound, her arms folded across her chest, her eyes cast to the floor. Candace picked up Agnes's chimp and set it in her lap.

"I didn't feel anything," Riley said point blank. He had been looking forward to something sensational.

Gus looked at him solemnly. "What do you mean, Riley?"

"I just didn't feel anything," Riley said.

"Well, that doesn't mean something didn't happen here tonight," said Gus.

"If it did, why didn't I feel it?" Riley said. He moved his sleeping sister's head from his shoulder so he could shift his weight on the couch. He seemed truly disappointed at what had not happened. Gus shifted in his own chair. Riley could see his eyebrow going up, his jaw tightening.

"Did anyone else feel it?" Riley asked, looking around at his sisters and brother.

"I did," said Cade enthusiastically. Slowly, everyone else nodded. Jody, always the one to smooth things over in the family, said she wasn't sure, that she had felt something but didn't know what it was. Joan struggled to get out of the rocker with the baby and excused herself. Riley looked at Lucy, who glanced at Gus and said, "Maybe it's because I'm not really a part of the family."

Gus cleared his throat. "There are a lot of reasons why we aren't given a witness," said Gus in sympathy with Riley. I could tell that would not satisfy Riley.

"You're just hogging all the spiritual experiences," he blurted out.

Gus looked at his oldest son, a smile rising so hard in him that his mouth finally opened and he let out a burst of air. Riley returned the gesture by staring back defiantly, his face reddened with shame. He looked at Jessica's head now in his lap and absently stroked her hair. Gus had stopped short of saying that the heavens become brass because of a lack of sexual purity, but he had implied it. Riley had read the handouts Gus had written and copied for his disciples, one of them titled "Sexual Purity and Recruiting the Spirit." Did Gus know about his oldest son's attic secret?

Gus explained that the SPIRIT would speak to them each in their own way. They all knelt while Gus poured out his heart in prayer. Riley chose not to shut his eyes as the extemporaneous but oh-so-familiar phrases filled the room. Family members lay nearly prostrate, spread out across the living room like exhausted hikers. Riley must have felt as rebellious as Lot's wife in the Bible, the woman turned to salt when she couldn't resist looking back on the destruction of Sodom and Gomorrah. How easy for Riley to show that he lacked faith. All he had to do was flick open his eyes during family prayer. His heart was pounding, but surprisingly he was not turned into a pillar of salt.

Agnes was the only other one with her eyes open. Too young to matter, she didn't know otherwise but seemed transfixed to see her suddenly collapsed family frozen on its knees like a scene from Pompeii. Sitting down amid her sisters, she absently pulled at her monkey's remaining button eye.

10 | TO ACT IN GOD'S NAME

When Riley was younger, before the family moved into its dream house on Snob Hill, he used to walk down the street under a black walnut tree and find part of the canopy underfoot and dried, an invitation to set about crushing each leaf he came upon. When he over-stepped one, he felt the need to return and thoroughly squash it before moving on, thinking it was a practice run for the exactness required to reach the celestial kingdom. The autumn leaves were a test of his willingness to be obedient, a task within his childhood reach. When Riley walks the streets today, he thinks of the leaves differently and ponders the randomness of it, as well as why it is he still has to resist the urge to crush every one of them.

The PLAN OF SALVATION was as systematic and methodical as the autumn-leaf stomping, presented to him at church as an elaborate system for the advancement of boys, like earning merit badges in Boy Scouts. At fourteen, he and his family assembled in Bishop Bowen's office. They were to witness Riley's advancement in the lower priesthood from the office of deacon to teacher, allowing him to visit church members in their homes, accompanied by his father, and to prepare the bread and water for the communion sacrament at church. He sat in a chair in the middle of the room and Gus stood behind him, resting his hands heavily on his son's shoulders. The bishop said something to his two counselors. As they gathered around in a circle, Gus moved his hands to Riley's head and the other three men followed suit, positioning one hand each on top of Gus's hands and another on the shoulder of the man next to him. As they closed the circle and bowed their heads, the room was hushed. Gus was concentrating, invoking the SPIRIT to be there with them. Almost immediately, his voice began to quiver with emotion.

Before ending the ordination, he blessed his son that his body would "grow strong in the service of the Lord," that he would study hard in school, go on a mission for the church in a few years, and marry in the temple. He thanked his boy for being a good son and brother. He promised that if Riley kept the Lord's commandments, the Holy Ghost would be his constant companion, that someday he would arrive at the point where he would never make a serious wrong choice again. That made sense to Riley because he had assumed his father was at that point. Finally, Gus reminded Riley that the priesthood was the power to act in God's name, to preach the gospel, to baptize, to heal the sick, and to minister to his future wife and his many future children.

The blessing ended in a different octave with the powerfully enunciated "name of the Savior, even Jesus Christ, who died and rose again that we might rejoice someday in the glory of the celestial kingdom with the Father, amen." Afterward, Riley stood and turned a full three-sixty, shaking hands with the men, including his teary-eyed father. Gus gave him a bear hug that took Riley's breath away. He whispered in his ear that he loved him. Riley said it back, and he meant it. How tender a father can be. Riley had a picture in his mind of his father sitting on the couch next to Candace, a few hours after dragging her down the stairs, and holding hands. Candace wept at the calm reassurance of her father.

Each of Riley's sisters dutifully gave him a light hug. Cade extended his arm to shake hands. Then Lucy, who stood beaming at him in her big-boned athletic way, said "Way to go, Rile" and slapped his back hard enough to make him jump, then grabbed his head under an arm and gave him a noogie. Riley yelped, breaking the solemnity of the occasion, the bishop looking on with wide-eyed consternation, and Lucy, standing there in her fitted dress and thick flat-bottomed sandals, suddenly seemed out of place and awkward. Riley's mother and daughters stood demurely by, decked out in Provo lace and bows.

I, Zedekiah, am here to report that in this supposedly last dispensation of time, people don't simply question whether angels are really "silent notes taking," as the hymn goes. The sinners feel like they can outrun the heavenly host. They leave us in the dust, our parchments and quill pens scattered to the winds. This is true for Riley as he walks down the streets of New York City. He marvels at how sins in modern-day Babylon seem to be taken in a boulevard stride, in great leaps and in the out-of-doors rather than small portions in subterranean alcoves.

Before people become free to do what they want, they take another journey. A guilt trip. Which returns us to our story. Riley was unexpectedly called in by the bishop one day for an interview, which wasn't out of the ordinary except that Bishop Bowen was a busy man. In addition to taking care of the Cascade Mountain First Ward, he was a stockbroker for Merrill Lynch. Riley didn't think much about the reason for the meeting because the bishop occasionally talked to the youth about their spiritual lives.

Riley waited in the small adjoining office where Brother Stinson, the ward clerk, opened envelopes and made marks in a ledger. He had three or four strands of hair carefully pasted across his bald and freckled head. When Riley arrived, the clerk gave him a quick clinical smile and then immediately went back to his work, absently sliding the eraser end of his pencil up one of his nostrils. It was hard to find someone who was good with numbers and socially adept, and when they found someone who was at least trustworthy and diligent enough, they kept him forever, mentally pigeon-holing him as a clerk. For some reason they never put a woman in that position.

Brother Stinson started punching keys on a large electric adding machine, his white bony fingers moving at a hypnotic speed while he recorded tithing contributions, attendance statistics, and the number of temple sessions people had attended. Riley wondered what in particular he might be adding at the moment? Fast offerings, perhaps? Maybe the number of children born to each family, or what sins people had confessed to. Whatever it was, Riley knew he was in the presence of the engine room of the PROGRAM OF SALVATION. He found himself staring until suddenly the clicking stopped and Brother Stinson glanced up over his narrow half-glasses balanced precisely at the end of his nose.

Riley smiled. "Lots of stuff to add, it looks like," he said.

"All in the service of the Lord," said Brother Stinson, returning immediately to the machine. Suddenly Bishop Bowen was standing in the opened door. His office had brick walls adorned with pictures of the prophet and the local temple. The floor was covered with indoor-outdoor carpet, his desk made of the oak veneer that was popular at the time. It was completely bare except for a box of tissues.

Whenever Bishop Bowen talked, a small globule of spittle accumulated on the middle of his top lip, a phenomenon of no small interest to boys Riley's age. The Bishop pulled a chair out from behind the desk so that the two of them sat knee-to-knee.

"Brother Hartley," he said, punching the air with both arms to get his shirt cuffs off his wrists, "I understand the teachers quorum is doing pretty well."

Riley nodded and said, "Yes. I think it is." Then before he could explain their upcoming service project to weed Sister Christensen's flowerbed, the bishop said something about how important it was for Riley to set an example for the other boys in the quorum since he was the son of Nelson and Joan Hartley and was himself president of the group. The bishop paused. Another globule had begun to form on the man's dry lips.

"I've received word that you have been involved in some activities that, well, let's say would displease the Lord."

Riley stared at him. What was he talking about? Was this about the incident last week when Riley and the other boys sang about what you could do when you're "stranded, stranded on the toilet bo-o-o-wl ... and you cannot reach the roll" while they were filling the sacrament cups? Sister Ohlander had overhead them and reported it. Riley turned his head to the side and squinted, trying to detect the bishop's meaning.

"Your body is a sacred temple of the Lord," the bishop said. He glanced at the wall and the framed picture of the nearby Provo temple. "The sex act is something that is holy and is intended to be done within the bonds of marriage. Do you know what I'm talking about?" The bishop's leg was bouncing up and down and the spittle had moved to the corners of his mouth and foamed slightly. He breathed in more deeply.

Riley was appalled. Did the bishop know about his self-abuse?

He wasn't sure what to do. Perhaps tears would be appropriate to the situation.

Bishop Bowen said someone had confessed to him about episodes of mutual masturbation involving Riley. It was true, then. The bishop knew something! One day Paris had called Riley from Maury Slaughter's house and said Maury wanted to get together with him. When Riley asked what he meant, Paris had said, "You know, that thing we do." Riley had taken off down the hill on Jody's ten-speed bicycle on the pretense that he was going to swimming practice. Instead, Paris and Maury—a boy with long hair and largely absent parents—and Riley lounged around listening to Emerson Lake and Palmer as a prelude to polishing the genie lamp.

In the bishop's office, Riley decided that tears were definitely in order. After all, the first step of repentance was remorse, which he could manage easily enough with Bishop Bowen sitting so close to him that, had he been inclined, he could have stuck a wet finger in his ear like they did to girls in the hallway. While Riley quietly wept and corroborated his growing list of accomplices, Bishop Bowen passed him a tissue and said soothing things.

"I'm sure this will never happen again," the bishop said. For penance, Riley would not be allowed to partake of the sacrament for two months.

When he emerged from the bishop's office, Maury Slaughter was there looking sheepish. He explained how he and Jason Morrison had given each other hand jobs at a sleep-over two weeks ago and let it slip that he had done it with Riley too. Jason, being the rat that he was, went directly to the bishop and behaved like a baby and cried his eyes out, according to Maury.

That evening the doorbell rang and it was Paris standing at the door. He and Riley walked around behind the house through the wooden gate Gus had put up when Joan started the ballet school. "The bishop asked me if I'd done it with you and Slaughter," he said, ashen-faced, then stopped and looked at Riley. "I didn't tell him anything. I didn't say a word," he said, breathing faster. "Even though Bishop Bowen said if I didn't confess, he'd tell my parents. He said I wouldn't be able to play the organ or the piano in church, but I didn't cop to it."

"He already knew, Paris," said Riley. "Jason told him everything."

Paris got a funny look on his face. "Well, I don't think it's any of the bishop's business," he said.

Riley moved to the backyard jungle gym and grabbed the chin-up bar. Paris stood without moving, feeling the cool canyon breeze that was moving north, seemingly at right angles from the broad face of Mt. Timpanogos. The entire bank of familiar rock massifs, bathed in the reddish glow of the setting sun, trumpeted their peaks overhead. "You just told him about the whole thing, just like that?" asked Paris plaintively.

"I had to," Riley said, looking down at the grass that was blurred by the slow motion of his swinging on the monkey bar. "What else could I have done?"

Unlike Lucy's conversion after she realized her wrongdoings and prayed for forgiveness, Riley's piety was the result of the bishop having scared him to death. His parents heard through the grapevine that there were boys in the neighborhood who had become homosexuals with each other. His parents were concerned enough to call in the boys for a talk. Joan was the one who led the conversation, actually. Ever since Riley asked Gus a question about sex and Gus had sketched out a picture of horses on the back of a manila folder, Riley had given up asking his father anything about the dark embers of stirring manhood. Gus was equally happy not to have to talk to his son about the topic.

On the other hand, Cade had no idea what his mother was talking about and kept glancing at his brother with a do-you-know-what's-happening-here? question on his face. Riley sat stone-faced like the prophet Joseph Smith in Liberty Jail. When his mother was done, he thanked her and escaped from the room, red-faced.

Riley stayed away from any priesthood assignments since the bishop had forbidden him to participate until he was worthy. One Sunday the opening hymn was under way and no one had shown up to usher people in from the forward chapel door. He could see his quorum advisor, Brother Tennyson, eyeing him and pointing to the vacancy, obviously unaware of Riley's interview with the bishop.

During the last verse of the hymn, Riley walked to the door, closed it for the invocation, and sat down on the metal folding chair placed next to it. He thought of every possible way to avoid being seen refusing the sacrament, but now here he was on the raised steps next to the door. He considered pretending to go out to investigate a disturbance in the foyer and coming back later. The problem was, the deacon might follow him or come back as soon as Riley reappeared.

After the bread was blessed, there was the deacon right in front of him, a clear-eyed boy one year Riley's junior who absently climbed the four stairs to Riley's station. When Riley indicated *no* to him from his chair, the boy misunderstood and was soon standing next to him, his fingers curled around the handle of the silver tray with the torn pieces of bread in it.

"No, thank you," Riley said. The deacon looked at him, confused. Riley said it again a little louder. Brother Stinson looked over to see what the disturbance was. Aware that there was an unexpected monkey wrench in the works, the deacon stumbled backward on the stair like a confused steer backing out of a slaughter chute.

Riley was sure everyone had seen him refuse the emblems of the Lord's suffering. In embarrassment he picked up his scriptures, which church members dutifully carry to meetings, and opened them. Gus liked to talk about the Book of Mormon and how Joseph Smith said it was the cornerstone of their religion. Maybe it was time Riley should read it, as he had promised Gus he would after being baptized at age eight. The humiliation of having to refuse the sacrament still burning his cheeks, he looked down and flipped through the columns of verses.

Up until then, Riley had only ever read the first page on his own, which began with Nephi lionizing his parents: "I, Nephi," it began, "having been born of goodly parents …" He had read that page about thirty times, and each time he had become bored and moved on to the book's illustrations of beautifully muscled men in kilts and no tops and svelte women in gauzy robes. He had written down a few words in his notebook from the captions but had neglected to look them up.

Now he turned to the Book of Alma, the longest section and one that Gus frequently talked about, wherein an ancient Nephite prophet worries about his son, Alma junior, who was in the business of persecuting believers. An angel strikes the son one day, so that "Alma the younger" is comatose for three days. When he wakes up, he explains that he had been in a purgatory "racked … with inexpressible horror," but now, after fully wrestling with his demons, he was converted to the Gospel of Christ.

This was *his* story, Riley thought as he re-read the passage. He was the oldest son of Nelson Hartley, a man of God currently at work on a book for Latter-day Saints. His father regularly lectured at the Lord's university down the hill, and he, Riley, had fallen into a sin that was second only to murder. Sex outside of marriage—with other boys, no less—was "heinous," the prophet had said.

Riley concentrated on the "inexpressible horror" phrase, the hardness of it, which summed up how he felt. He began to sweat. By the time the bishop announced the closing hymn, he was convinced he had hurt every member of the congregation in some metaphysical way by his egregious misbehavior. The congregation was enveloped in a dark shade, tainted by the disembodied presence of his foul deeds.

As the ward sang *The Spirit of God Like a Fire Is Burning*, Riley felt like an outsider. Brother Tennyson had advised him to set goals. He would read the Book of Mormon before he got out of eighth grade, he decided. He would pray when he was tempted to abuse himself. "The natural man is an enemy of God," the Book of Mormon read.

He soon found that praying to resist temptation placed the temptation forefront in his mind. Plus, being in the attitude of prayer not only put him inconveniently doubled up so his eyes were near his crotch, he sometimes poked out of his boxer shorts when he knelt down. When Brother Tennyson gave them a lesson on morality and distributed a pamphlet titled *For Young Men Only*, Riley learned that sperm production speeds up when you tamper with the equipment, like opening and closing the valves at a factory. The pamphlet instructed boys to imagine their thoughts taking place on a stage, their job being to keep uninvited characters from showing up and upstaging everybody else. They were to memorize a favorite hymn and sing it to themselves whenever they felt tempted by those shady rogues who shamefully emerged out of the wings to turn a church production into a burlesque.

Riley decided to write every verse of *I Need Thee Every Hour* on a poster board and tape it to the wall opposite his bed.

"I liked your ski poster better," said Cade as he looked at the new handwritten addition to their decor. "Why not something from *Saturday's Warrior*?" he complained, referring to the local musical he had been cast in that had the snappy score. Suddenly Cade was feeling both spiritual *and* hip, Riley noticed.

Cade would not be given any information about why Riley took down the Rossignol poster. It was enough for Riley to know for himself that this was his contribution to his forever family. He felt like he was doing pretty well with his abstinence until one Saturday in May just before school got out when he was at Eric's house, playing with a new portable cassette player, and his friend's sister, Trenese, asked them to hold a sun lamp over her and her big-breasted friend, Carolee, and move it from feet to heads at thirty-second intervals. The girls positioned themselves on the floor in slight bikinis, with wet cotton balls on their eyes.

The exercise produced an explosion of hormones, and Riley had to excuse himself to go to the bathroom, but not to read the Book of Mormon. When he got home, he lay on his bed and wept. In his mental theater, he had been upstaged by Carolee's breasts, and afterward every indiscretion of his past life had flooded into the orchestra seats to heckle him. "No unclean thing can enter the kingdom of heaven," he heard someone say from First Nephi chapter ten.

Riley needed an intercession, I decided, so I brought in his great-great grandfather from Old Mexico and left the old bearded fellow in the living room where Riley would dream about him papering the walls. When the modern Riley appeared, the former Riley would hand him a brush that was oozing with paste. "Get to work," he would say, before turning back to his own wall. "What would it be like to accompany one's great-great-grandson in a task as simple as that?" I asked Verus, but he thought I was meddling again.

"You shouldn't care," Verus said. "It will only come to grief. Hang it up, Zed."

I wish I could, but I know I can't. I've become fond of the kid.

13 | VIRGINS AT THE TEMPLE DOOR

Grandpa Charles, "Chaz" as Gram liked to call him, was a bald widower-in-shining-armor from Portland who, with a post-polio leg, had limped into Gram's life, and into the lives of the Hartley family, with the good-humored generosity of a TV dad. He wasn't exactly jovial, but he had a dry sense of humor that made Gram smile.

"The Brethren aren't pleased when a woman remarries after her husband's death," Gus confided his reservations about his mother-in-law's plans to his son. "A man can have another woman sealed to him in a temple marriage, but not the other way around." It was because polygamy was the law of heaven, Gus explained to Riley.

The temple was the family's Mt. Sinai—not where they went to church on Sundays, but the edifice that hosted special secret ceremonies. The one in Provo was practically in their back yard at the mouth of the canyon below the cliff where legend had it an Indian from the Timpanogos tribe threw herself off a ledge to appease the gods. The temple was built in a modernist style in the early seventies to look something like an inverted thumbtack, its huge glass-and-concrete panels forming an oval that brought to mind the tier of a wedding cake. It had an enormous gold steeple on it that, at night with floodlights on it, looked like a radioactive carrot. This was "the House of the Lord," meaning where Mormons believed the Lord dwells when he comes to earth and where rituals are performed in his presumed presence.

Lucy was sitting outside with Riley and the younger children the day their new grandpa and his bride, their grandma, got married inside. A water fountain sprayed in a timed sequence like the fountains at Caesar's Palace in Las Vegas. Riley had been allowed into the temple once, at age twelve, to be baptized for deceased non-Mormons who had not had the opportunity to be baptized when they were alive. Dressed in white, he had held the arms and hands of the officiator who, in the presence of two witnesses, had immersed Riley sixty times at a fast pace for sixty different dead people. There were stories of spirits of the dead observing the proceedings, but tragically Riley couldn't get the water out of his eyes long enough to see if it were true.

Adults who had received another temple ordinance, the mysterious endowment, were the only ones who could witness a marriage, so the three older girls had gone to pick flowers despite Gram's half-hearted protest at being treated like a young bride. Lucy—who was a temple virgin like Riley—was telling him that prior to receiving one's endowments, you had to be washed and anointed, some married girlfriends had told her.

"What do they wash?" he asked Lucy. She seemed especially radiant that morning in the July sun.

"Your body of course," said Lucy.

"Every part of it?"

"It's a symbolic washing, Riley. I'm sure they don't get out a bar of Lava soap and scrub you down." Riley winced.

DREAM HOUSE ON GOLAN DRIVE

Lucy looked over at Jessica sitting on the lawn and piling grass on top of Agnes's head. "Jessica! I told you not to sit down when you're in your poofies!" she said, poofies being the little girl's formal dress with poofy sleeves. Agnes looked up with a grin, a wad of grass the size of a softball balanced on her head. A single blade stuck in a stream of mucous that glistened below her nose.

"What is the anointing? Is that like when Dad uses oil on people's heads when they're sick?"

Lucy straightened her own dress, a shirtwaist acetate-and-polyester garment that barely contained her strong figure. She wasn't comfortable dressing up. If sandals and a robe were good enough for Jesus, they should be good enough for everyone, she liked to say. She changed the subject and pointed out a rock climber on Squaw Peak.

Riley looked up, squinting, but couldn't see anything.

"You're such a DRAG, Riley." She shaded her eyes with her hand. "He's wearing climbing pants that come down to the knees … and a helmet."

Riley noticed his brother and sister on their way back from a walk around the temple. Cade had taught Winnie the songs from his musical, the first act of which took place in the pre-mortal state, everyone dressed in ghostly white. The show had turned out to be such a hit that there were rumors it would move from the high school auditorium to a regional tour. Cade and Winnie had been singing for weeks. Jody taught Cade how to apply stage makeup. For some reason this newfound sophistication made him more annoying than usual.

Lucy was still enraptured by the climber, who was using a rope and crampons. With her hand shading her eyes, the breeze threading through her hair, she looked like she was about to take flight.

Riley missed having her live with them even though she was loud and competitive and sharp. She was also indisputably her own self and not afraid to show her flaws, like the time she dressed up like a man for the BYU homecoming dance. She wanted to protest the differences in dress standards, that men didn't have to "prettify" themselves with special hairdos and makeup. She asked Riley his opinion on perplexing things sometimes. He rarely had an opinion unless it was something his mother had said about a topic. It flattered him to have Lucy around, like having an older brother, but more than that.

"Riley, do you think I should marry Leslie?" she said, referring to a long-time friend who wanted to be a geologist. She lowered her hand and sighed, looking back the opposite way toward the valley.

"I don't know," he said. "He seems a little weird."

"I've told him that maybe, if he changes his name, we can talk about it," she said.

Riley shook his head and felt like he was shaking it for everyone in the family. They had argued with Lucy about how superficial it was to reject a man's proposal because his name was Leslie. What Riley wanted to say, but couldn't, was that she was too good for him. His interest in rocks was boring. What could he contribute to a relationship with Lucy?

"I'm serious about that," Lucy said. "I would rather throw myself off Squaw Peak than marry a man named Leslie." She looked at him and laughed. "If I can change my name from Bertha to Lucy, well … so can he, I guess. I wonder if Iron Butterfly is still around? Do you think Neil Diamond would come here to perform?" She started singing, "I am, I said. I am, I criiiiied" in her best Neil Diamond voice.

Riley could not speak. It was hard to keep up with Lucy's distracted interests.

"I've never really told this to anyone, Rile," she continued. "You know how Nelson says marriage is so important, the Lord … you know, the Lord will give you some kind of confirmation on who is Mr. Right? Well, that hasn't happened. I keep thinking eternity is a long time to be with someone, especially if they turn out to be a DRAG. I've been praying for it, but …" She smiled and took his hand in hers. "Will you marry me, Riley?" she said. "Even if you do think it's too expensive to feed me?"

Riley stood there holding her hand like he was conducting an experiment with electrical currents. It was in jest, but it made his heart assert itself against his breastbone to think she had remembered his comment about feeding her. He felt sorry for it, sorrier than for anything he had ever said or done up to that time, including getting caught by the bishop being intimate with Paris. And the other issue too: Lucy as his wife?

She laughed at Riley's confusion. He looked down embarrassed.

"You're a good kid," she said. "Your father and mother are proud of you."

"They are?" he said, looking back at her.

"It will be a lucky girl who marries you," she said. "You're going to be even more spiritual than your dad. I wish my parents were like yours. I tease your parents, but they're my models for living. Did you know that?" She had never been this serious with

Riley before, and he was unsure how to react. It felt like he was off-script and ad-libbing.

"I guess Leslie's not bad," he said at last. "I'm sure he'd make a good husband for you, even if he's a little quiet." Lucy raised an eyebrow at him and frowned. He added a little sheepishly, "For you, I mean."

"Who, me? Are you saying I'm loud?" She let go of Riley's hand and mocked herself in an exaggerated way with two pointed fingers.

Now *he* laughed out loud. "You're not obnoxious, Lucy Barclay," he blurted. "You're … wonderful, you're one of the best things that ever happened to our family. To me."

Now it was her turn to be startled. "Why is that?" she demanded.

"I don't know." He looked away. The screams and laughter of his sisters punctured the steady hissing of the fountain. He loved his little sisters. At the same time, he pitied them, they were so tiny. There was no way to keep them from getting older either.

"You make me feel like it's okay to be myself," he ventured, "that I don't have to be perfect." He looked at her face, framed by a borealis of hair pinned behind her ears. She listened intently. She had pegged herself as obnoxious when really she was intrepid. This was why he loved her. She spoke the truth about herself and other people and got away with it.

Suddenly Winnie started jumping up and down, pointing at the temple door where Gram was waving, her face aglow between her clip-on earrings. Grandpa Chaz, with his funny little face, was ambling along the sidewalk, Joan and Gus in tow. The three older girls were pulling into the parking lot at that moment. Candace irreverently honked the horn when they saw Gram and her new husband. The younger girls and Cade all ran to greet their grandparents. Riley began to walk in that direction until he noticed that Lucy hadn't moved.

"Aren't you coming?" he said.

She held back, standing there in her flat sandals and plain dress that was pulled up too tight under her arms. The sunshine filtered through the fountain water and sprayed behind her like a bridal veil. "In a minute," she said. "I can watch for a minute."

14 | ON HIGH

Every year at least one of the out-of-state college students becomes enraptured by the beautiful mountains surrounding the valley and heads to the cliffs, only to fall to their death. Crumbling and unreliable, the rock face can be treacherous for the uninitiated. The glacier on Mount Timpanogos is equally dangerous. One year three students fell into the same crevasse on successive days—plop, plop, plop like billiard balls in the corner pocket. I ministered to the first two but gave up after that. Foolish people!

I became obsessed with the theater in New York when I was living there in the late 1880s. Since then I've subscribed to the *New York Times* to keep up on things even though I'm originally from Central America. There's a story today in the city section about a man who was holding his baby niece next to a window on the fourteenth floor and leaned too heavily into the window. It gave way, and *whooosh*, they both fell to the ground. The cause of death was the verticality of New York City. I guess you can hardly blame people for wanting to get a nice view. Gus liked to tell Riley, when they inched along the ledge at the top of Mt. Timpanogos, that "if you slip, remember to look to the left because that's where the view is."

Eventually, Lucy could no longer wait for the loftier view of a marriage confirmed by the SPIRIT, so she married Leslie based on her best hunch. She confided to Riley a little later that part of the temple ceremony involved receiving a secret name that God would know you by when you died. For married people, the husband was forbidden to tell anyone, including his own wife, what his new name was, but the wife disclosed hers to her husband. Leslie had assured Lucy that his temple name was "kind of sexy." She would have to take it on faith.

As for Riley, it was time to begin the mid-day religious instruction called seminary that Mormon youth received in a building across the street from school. Seminary was like Sunday school—the curriculum was similar—just less stuffy. The teachers were men who had served missions and believed that "learning the gospel can be F-U-N!" The cheery advertising for the elective classes ranged from bulletin boards that turned on pop bromides to afternoon barbeques in nearby Provo Canyon. There were the screenings of religious movies like *The Ten Commandments* and scripture chase, a frantic competitive game in which teams raced against each other to locate chapters and verses of key scriptures in their red-penciled copies of the holy books.

The teachers were the most seductive part of the program. They were all sensitive, sympathetic men whose job was to help angst-ridden adolescent students understand that when you heard something religious and cried, it was due to the prompting of the Holy Ghost. Sometimes these blustery men would mention outrageously apocryphal stories about, for instance, three Nephites who supposedly wouldn't taste death and performed heroic deeds for needy mortals. Stories that made me blush. You would think I'd sleep through seminary, but I had to be on guard, for the good of my young charge, due to the effervescent siren songs of those teachers wooing young people like they were signing up recruits for the military.

In ninth grade Riley had Brother Bestor, a rookie who was full of innovative ideas to make the Old Testament as memorable as possible. When they studied Noah and the flood, he walked into class bare-footed and led them outside to show, based on trees and building tops, how large the ark would have been. Other times he would play songs from rock groups like Bread and talk through misty eyes about the meaning of friendship and the regret one can feel for mistreating someone, especially if that someone were to suddenly die.

He explained that the world was six thousand years old. The reason for this was because it was the reckoning of the Old Testament, and there were fossils and dinosaur bones because God had put the earth together with chunks of material from other planets. Sometimes Brother Bestor would play a saxophone and tell jokes like,

> *When are cigarettes first mentioned in the Bible?*
> *When Rachel lit off her camel.*

He explained that the SPIRIT gives you a tingling sensation, a chill up your spine or, as the Doctrine and Covenants says, "a burning in your bosom." Every few weeks students were asked to bear testimony to their feelings in extemporaneous outpourings of emotion, often accompanied by tears.

"How many of you felt the SPIRIT during Angela's testimony?" asked Brother Bestor one day after Angela, still sniffling in her seat, had concluded her stirring narrative about a cousin's recent

DREAM HOUSE ON GOLAN DRIVE

death. The students looked around the room at each other, then back at Brother Bestor, who was sitting on the edge of a table, his shirt sleeves rolled up, the scoop-neck of his temple garments luminous under his shirt. He looked so scrubbed, his ears glowed. Slowly, a girl to Riley's left raised her hand. Brother Bestor looked at her thoughtfully.

"Tell us what you felt, Stacey," he said in a hushed tone. Stacey swallowed hard and explained how, when Angela reported that she knew her cousin had been called home for a reason, there was a tingling in her hands and up the back of her neck, almost like a shiver.

"That was the Holy Ghost, Stacey! Thank you for sharing that," said Brother Bestor, casting his eyes about until he fastened his gaze on Riley, who had recently lost respect for this man. The week before, Brother Bestor had found a Winchell's donut bag in a toilet stall and had laughingly mimed how he imagined some lost soul had eaten jelly-filled donuts while using the bathroom.

"Riley, how about you?" Brother Bestor said. "Have you felt any special things during our meeting thus far?"

Riley was not feeling particularly cooperative. In his biology class that morning, during a discussion on anatomy, he raised his hand to say his sister was born with three kidneys. The teacher, Mr. Stone, explained how an adrenal gland was attached to each kidney and asked if Candace got extra excited over things for that reason. Hyrum Calder, who was in Riley's ward, piped up and said, "She gets real fired up, depending on who she's with." That drew laughs.

Riley looked at Brother Bestor, whose first name was Ben. "I've had those feelings when I listen to music, Ben," he offered. Brother Bestor nodded appreciatively.

82

"Music does have that effect on us," he said. "Remember, the Lord says in the Doctrine and Covenants that 'the song of the righteous is a prayer unto me.'"

"I was thinking of the Doobie Brothers," said Riley. The class laughed. Brother Bestor's ears turned red as he gave Riley his forced "isn't the gospel F-U-N" smile. Testimony time was suddenly over and the closing prayer was given.

"Riley," Brother Bestor said as the class was dismissing. "Would you mind slipping into my office for a minute?"

"You know, I was just kidding about the Doobie Brothers," Riley told him. He stood and collected his books.

"I know you were upset with me last week when I was joking about the donut bag." He was right, of course. Riley had been upset. "Riley, we all have to laugh once in a while."

"Well, I thought it was crude," Riley countered, some boldness spiking in him.

"I don't think a seminary teacher needs to act too prissy."

"You're supposed to be an example," Riley said, calling up his best effort at righteous indignation.

Brother Bestor unrolled his shirt sleeves and buttoned his cuffs. "I know it must be hard to be Nelson Hartley's son," he said. "People think your dad is about to be taken to heaven any minute." He folded his arms across his chest and watched the last student exit. Gus had recently landed a half-hour radio show in which he delivered shortened versions of his talks.

"He's just a normal person."

"I know, but some people perceive him to be special."

"People are hungry for what the gospel is all about," Riley

continued, a mantle of hot purpose descending on him. "We should be getting revelation, like the prophets. That's what he says."

The words he was quoting from his father expanded in the air like a challenge. Goose pimples popped up on my arms and neck as if I were in a sudden chill myself. The kid was good! He would have done well in Nephite times.

Brother Bestor sighed. "Riley, this morning before school, Paris Carter came in to talk to me."

Riley looked at him closely. Kids sometimes confided in teachers like Brother Bestor, the closest thing they had to a professional clergy. Riley stood still in his new-found armor and stared back at his teacher, his heart beginning to pound. "Paris has problems," Riley said.

"I know you're friends with him."

"We're not that close."

"He said that when he first got involved sexually, it was with some boys in his ward." Brother Bestor paused for a minute.

Of course, Riley wondered what Ben knew. Ever since the bishop talked to them, Paris had remained distant. One day they were working together on a poster for a health class and Paris confessed that he had fooled around with some BYU students. Riley asked him if he was scared. He said no. He said he liked it, that they did a lot of kissing.

"Is there anything you'd like to talk to me about?" Brother Bestor finally asked. "I told Paris I want him to bring in his magazines and I'd help him dispose of them." Two students for the next class suddenly appeared in the room.

"I have to go," Riley told him.

"Riley, I think you're right about Paris being a troubled young man."

Riley walked out the door, down the short hall and outside, crossed the street, and entered the school yard. He could feel his ears burning up.

As I traipsed after him, I felt even airier that usual, sort of proud that my charge had the nerve to stand up to his teacher. I think he felt lighter too, as if he'd just dropped his books and might lift off the ground any second and float like a helium balloon past the windows of the junior high school, over the tarred roof where I could see a Frisbee, a flattened volleyball, and a pair of girls' faded pink panties. I could imagine Riley floating off toward the Wasatch Mountains to hover in the air like the Angel Moroni in Joseph Smith's bedroom and admire the view from there.

When Riley's sister Candace got pregnant, she was crushing her own bed of random leaves right along with her brother. Where Riley's voodoo leaf-stomping would guarantee exaltation in the celestial kingdom, hers was an attempt to guarantee her mother's love. She would be a mother, too.

The baby's father was Sam, a boy in the same high school class as Candace. Since fornicators are not allowed to marry in the temple, their marriage was solemnized behind the dream house in a garden wedding. Candace exhibited a curious fortitude through it all. During the ceremony, through the warmth of her beaded bodice, she emitted a look of satisfaction as if to say to Joan, *I can be just like you.* The fact was, however, even when grandchild number one came screaming through THE VEIL into the second estate that was earthly life, Candace was still only one tenth of the former Miss Utah, mother of ten.

For Labor Day the forever family went to Kiwanis Park to have a picnic. Even though they numbered seven in all, the family felt decimated. Riley was the oldest of the siblings now. Candace was with Sam. Muriel and Jody were old enough to be elsewhere working, studying, dating. Gus was in Mexico as a guest lecturer for a touring group. The outfit he was with believed the ancient utopian city of Zarahemla spoken of in the Book of Mormon was in present day Chiapas.

Joan told Riley about a little girl who fell recently at Dead Horse Point and how Brother Stewart, a ward member, had witnessed it. "There wasn't a scream or anything. There was another little girl there, around seven or eight, who looked just like the one who fell. Brother Stewart didn't know if the two were twins, but they were both dressed in little German dresses."

Riley wasn't sure what a German dress looked like, but he nodded anyway. He knew the drop at Dead Horse Point, down to the Colorado River, was about two thousand feet.

"He actually got there moments after it happened," Joan continued, caught up in the horror of her own story. "They had to keep the mother from going over the rail herself." She and Riley were sitting at the table while she poked at the last of the potato salad with a plastic fork. Nearby, Cade was trying to teach the younger girls how to throw a Frisbee. "I don't know how long it took them to find the body," Joan said. She put down the fork and stared into space.

Riley's mother had never been the energetic type, as long as Riley had known her, but with eight of ten kids home and the Tutu Ballet School she and Jody ran downstairs, she was exhausted now most of the time. It had been a particularly hard year. Riley came home from school most days to find her lying on her back in the middle of the living room floor. "Cade, could you watch Susan for the next hour?" she might say, directing traffic from her back. "Riley, would you help Winnie with her science project? Does anyone know where the masking tape is?"

Joan looked at her own two girls on the grass. Jessica threw the Frisbee perpendicularly at the ground. Even at her better attempts, she looked like she was bowling. "Imagine what a tiny body looks like after falling from that height," she continued. Riley shuddered.

"Would you like some more potato salad?" she said, as if food and the mangled body of a girl were a good pairing. Since Candace's pregnancy, Joan's longstanding interest in morbid stories had escalated. Two days earlier she had talked about a woman in Grandview who left her baby in the car while she ran into the post office. The baby got tangled in some dry-cleaning plastic and suffocated.

"How is swimming going, Riley?" Joan asked off-handedly, as if she were still addressing the accident at Dead Horse Point. "Your dad and I hardly see you anymore." While she spoke, she surveyed her younger children playing. "Agnes! Stop that right now!" she shouted. "You're going to tear your little sister's arm off. She's not big enough for that."

"It's okay, I guess," said Riley.

"When's your next race?" she asked, picking up the fork and stabbing it at the salad again.

"On Thursday at South High."

"Agnes, that's it," she yelled. "You come over here right now and sit down. I mean it. Get over … Oh just forget it. Chums, bring Susan here, will you?" The uncooperative Agnes began twirling around, her arms outstretched until she fell down on the grass and lay there looking up at the sky. Her mother returned to the conversation with Riley. "Isn't it the High School Olympics?"

"The *Junior* Olympics," he said. He had joined the team two years earlier and worked out with a team sponsored by BYU's indoor facility where they swam during the winter. He wanted to be the next John Nabor, the backstroke champion, except that his best event had proved to be the breast stroke.

"Well, I just wish we could go to these swimming things more often. Maybe I can go to the one in Murray. Chums, where's Susan?" She stood up again. "Chums, I asked you to keep an eye on her."

Riley caught a glimpse of his mother's underwear with the Masonic marks stitched into it. Receiving temple garments was a rite of passage he would undergo in a few years. He considered his mother, standing above him, her blonde hair frazzled and shining at the edges in the sunlight. He treasured his time alone with her, especially since she seemed genuinely interested in what he was doing, as opposed to his father's cursory interest. He wondered how long the conversation with his mother would last before he fell off her radar and she was pulled in another direction entirely.

"Have you heard from Lucy?" he asked her. Back on the radar screen, he had returned as a momentary pulsing blip.

"She called last week. They're moving to Orem because they get more for their money there," she said, followed by, "Chums, I can see Susan over by the restrooms." She pointed her finger and pumped her arm twice in the direction of the low-slung building. "Bring her back, will you? Riley and I will keep an eye on her."

Joan was in her element, in Mormon *medias res*, plugging holes in domestic dikes while appearing ever-so-lovely in her middle-class fashion sense. Unlike the scowling grandmas from Eastern Europe who wore babushkas, women here had to look smart in polyester while they managed old-world-sized families on traditional-sized budgets. In her giant Miss Utah scrapbook at home were pictures of her in bathing suits with a little fabric panel where her legs came together. She looked more like a movie star than a mother. Did she ever wish she still looked like that? Did she wish she had shoulder-length hair, eyebrows done up, her feet in high-heels and placed carefully in fourth position, her smile so assured she assumed she would look fine if the whole world were looking at her?

He turned around just in time to see Chums, the retriever, tugging at Susan's arm.

"I told you not to make her cry!" yelled Joan.

Every time Riley thought his mother was about to lose it, he could see her steel herself resolutely. It was as if she were driving her emotions into a deep bed of hidden coals that had nowhere to burn except down into a kind of bedrock. It made him want to protect her, and he felt guilty for wanting to monopolize her attention.

She sat back and sighed, looking at the hastily eaten meal lying in ruins, a chicken wing stuck to a paper napkin and fallen off the table.

"They're in Yellowstone right now, aren't they?" Riley asked.

"Yes, and she's due the same time as Candace."

This was the first time his mother had mentioned the impending birth of Candace's child. Riley understood that she was angry at Candace for embarrassing the family because Riley felt that contempt too. He could hardly talk to her when she came over, and he wondered why they had even bothered having a reception. The Doorly boy didn't have one when Eddie's girlfriend became pregnant two weeks before he was supposed to enter the Mission Training Center. The stake president had asked Gus if he should release him from his student ward responsibilities "until the whole thing blew over." "No, we're getting through it," he had said, but reputations had been imperiled.

"Leslie wants to finish up at school next year," said Joan. "He'll go on for a master's degree. Lucy says she wonders if she'll make a good mother. She calls to ask what I think the future holds every time she hears something on Paul Harvey or reads another book."

"She listens to Paul Harvey?"

"She was telling me she doesn't know what she'll say to her baby when he starts dating."

"What? It's not even born yet!"

"You muck your way through it, is what you do," his mom said. "You just keep the commandments and hope for the best." Riley could tell his mother was thinking of Candace. "That's what it means to have a testimony."

The conversation was turning into a catechism, which wasn't what Riley wanted. "Lucy thinks you and Dad are perfect."

"Not true, although that's what we're striving for."

"She wasn't happy when her parents couldn't see her get married. She thought that being Presbyterian wasn't any reason for them to be kept out of the temple."

"She knows the rules," Joan countered.

"It doesn't seem fair," Riley said. In fact, he was the one who thought Lucy's parents should have been allowed to see the wedding. It was a moment when Lucy could have shined in the presence of her disapproving parents. Locking them out of the building added to their pique, and there wasn't even anyone there to answer their questions about what was going on inside. Riley had to stand with them and look dumb while the girls chased each other around the grounds.

"Well, if that's the way Lucy feels about it, even *after* being to the House of the Lord, then something's wrong. She was always a little headstrong."

"I like her."

There was a pause. Then his mother turned to him and said, "Lucy has had a troubled life, you know. She had an afro, sandals, and everything that goes with it before she joined the church."

"It shouldn't matter after you're baptized."

"It's our job to be good examples," Joan continued. "She's a good woman, don't get me wrong, but she needs direction. And she needs to remain teachable."

His mother was right, although instead of "teachable" she meant "tractable," controllable. Lucy wasn't anything a mother should be. She was distracted and brash in expressing her objections to things. She should be more dutiful, thought Riley. As a member of the church, she shouldn't let the church look foolish. She should protect it, not criticize it. Gus told Lucy she was trying too hard to merge the gospel with the world. *The Lord wants us in the world but not of it*, Gus said to her.

"It has to be grounded in reality," Lucy had replied, forcefully. Riley didn't understand that. To him, the gospel was the *real* reality and everything else was counterfeit.

When they loaded up the car, Agnes was cross and started crying incessantly. Chums was out of sorts too because she wanted to sit in the front, but Cade had gotten there first. Chums was taking it out on Jessica, who was preoccupied with repeatedly pulling her gum out of her mouth in a long string.

"Don't!" Chums said every time Jessica swung the gooey strand near her face. Cade was trying to get KRSP on the radio. Winnie was pouting over not having been allowed to go to her friend Kristin's house for a sleepover. Riley was in the second row of the van, the family Volkswagen they called the Green Loaf. It was cluttered, noisy, and humid with family needs. Baby Susan had crawled into Riley's arms and fallen asleep. Her eyelids were still partly open so that he could see her vacant eyes, as if they were marbles.

He wondered how Gus was doing in Mexico. Was he near Colonia Juárez, where Grandpa Riley had taken his wives to hide? Gus showed him on a map, his thick finger tracing his route. Riley had forgotten where Colonia Juárez was, but he remembered his father's finger pointing it out.

Once Gus took Riley and Cade to San Diego to a beach that turned out to be nudist. A topless woman with nipples the size of silver dollars strolled by while they were spreading out their towels. The family was in southern California so Gus could speak to the wards that had invited him. Evenings were spent dressed in Sunday clothes and sitting in chapels smelling of varnished wood and people's cologne. Gus had grown up in Arizona on a farm where he used to dangle his rubber boots into the irrigation canal to keep his feet cool. He was probably telling stories like that right now, Riley thought as he shifted the baby's head to the other arm. Gus inspired everyone with his stirring testimony and his tears about how the Book of Mormon had changed the life of a young farm boy.

They ascended the hill to their neighborhood, and Riley noticed the almost inaccessible Squaw Peak overlook. "Mom," he said, "how would they retrieve someone's body after it fell off a cliff? Like the girl at Dead Horse Point. How did they get her back up top?"

Joan was resting her hand on the knob of the long stick shift that rose from the floor of the van. She looked ill-at-ease and sometimes pumped the clutch and ground the gears with the same ineptitude Riley had suffered during his weekly piano lesson with Sister Bennett. Despite his mother's determination at the wheel, she still looked pale and fearful.

"Helicopter, I guess," she said. "I don't know."

Candace delivered baby Clayton four weeks early. The proud father thought it was funny to show up at Primary Children's Hospital with bubble gum cigars. The Hartley kids posed with them like Groucho Marx until Joan discretely, when Sam wasn't looking, gathered up all the cigars and disposed of them. Riley noticed that Sam had started calling his wife Candy and that he used words like *hellacious*, which Riley couldn't find in the dictionary. "She just slays me," was something he said, which didn't seem to make any sense at all. Once when Gus's Chevy was on the blink, Sam, who since the baby had gone full-time at his father's auto shop, popped the hood, groused around for a bit, and exclaimed that it had "pretty good chops for a six banger."

Riley was the family's one-man taxi service and one of the best swimmers on his high school team, as well as a collector of words and phrases that now filled an entire notebook.

Lucy delivered her child nine months after the honeymoon. The infant was hardier than Candace's preemie, its fat legs pumping up and down when Lucy changed his diaper. He had a head of black hair like Lucy's. Almost every day Lucy came by toting Dryden and sat at the family's oval dinner table to breast-feed him. There were special temple garments under her blouse with slits for nursing. Between burpings, she had Riley give her samples from his word collection—*amanuensis* (a secretary who takes dictation), *arriviste* (a French word for someone who is ambitious), and *anomie* (lack of purpose, identity, or ethical values).

"One of my favorites is *lofty*," Lucy told him, a cloth barely covering her bosom, to Riley's stunned gaze as the upper curve of her breast rose and fell as she breathed. "Not necessarily because of what it means," she continued after making sure Riley couldn't watch, "but because it sounds like the nape of Dryden's neck." The baby could be heard slurping under the towel. "*Lofty* sounds like a hot air balloon flying in front of white billowy clouds. I even like saying the word," she said. "What else do you have for me, Rile?"

He opened the notebook to the first page. "Agitprop," he said, looking up.

"Which means?"

He read, "Serving to both agitate and propagandize, to excite public opinion."

"The anti-Mormons do agitprop all the time. What else?"

"Atavism."

"Meaning? No cheating, now close the book."

He closed it. Under the cloth, he could tell, Lucy was pinching her nipple like mothers do to improve the flow of milk.

"Resembling a remote ancestor," he said slowly.

"Is that it?" she interrupted.

"Just a minute. Resembling a remote ancestor," he repeated, "in some characteristic that nearer ancestors do not have. Reversion to a primitive type."

"Do you understand that?"

"Not really."

"Maybe that's why Dryden doesn't look anything like me or Leslie," she said, looking down at the baby, "except for the hair. Maybe his great-great-whatever had a ski-jump nose and fat legs. Maybe my Dad looked like this when he was born."

"That's hard to imagine."

"People are funny the way they coo and make a big poo-poo over infants, aren't they? Babies are pathetic looking—all red and squished and with that constipated look they have. They probably *are* constipated," she said, turning to Dryden, "aren't you, my little smudge of love with an overbite?"

The truth was, Dryden wasn't cute. He looked like Red Skelton, but Riley felt it was in his best interest to lie. "I think he's cute," he said. He put down his word book and thought about what it meant to create a person, to push a body out of one's own in a twisting helix of mind and body, like a prayer or a poem, spoken into existence. There had been so many pregnancies in the house, so many babies brought home to nurse, that Riley was used to it. But the picture of Lucy and her alternately sharp and warm comments endeared her to him and prompted a sense of wonder in Riley that spoke to the question that was life.

"Does it hurt to nurse?" he asked.

"It hurts wonderfully. It feels like a sprint at the end of a race, when you can't breathe—or when you have a sunburn and don't want anyone to touch your skin."

"It feels as lousy as *that*?" he said.

"Sometimes it's more like the memory of something, like you're on deck at the pool after a race and you think about the meaning you just gave to the lane, because otherwise it would just be an empty lane. It was so hard to do, you're not sure how you should feel."

Lucy carried Dryden into the living room and placed him on the flowered couch with the pink corner pillows, then adjusted herself under her shirt. Riley followed her and stood looking at the little form with its arms at right angles, fists like cream-colored knots in a maritime rope. "It's amazing to think he's going to grow up someday," she said, "and be big enough to go on a mission."

Lucy had changed since she gave birth. She sounded like all the other mothers now, with her cloying words like *special* and *blessed*. "Don't give me that face, you little Laman and Lemuel," she said, looking at Riley.

Riley rolled his eyes. He had said in seminary recently that he didn't know if he wanted to go on a mission. That statement alone elicited shock from the girls and produced its own reward in the amount of attention it generated. Everyone had just seen his father star in a church film that showed him mentoring a young man preparing for a mission, so it was a tender subject to Riley.

"I'm sure you're going to go," Lucy said.

"Not everybody goes. Look at Donny Osmond. He didn't," Riley said, standing his ground.

"Donny had a greater work to do through performing. What are you going to do instead?"

"The Osmonds suck," he huffed. He looked at Lucy to gauge her reaction. "I'm sick of hearing about mission calls," Riley added and walked over to the plate-glass window. It was mid-May and the leaves were still emerging on the Lombardy poplars Gus had planted along the back fence. Long lines of trees like that were sometimes the mark of pioneers who broke up the monotony of expansive farmland with visual aids. The trees on Golan Drive were more recent. Gus had planted them simply because he liked the way the tiny leaves sounded in the wind. For him, they recalled his family's ranch near Thatcher, Arizona, where every ditch and every road seemed to be marked by the tall thin sentries with the hiss of the ocean in them.

In front of the trees, Riley could see Agnes's Big Wheel half buried in the sand box. He wondered what little girl drama had brought the tricycle to such a state.

"Someday Riley, you'll be sitting on a cloud with your harp ..."

"On a cloud?"

"I'm speaking figuratively. You'll be sitting there and an angel will float by and ask you where you went on your mission, and you'll feel dumb. You'll have to say, oh I didn't go because Donny Osmond didn't."

"Why did you join the church anyway?" he asked Lucy with a start, turning back around. He was finished talking about missions.

"That's a funny question. Because it's true, of course."

"And now you live the PROGRAM, right? Whatever they tell you to do, even though you didn't before?"

"You have to live your life. It makes sense to me now."

"What if you don't fit in?" Riley was thinking of Paris Carter, whose life had gotten more difficult since he started seeing doctors to cure him of his homosexuality. He had been replaced as the ward organist and had moved in with the Jensens down the street. Paris and his dad weren't getting along. Riley had seen the small bottle Paris's psychiatrist had given him, with an unguent he was supposed to sniff when he got aroused. The doctor said it would help him resist temptation. In February, Paris had dropped out of school. Riley could have been like that. He could have gotten mixed up with some college students and turned out like Paris, batting his eyes like a girl.

"If you don't fit in, you change, you repent."

"That's not what you did. You've always questioned everything. You said they kicked you out of a religion class at BYU."

"Brother McKinney wouldn't answer my questions," she said, then more abruptly, "You want to know why I joined the church, Rile? Because I heard something true. Where did our spirits come from, for instance? What's the point of everything?" She walked toward him. "Do you know how lucky you are?" She stopped talking for a minute, breathing hard. "Every time I wonder if the gospel is … a *hoax*," the word taking her breath and causing Riley's heart to pound, "I try to imagine what it would be like without it. There is a *feeling* of belonging I can't get anywhere else. I know you and your family aren't going to give up on me."

"What *feeling* are you talking about?" he demanded. "And don't give me that story about a tingling up your spine, some natural feeling everyone thinks is supernatural," he said, his voice rising. Dryden started to cry. Riley had forgotten about him. Lucy walked back to the couch and bounced the baby on her shoulder for several minutes while shushing him, keeping her back to Riley. The tiny body shuddered as it fell back into a fitful sleep.

"A lot of times I don't fit in, Riley. I feel awkward and wonder why I can't just see things the way Mormons do who were born into the church," said Lucy. "Then I start asking questions, all kinds of questions, anything that pops into my head. I believe the Lord provides answers, usually through someone else. Someone like your folks who have more faith than I do." She turned around and faced him. "When I was trying to decide if I should marry Leslie, I finally realized I wasn't going to get a clear confirmation, so I did what I thought was right. That's when, as you say it, I got the feeling in my spine."

"You got the answer *after* you married him? Well, that makes perfect sense."

"It's true, though. Nelson reminded me of the fact that 'faith precedes the miracle.'" She paused for a moment, cradling the infant in her arms. "I never told anyone in your family this, not even your Mom, but when I was …" she swallowed hard, "… on the road with Monk, I had missed two periods and we went to a clinic in Philadelphia, and I let them take care of it." Her eyes were misting over.

Riley felt angry at himself for pushing the issue.

"I came here to find myself, but I felt lost until I heard Nelson speak at a fireside meeting. It was like a light turned on in my head. I thought maybe I could be pure again. That maybe there was hope." She put her cheek next to the sleeping baby's and gently rocked. She seemed transformed.

"Your life isn't over when you decide to be a Latter-day Saint," she said. "If you live the gospel, it *is* life, it's day-to-day like for everyone else, or at least that's how it feels. I don't know what I'd do without the church, though," she said, wiping a tear from her eye.

There was a brief pause. Despite his discomfort at having rattled Lucy, Riley was still annoyed to hear her talk to him as if he were a lost soul. One time he had a fantasy that she had come into his room and kissed him while Cade was asleep. Her mouth tasted like concord grapes, the tough dusty jackets that, when crushed between your teeth, gave forth a burst of tart, then sweet juice before you hit hard seed. What did Leslie know about this woman who had slept in the bedroom adjacent to Riley's for over two years before her marriage?

Lucy sighed. "Someone told me it can be harder to live by what you know than to fly to something new. It's easier to keep looking for something because you're not responsible for what you already know is true. It's good to be loyal to what you know."

Everyone at church was always talking that way, about what they *knew* to be true, when what they actually meant was that they *believed* these things. When they stood up and said they knew *beyond a shadow of a doubt*, they didn't! At least Riley didn't. One thing Riley did know. If he didn't have a "testimony," if he was not valiant in this life, he would pay some kind of terrible price for it. And not just in the hereafter.

It was several months before the first grandchild could be named and blessed at church. While Clayton was improving and stabilizing, Candace had to explain to her younger sisters what the extra part was between the infant's legs. It had been some time since the house had seen a baby boy. The girls looked on in wonder, as if Clay were the baby Jesus himself, except anatomically correct.

The blessing took place at Sam's and Candace's ward where theirs was not the only extended family to witness a begowned and wailing offspring blessed. But at eighteen, Candace was the youngest mother there, only two years older than Riley and already fixed with a quizzical look that would deepen into a persistent sadness over time.

At the appointed moment, she handed Clay off to Sam, who was dressed awkwardly in one of his father's wide patterned ties. He and Gus walked to the front. Sam held the bundle like it was a football he had just intercepted. At the podium, to the side of the lectern, some other men joined in forming a circle, each one with a hand under the infant and another hand on the shoulder of the man next to him. With their heads bowed in prayer, the suited group bounced the baby up and down to keep him from fussing while Gus offered the blessing.

Afterward they patted each other on the back and parted so that Sam could hold up the child for everyone to see. The congregation warmly *ahhhed* at the new arrival, fresh from the presence of God. Sam returned to his seat in the back pew and wept, his tears streaking his face. Gus smiled approvingly, and it seemed that almost as quickly as Sam had been judged, he had been forgiven. It had been nearly a year since the civil marriage. If Sam and Candace passed their worthiness interview with their bishop, they could proceed to the temple soon and all would be forgotten.

Joan invited everyone to the house after the service, where she had a ham and hard rolls, potato chips, a relish plate, and two kinds of Jell-O salad. Grandpa Chaz and Gram were buzzing about the new condo they were decorating. Then there were Leslie, Lucy and Dryden, the whole little family having taken on Lucy's scuffled and chronically out-of-step look. Leslie was lanky, had a slight over-bite that made him look drifty, and had a nervous laugh. Even Dryden seemed out of place in nothing but a diaper and his drool.

Riley had so many words in his notebook, he had to buy a new one. He and Lucy would often share his new discoveries: *inchoate* (in partial operation or existence), *profligate* (abandoned to vice), *obfuscate* (to obscure or confuse), *unctuous* (oily, greasy, smug, given to a pretense of spiritual feeling). He decided the notebooks were embarrassing, something a child would do, and lacked context. He couldn't remember why he had written down any particular word or where he had encountered them. They were freestanding symbols. Yet, while reading a new book, he could not proceed from a page to the next until he learned the meaning of each unfamiliar word.

"I find it comforting," Lucy once said to him, "that God created the world by speaking it into existence, not by some seismic or evolutionary burp. When he said something's name, it appeared. At least, that's the way I like to think about it."

Even with the ballet lessons downstairs, the family was still seriously in debt. Gus had backed off of peddling insurance fulltime to work on his book. Two days after Christmas, he stood next to the sink in the kitchen and remarked to Riley and Jody that the family had overspent. God's promise to his tithe-paying children was that they would be provided for, he said, but he was still waiting for his return on the investment.

"Maybe we can take some of the presents back," offered Jody, thinking of Cade's forty-pound bow and Riley's stereo. She looked at Riley, who looked at Gus. At nearly twenty, the oldest yet to marry, Jody had become the arbiter of such things. Even Mom and Gus relied on her.

Gus looked down thoughtfully, his arms folded across his chest. "Would you be embarrassed if you had to give the stereo back?" he asked Riley. It was something Riley had wanted for more than a year. He was thrilled when he saw it in the living room on Christmas morning, in its square plastic dust cover, all set up for him and sitting on the Postum table with Elton John's *Greatest Hits* album. He had shown it to his friends.

"It would be humiliating for him to tell people he had to give it back," Jody said.

Gus didn't say anything.

Later that week Joan called an emergency family meeting while Gus was at work. She rarely cried, but this day she did. Her father, she said, had died early because he was always worrying about money, and she was not going to let that happen to her husband.

Riley thought, while he boxed up his new stereo, of scratching one of the wood-veneer speakers so Sears might not take it back. Then he remembered his mother in the rocking chair, her eyes clouded with tears. How could he let his forever family down? What was right to do was what Mom wanted.

That spring, when his book was accepted for publication, Gus called the family together for a special prayer of thanks. He hoped the book, which explored how every Latter-day Saint should be open to personal revelation from God, would lift them out of debt. Everyone was there, even Sam, Candace, and the baby. Jody had decided to quit BYU because of its draconian insistence that coeds not wear pants and inflexibility on class options. "I marched in there and told them I hated it and wanted my money back," she reported to Joan earlier that week. Jody laughed about the woman behind the counter who couldn't believe an LDS girl would say such things about the Lord's university. Jody was feeling better, having made up her mind, but as they assembled in the living room to pray, something was wrong with her. She was animated, but her thoughts were elsewhere.

Riley had once clocked Gus's praying at a record that was just shy of nine minutes. This time Gus was absorbed even more than usual and used extravagant words like *similitude*. How strange that every book and every sermon—every person's speech—was comprised of the same words in a different order, from the prophet's sermons to a prostitute's proposal. Everyone drew from the same lexicon. Something as profound as *Othello* was made up of a string of words like the ones his father used.

In Gus's book, *Christ Talks to You*, he expressed every hope he had held for the Hartley children. The book itself was their ticket out of debt. It was the way Cade and Riley would be supported on their missions. It was going to be the family college fund. Riley hoped some of the royalties would go toward a vacation, that they would take pictures of themselves in front of the Taj Mahal. For Joan, Gus's book would mean that after four years, she could close the Tutu school for good.

The day after the celebratory prayer, Jody announced to her mother that she was going on a mission. "I've talked to the bishop about it," she reported, "and I'm preparing my papers."

Riley had just made a bologna sandwich and was passing through the front hall when he overheard this.

"Your papers?" said Joan, nearly dropping a pile of little girl parkas she was going to hang up.

"He said I'd be a good missionary," Jody said.

"But," Riley said, stopping to pick up a pickle that had fallen from his sandwich, "I thought I was going to be the first one on a mission." Joan was silent. She hung up the coats one-by-one in the closet hall, fingering the last one as if it represented every last bit of control she held over her family.

"What Riley says is true," Joan said finally. "You'll need financial support." Missionaries were supposed to finance their own missions. "We don't have any money from the book yet," she said, "and it may not go far."

"I have a year before I'm twenty-one," Jody said. "I can get a job that pays better than ballet."

Riley thought about lady missionaries. They were older single women. He looked from Jody to his mother, wondering what she would say.

"Have you talked to your dad about this?" Joan asked, and hung up the last coat.

"He told me to pray about it," she responded, waiting for Joan's reaction. Riley took a bite out of his sandwich and munched thoughtfully.

"Riley, go eat that in the kitchen," Joan said with irritation. "I don't want it getting all over the living room." She turned her attention back to Jody. "What about Blaine? What happened to him, Jody? He was such a nice boy."

"He's a wimp," she said. "He can't make up his mind about anything. He doesn't know if he wants to go back to college or get serious with me or what. Ever since his mission, he doesn't do anything except read his scriptures and write to his missionary buddies."

"Maybe he doesn't like women," said Riley, his mouth full.

"Riley!" yelled Joan. "Go back into the kitchen or your name's mud."

Riley passed through the kitchen and continued out into the garage, and around to the back yard where Cade and Winnie were. She didn't have to yell at me, he thought, suddenly losing his appetite. Cade and Winnie were bouncing on the huge inner tube Gus had brought home one day from a gas station.

"Shistle," said Cade, playing the word game where you tried to make your opponent say a cuss word.

"Pit," responded Winnie.

"Shistle."

"Pit."

Shistle."

"Pit."

"Pistol."

"Shit. I mean pit!"

The first night Jody didn't come home, Joan assumed she was staying with her friend Cathy who had just started a job at a dental office. When two days went by without a word, and Cathy said she hadn't seen her, Joan called the bishop, who announced a twenty-four-hour ward fast. Then she called the police.

Muriel was the last one to see Jody, three weeks after Muriel's wedding. The younger sister had come for dinner at Muriel's and Scott's new apartment, where she had talked about how, for the first time since graduating from high school, she knew the SPIRIT was directing her in the path she should go. When they asked her how her missionary papers were coming, she brushed it off.

"I was just afraid I wouldn't get married," she had said, "and that I didn't have what it takes to finish college. I was gaining weight. Those aren't the right reasons to go on a mission." She talked about a new guy she had met, Al, who she said was like Gus. She hoped the family would soon meet him.

When the police arrived at the house, it felt like an invasion, like when Candace's boyfriend had shown up drunk. The family took on a new shape around the sudden presence of men in navy-blue uniforms, belted, with heavy gear that clanged and beat against their legs, contesting with the family's only armor, that of a practiced superiority.

Gus sat immobilized while Joan answered the officers' questions. The week before she had been talking on the phone with Sister Pratt about a four-year-old who was propelled onto Interstate 15 because he had leaned against an unlocked hatch door. To Joan, children weren't necessarily the objects of joy, as much as targets for misfortune.

When Lucy arrived, she was loaded for bear. "Who is this Al guy? Who had Jody talked to besides him? Is it Albert or Alfred or what—we don't even know his name!" she gasped.

"You're upsetting the girls," Joan told Lucy. "Sit down." The police wanted to know who Lucy was. "A friend," Lucy replied, and when they asked how she knew someone was missing, she told them Riley had called her. They looked at Riley, one of them with a notepad suspended in air, but he said he didn't know anything. Lucy paced.

Jody was over eighteen, so she was a missing person, the police explained, not a runaway, and there wasn't much they could do. The moment the door closed behind them, Joan dropped her face into her hands.

A week later Joan and Gus called a family meeting. Gus had met with Jody and her new husband in a coffee shop. His name was Al, and he was someone who had two other wives. The *zzz* at the end of the word *wives* filled the room like a fog. It had never occurred to anyone that Jody would have gotten married, let alone to a polygamist! When they all started breathing again, Joan spoke, the force of steel in her voice. "Jody is confused. This man approached her at Temple Square, and he's been working on convincing her ever since."

"Convincing her of what?" Riley asked. Now, as the oldest at home, he would be the one left to figure out what parts of the story his parents weren't telling them.

"Fundamentalists have persuasive arguments," his mother continued. "I don't know what they are exactly, that's not important, only that they've convinced Jody that this is her calling in life, that she has a special role in preparation for Christ's return."

Gus sat looking at the ceiling before clearing his throat and saying, "Riley, when the church gave up plural marriage in 1880, some of the members were told to practice it secretly to keep it alive."

"They don't need to know those kinds of details," said Joan.

"This Al guy is actually pretty likeable," Gus added. "He's kind of handsome too. He has a sense of humor." Joan looked at her husband like he might have just been teleported in from another planet.

"Can't she divorce him?" asked Riley, turning to his mom, who for the first time looked old enough to be a grandmother.

"She doesn't want to leave him," said Gus. "She's convinced this is a higher order of marriage." Riley couldn't imagine what *higher* order there could be other than the one his family was currently living. How many more commandments could there be? Already it seemed everything you might actually want to do was taboo, but to think that there were other people living by other rules, and that … it was okay. It seemed to him his life ended when he was baptized and told he would be held accountable for his actions. What other lifestyle could there be?

"Are we going to see her?" asked a plaintive Cade. Jody had spent hours rehearsing lines from *Saturday's Warrior* with him. Riley remembered seeing his brother dressed in white to represent a pre-mortal existence, singing happily with the others in the musical, his expressive face highlighted with make up. It had made Riley blush to see his cheesy enthusiasm.

> *Without a doubt, we can work it out*
> *Pulling together, we can work it out!*

"Not for now," said their mother matter-of-factly. She took a deep breath. "Your sister has made it clear that she's not ready to come …"

"Come here, son," interrupted Gus. He extended a hand to Cade, who ran to him. Gus cradled him as best he could, pressing his lips into the top of Cade's head. As he did so, Gus revealed a painful grimace. Their tears were romantic, almost. Joan looked on vacantly. The sisters sat still, not knowing what to do.

How could Jody have done such a thing? Riley wondered. His confusion was turning to anger.

Joan explained that no one in the neighborhood needed to know about Jody's becoming a polygamist, even though the Sperrys, two blocks away, had two daughters in polygamy, according to what Sister Pratt had said. The Sperry girls had even moved back to Missouri where, according to Joseph Smith, Christ would appear on his return. Sister Pratt thought this information about the Sperrys would comfort the family in light of Jody's disappearance.

When Riley asked his mom what they were supposed to say to people, she suggested they say their sister had married a man who had several children already. That much was true. "Tell them she's too busy getting settled to visit right now."

Jody may have been indisposed, but that didn't mean Riley couldn't visit her. He had his driver's license. It couldn't be that hard to get to Logan, about three hours from Provo. You got onto the interstate, he imagined, and drove north. He asked Lucy if he could borrow their car for the day.

"Nelson and your Mom would kill me."

"Tell them you didn't know."

"But I do know."

"Leslie can tell them," he said, turning to Lucy's husband.

"I don't need the car tomorrow," said Leslie.

"You don't understand," said Lucy, who was pregnant again and was feeding Dryden orange baby food. Dryden had spread it from one ear to the other and looked like a melting clown. "Fundamentalists are crazy. Never mind that they're breaking the law. They wear buns in their hair and horrible shoes—worse than mine—and act like they're slaves to their husbands."

"What will you do if you find her?" Leslie asked, turning to Riley.

"I don't know. I just want to ask why she did it. She's going to be excommunicated."

Lucy and Leslie were quiet. They knew that church members were given the boot if they were caught living *the Principle*, and they knew Riley's great-great-grandfather had been a polygamist-in-hiding in Mexico after the church told people to stop it. Dryden goo-gooed and looked at one of his hands so closely he went cross-eyed.

"I can't believe this is happening," said Lucy. She put down the spoon and looked out the window. "What would possess

Jody to become such a fanatic? She must know she's jeopardizing everything."

She was mostly jeopardizing the reputation of the forever family, I told Verus over drinks. It was not individuals, but families that were the irreducible unit of heaven and earth, according to Mormons. The Hartleys were chosen for the last days, to clear the way for the blessed return of Christ. "I've catalogued these myriad theories about how human actions will force an early return of Christ and put an end to our respective wanderings. As ridiculous as that sounds, I still like to think one of the theories might be true," I said, while Verus shook his head in disbelief.

"You're insane." Verus said. "And so are they. What is this 'chosen' thing? I thought everyone had given up on that idea."

Leslie thought it was a good idea for the boy to drive to Logan and shrugged and raised his eyebrows in an *I dunno* gesture when Lucy turned to him for advice, at which Lucy consented. "Okay, you can take the car but be very careful. You hear me, Riley?" she said.

What I thought was that finally, my little charge was taking charge, showing some initiative on his own accord.

Riley didn't mention that Cade was going with him because he knew Lucy would think he was too young. Cade was two years younger than his brother and looked even younger, his arms still like a girl's. At his mother's encouragement, Riley had invited Cade to join the swim team, and when Cade walked out of the dressing room that first day in his Speedo, he looked like he had stepped off of Sesame Street, his penis twisted up in a conspicuous way, his goggles already on, the long white elastic band pushing his hair up into a loop. Even so, and despite the fact that

Cade was an eternal pest, he had become Riley's audience for stories at two in the morning about how Eric Whitworth and he had run from the police after toilet-papering the house of a girl in the junior class.

The trip north was going to be Riley's big adventure, and Cade would be his witness to it. Besides, when Riley saw his brother cry after being told about Jody, he had felt sorry for him.

The bus dropped the boys off at school with the other students, and they acted like they were consulting about something while they waited for everyone else to leave and the bus to pull away, then hightailed it down University Avenue to Lucy's and Leslie's apartment. Cade waited for Riley around the corner of the building. Lucy was in her nightgown, her hair even crazier than usual. She gave Riley some cookies and a bottle of ginger ale. "Do you have enough money for gas?" she asked. Riley nodded. She handed him the keys. "Be careful."

Just like that, the three of us were launched on a dangerous mission that Riley was sure they could accomplish until he saw the road reflected through the windshield of Lucy's Toyota and decided it was unlikely they would meet with success. They became silent, listening to the talk of the morning DJs on the radio.

"How are we going to find out where they live?" Cade said when they entered the freeway. It sounded funny when he said "they," as if Jody were now something mysterious and beyond their parents' winsome creation.

"His name is Baines, Alvin Baines," Riley said, not telling Cade he had seen it written in a journal Gus had left open on the dining room table.

"The phone book?" he asked.

"Yeah, I guess."

To the right, the sun was coming up over the Cascade Mountain peak, making the entire Wasatch Range uni-dimensional. Ahead of us lay the flanks of Mt. Timpanogos, frozen and cyanic in the still morning air. We passed the steel mill, the lights on the rectilinear smoke stacks blurred by fluming steam. By the time we reached the Point of the Mountain, the day was upon us, the Salt Lake Valley spread out like another world, which it was—self-consciously hip with its international airport to the northwest and the buzzing ski resorts in the eastern canyons.

The family drove to Salt Lake for two reasons: either to visit Temple Square for some kind of church event, or to take Gus to the airport where they watched the outside world collide with Zion in a place that had the stale aroma of cigarettes and gift shops selling souvenir shot glasses, which just confirmed the worldliness spoken of in the Book of Mormon.

The signs near the junction of Interstate 80 announcing Cheyenne and Reno showed how easy it would be for us to turn the wheel ever-so-slightly and find ourselves in an instant hurtling toward some other place in Wyoming, Nevada, California, or Canada. For now the freeway took us out of the Salt Lake Valley, past oil refineries and a tangle of railroad tracks, and onto the mountain bench, a remnant of Old Lake Bonneville that once covered the entire area, before shrinking down after the ice age to the shallow and stagnant Great Salt Lake. From this temporary vantage point, we could see to the west the lower-rising mountains, at the foot of which lay the lake, a pale blue ribbon that widened and pooled beside the interstate at Willard Bay. In the main lake, the water was five times saltier than any ocean, a sea with no outlet except for the sun's reverse drainage heavenward. Sometimes one could make out the blanched sail of a boat, but on this day the lake was empty and angry, a mirror of the winter sky.

This was the length and breadth of the kingdom established, as the apocalyptic Isaiah prophesied, in the tops of the mountains, a striking physical enclave anchored by a dead sea. It was a theme Gus liked to talk about in his impassioned lectures. It was where Zion was to put on her lovely garments and rule in power and glory until the second coming of Jesus, who would reign in peace for the millennium. It was the revenge Latter-day Saints harbored against a sin-sick world destined to reject the message of the restored gospel and destined to burn at the Lord's second coming. To speed along the corridor, you could almost hear this collective reverie, tethered to a secret ecstasy. It was an epic vision that could arrest even an ancient one.

We slowed to exit.

"That says Logan," said Cade, pointing to a small sign indicating a town rather than a freeway junction. We turned off onto U.S. Route 91 and drove into the mouth of Sardine Canyon, away from the sun-spattered valley and into the dark clouds hedging the mountains where we were going to ascend. Cade read every sign as we passed them. "Watch for falling rock," "Deer Crossing," "Chains required when lights flashing," "Logan: 14 miles."

It began to snow.

19 | THE PRINCIPLE

A few days after Jody's disappearance, Riley thought he saw her near the swimming pool while he swam laps. He did all his obsessing in the pool, in tandem with another boy, Gil (appropriately named), in twenty-five yard increments. He couldn't tell Gil about his sister without having to hear jokes about polygamous threesomes. In the steady beating of the water, Riley fashioned the exchange he would have with the man responsible for his sister's disappearance. As he was thinking about Alvin Baines one day, forcing his arms and legs to push harder through the water, he looked up through clouded goggles, his heart pumping like a hammer, and could have sworn he saw Jody sitting in the bleachers, watching him, her hair out like Ali McGraw's.

By the time we reached Logan, there was an inch of powdery snow on the ground. The boys stopped at a Sinclair gas station so Riley could look up Al in the phone book, but found nothing. He asked the older man at the desk if he knew a Baines family. He didn't. Riley told him the Baineses were polygamists, and the man, after looking at him in a funny way, said they might be at the farm two miles down the old Smithfield Road. First they stopped for hamburgers and tried to blend in with other teenagers just out of school, but compared to the young people in cowboy boots throwing French fries at each other, Riley and Cade seemed out of place there.

They got to the farm house in mid-afternoon and a middle-aged woman in an apron opened the door, while two young children pushed past her. "Is this the Baines house?" Riley asked, feeling immediately awkward at how formal his question sounded.

The woman didn't say anything.

The children pressed their faces into the screen door, noses squished white, then skipped away laughing into the yellow light of the living room where they tumbled into a large pile of fresh laundry.

"Is Jody Hartley here? She's our sister. Is she here?" he repeated.

The woman opened the screen door so the boys could step into the front hall, then she picked up the phone in the kitchen. There was a smell of peanut oil in the house. On the wall was a color print of the Logan temple. The children sat in the laundry and stared.

Cade fidgeted, humming nervously, while Riley thought about swimming fifty yards freestyle, which takes about thirty seconds. They could hear the woman talking. Riley imagined himself finishing the interval and climbing back onto the starting blocks, shaking out his arms for the next one, when the woman hung up and motioned for them to sit down on the couch.

She crossed the room and shooed the children out of the pile of clothes, then knelt and began folding, but still said nothing.

The boys sat, their breathing shallow. They could hear a pickup truck arrive, the engine cut, and saw how, when Alvin Baines entered, instead of seeming foreign, the room instantly re-built itself around him. His thick coveralls had the smell of cold air and salt. He removed his vented baseball cap with a clean snap, his hair oily enough to retain the hat's shape. He had the same blocky build as Gus, but more grizzled, his dark eyes close together behind a hooked nose that made him look as severe as a scowling bird. The boys stood. Baines looked at them for a long time before saying, "Liza, these men might like a soda. Men?"

"No thank you," Riley said. Baines did not offer to shake hands. The woman stood up with the folded clothes and walked out, calling to the children, who stumbled over each other as they backed out of the room giggling. Riley wished the woman would stay.

Baines unzipped his coveralls to reveal a denim shirt buttoned to the top. "I was wondering when someone would get here," he said. "Too bad it wasn't last week before this front moved in. It's not safe driving up Sardine Canyon in the snow."

"We're not here to do home teaching," Riley said, realizing his response sounded scripted, which it was. "We're here to see our sister."

Baines smiled. "How old are you, Riley?"

Riley flinched to hear his name mentioned, to realize that Baines knew something about him—this man whom he had never seen before.

"Where's Jody?"

"I thought you'd come in the Green Loaf. Where's that?"

Cade turned to his brother with a look that said, How does he know about that?

Riley didn't take his eyes off Baines, who seemed calm and almost sympathetic behind his beak nose.

"I guess those VWs don't do all that well in the snow," said Baines.

"You're breaking the law," Riley said, barely able to contain his anger and fear. He stepped toward the staircase in the front hall, but Baines stepped in front of him. "I want to see my *sister*!"

Baines folded his arms across his chest. Riley fully expected to see Jody standing behind him.

"I have something to show you," Baines said, waiting for Riley to step back, which he did. He reached into his rear pocket. "You've probably never seen one of these." He produced something encased in what looked like a plastic bag. "I doubt in Sunday School you were told about this." He extended the bag to Riley. "Take it. It won't magically turn you into a polygamist."

Riley reached for it. Baines kept his grip on the other end long enough for Riley to have to tug at it.

"Take it out. It's money from a long time ago," Baines said.

Riley removed the note, his hands shaking slightly. Cade moved in to get a look himself. The note was soft, like cloth, and the printing on it read BANK OF DESERET.

"It's a ten note bill," said Baines. "When your grandfather Riley came out west, the Latter-day Saints had their own currency. They even had their own alphabet."

Riley handed it back to him.

"Keep it," Baines said.

"I don't want it." Riley replied. "I just want to see Jody."

Baines shrugged, took back the note, folded it into its plastic bag, and returned it to his wallet. He stepped aside and nodded in the direction of the stairs.

Riley started for them and put his hand on the railing, Cade behind him.

"Her room's up there, but she's not here at the moment," Baines said. "She's in Ogden with one of her sister wives doing the shopping. They're staying overnight with relatives."

Riley began to pant. He felt as if he'd just finished a grueling 200-yard race, his legs wobbly. He turned to Cade, who was white, his eyes moist.

"*Now* will you sit down?" said Baines.

Riley hesitated, his hand moving from the railing to the wall. Suddenly there was nothing left to do, no technique learned from training. He and his brother returned to the couch and sat down defeated.

Across from them, Baines lowered himself into a large upholstered arm chair. It was worn, like the rest of the room. "I like your persistence, Riley," he said. "Perhaps there's some of the old Reid spirit in you. I wonder how much you know about your ancestor? Jody didn't know much about him."

Riley didn't say anything.

"For all the talk around here about our heroic past, not many folks have any idea what their ancestors were like. So that's my question, Brother Hartley. How much do you know?"

Riley stared back with a look of contempt.

"Your sister admires you. She says you're smart and that you collect words. Maybe this afternoon I can give you a few new ones."

Riley noticed that Cade had a glazed look in his eyes, like he was trying to decipher Baines but found him mesmerizing.

"You're not even a member of the church," Riley said, a little too abruptly.

Baines leaned back in his chair and looked up thoughtfully, as if he had discovered a new crack in the ceiling. "I won't bore you with all the arguments about why plural marriage is still a commandment," he said. "The Brethren know the doctrines, and yet they are the most ardent foes—even though they still practice polygamy, in their own way."

"No they don't."

"You're wrong about that, Riley. They want it both ways. Monogamists in this life and polygamists in the next."

"Mr. Baines," Riley said, rallying, "I think you're unstable."

Baines looked at him with surprise, his eyes widening until he burst into laughter. He laughed so hard that his head cocked back, the roof of his mouth obscenely pink.

Cade put his hand on Riley's leg and squeezed. Riley could tell his brother was trembling.

"I think I might've met my match," said Baines, catching his breath. He took out a bandana and wiped his eyes.

Even if it wasn't going well, Riley thought, he had to be strong for his brother. He had to do *something*.

Baines stood and went to the bookshelf on the other side of the room. There he retrieved a large sheet of paper and unfolded it to reveal a map. Reverently he spread it out on the floor, its edge nearly touching Riley's foot. It was a map of the western United States.

"This was Zion," he said. "Present-day Utah is a tiny piece of what was supposed to be the State of Deseret. This is your heritage, Brother Hartley. This is what your ancestors gave up. Did you know that? Look at it, son. This is what we were."

Riley saw there was a red line drawn from San Diego

southeast into what looked like northern Mexico, north through the middle of Colorado and Wyoming. Then it dropped sharply into Idaho and Nevada, then back into California to slide through San Bernardino, closing the loop south of Los Angeles. It was about a third of the United States, including San Diego, Las Vegas, and the entire Rocky Mountains.

"It wasn't morality that the U.S. was after when it pressured the Latter-Day Saints to abandon celestial marriage," Baines said. "Polygamy was a bogey man, paired by Abraham Lincoln with slavery to scare everyone into declaring war on us, which they did. And it was a smokescreen for what they really wanted. It was milk in the Mormon coconut they were after. It was this," he said forcefully as he thumped the map so hard it left an indentation in the paper.

Baines sat back down in his chair, the map still on the floor. Riley thought this must be the kind of conversation Baines had with Jody. He was drafting an entire universe, bent intently as he was, like Newton, on establishing a new galactic order.

"Who do you think America's biggest fans are now, Riley?"

The question hung in the air. Riley wasn't sure if Baines wanted an answer or if he was just asking for dramatic effect.

"Who are the most loyal Americans in the United States?" Baines repeated, followed disdainfully by, "Mormons! They've become nervous little spaniels, chasing after approval and pissing on the floor. Church members even fawn over God-forsaken Hollywood these days." He stopped for a moment and shook his head. "The church gave up a kingdom bigger than the Republic of Texas for this pathetic little square, even Wyoming taking a bite out of it!"

"I thought you weren't going to talk about polygamy," said Riley, lifting his chin.

Baines stared at him uncomprehendingly for a moment. "You're right," he finally said and stood up to pace, hands on his hips. "I don't want to upset my new brothers-in-law. This isn't my battle anyway. It's God's plan." He stopped. "Why do you think Abraham Lincoln was finally removed from office? Because God will not be mocked."

Riley looked at Cade, who was too young to be hearing this. But Riley was also intrigued with the possibility of learning something his mom and Gus couldn't tell him. "In the Book of Mormon," Riley said softly, "*deseret* was Hebrew for the honey bee they took with them to America," he said. "But I can't find that definition in the dictionary."

"That's all been removed," Baines said in quick retort. "Deseret was once an entire country, named after the industrious bee. Now it's just the name of a daily newspaper and a thrift store."

"And a cement company."

"Yes, that too." Baines sighed. He walked over to Cade, who was as close to Riley on the couch as he could get. Riley started to rise in protest, but Baines reached out and cupped the back of Cade's neck, at which Cade's eyes closed and his head lolled to the side, his neck stretched long against the dingy afghan covering the back of the couch.

"What are you …?"

"*Shhh*" said Baines, and gently tipped Cade so his head rested on the cushion. Baines moved the afghan to cover Cade, who nestled into it, his mouth falling open. There was a pause as the older man looked at Cade and confessed he saw something of his own sons in him.

Watching all of this transpire, I felt sorry for the polygamist. He was right that people didn't know what had motivated their ancestors. I wish Verus had come to keep me on track because Baines was like an LDS missionary redefining "true."

"My boys are the young lions of Zion," Baines said. "They're just like you and Cade. The Lord is merciful to us. I want them to be just as happy as God wants us to be. At your age, I remember, the sex drive became all-encompassing … I don't mean to embarrass you," he added.

"Why would I be embarrassed?" said Riley, looking up at him with a determined gaze. "I'm old enough to know some things."

"It will either redeem you or destroy you. Where will you take it if it's not embraced by the Lord's plan?"

Riley was, in fact, embarrassed. He began to feel the way he did around Brother Bestor. "It's none of your business," he told Baines.

"I shudder to think of your manhood being wasted. Monogamy is a Roman invention, more political than sacred. That's all. I'm struck with the lost potential, and it saddens me. The sex act was meant to burnish the prince into a king, make him responsible, to settle in him the glories and comforts that come with sexual intercourse."

Suddenly Riley could hear the woman in the kitchen, who had probably been listening to them the whole time. He stood up, flustered. "I'd like to see Jody's room," he said. He felt he might have a slight psychological advantage now. "I want to see where my sister sleeps and know she's okay."

Baines nodded. Cade was still asleep. Baines tried to insist that the two stay overnight because of the weather, but consented to help them put chains on their tires and release them. Riley climbed the stairs alone, glad Cade wasn't there to see Jody's narrow bed, situated behind the folding door to another room. She had thumbtacked a picture of the family on the wall above her dresser.

As they departed, the snow crunched under the tires and the car slid when Riley applied gas. He pumped the brakes for traction, as Gus had shown him. He kept thinking of what Baines had said about the angel threatening to cut Joseph Smith in half with a sword if he didn't live THE PRINCIPLE. "It was an upraised sword, Riley," Brother Baines had said after Cade was put down. "Sanctioned by the Holy One of Israel." The sword was a sexual metaphor and not of this world, he explained. It was the joining of temporal and spiritual. It was glory, a concept that stirred something in Riley's head, heart, and groin all at the same time.

"We should have blown up his barn," said Cade as they distanced themselves from the man who had taken their sister away. "Set his truck on fire or something, killed his cat."

"His cat?"

"There was a cat there that looked like Squirt. Kind of fat."

"I thought you liked Squirt."

"Don't you feel sorry for Mom and Dad?" Cade said.

That was the question that stopped me from my eternal, ineffectual musings, and I wished I could have been a visible friend riding alongside them to talk them through it. It was probably the first time Riley Hartley realized he didn't know what he felt toward his mother and father, who suddenly seemed less than what

128

they had claimed. Alvin Baines was certain of his position, just like Riley's parents were of theirs. Gus and Joan had shown their love for each child, despite the fact that there were ten of them. Baines showed love for Jody even though she was one of three wives. What became clear to me that night was that Riley and Cade, in coming to realize their parents' vulnerabilities, fell more deeply in love with them. Riley wanted to protect them from Baines and from the pain their children caused them. That is why he went to Logan. Even though it inevitably meant the children came to question their parents, this old jaded Nephite wished he could have been as loved as Joan and Nelson Hartley were.

To Riley's surprise, Jody returned home after three months. It was the last day of school. When he walked into the house, she was sleeping on the living room couch, dressed in sweats and lying under an afghan as if she were sick. She was surrounded by Muriel, Candace, and Lucy. Riley couldn't believe it. Every day in his water-logged solitude at the pool, Jody had become the woman folding laundry in the Baines farmhouse. He assumed she had bunned her hair, renounced makeup, and limited her enter-tainment to scripture reading. Now here she was in the flesh, the television on in front of her, now and then twitching in her sleep.

He heard his mom say the word "miscarriage." Cade and Gus walked in carrying groceries. Cade smiled, his face cracking with excitement. "Riley, did you see Jody?" he whispered.

It turned out Jody was home to stay. The bishop put her on church probation, but that was nothing. Her reappearance was a miracle. No one brought up Alvin Baines to her or how she had gotten away. Everyone blinked and there she was! She had escaped the rigid borders of their lives to experience the kingdom of God in miniature, and she had chosen the Zion of their home.

When it was Riley's turn to extend past the horizon of the familiar, he realized how comfortable his life on Golan Drive was.

Whenever he needed to get away, he swam laps in his head—
thirty seconds per fifty-yard freestyle including one flip-turn.
It was one of the few attributes that later would survive his trip
east when he submerged himself into his new world. A fifty-yard
freestyle race got him between subway stops on a good day. A
hundred-yard individual medley bought him the amount of quiet
one could expect between car alarms in late-night Brooklyn.
Mind swimming, he has learned, helps him avoid letting the past
swamp the present.

Before deciding what kind of future he wanted, Riley got
a job as a lifeguard at the Provo City pool. It was idyllic, he
thought, the radio wafting songs from Boston and Styx across the
water, the entertaining chatter of disc jockeys. Life guarding nur-
tured a sensuous side, the lazy sun penetrating his skin after the
rays bounced off the pavement, the consciousness of an empty
pool at the end of the day quieting his thoughts. He guarded
people's lives and protected the interior space of his mind where
his world consisted of little more than the swing of his whistle
on a braided cord around two fingers, which he liked to coil in a
clockwise direction and then backward, counterclockwise.

By the end of summer, he was thinking about becoming a
career lifeguard. He could move to Los Angeles. He could work at
the beach. He would live in a swimming suit and not have to wear
temple garments under his clothes like his parents did. He would
be the Tarzan of Huntington Beach. He would develop rippling
muscles like he saw in magazines. Maybe his hair would turn blond.

But who was he fooling? Another year of high school, a year
of college, a mission … everything was set in granite for him. It
was always the same refrain: mission, marriage, kids. It was like

getting on an airplane and knowing you would eat the pre-pre-pared meal, see an in-flight movie, look at the magazine, and take a nap in that order. Unless you crashed. A mission could be fun, right? Japan, Germany, South Africa. Lance Bennion was sent to Albuquerque. "We're learning to love the people down here," he gamely wrote. The bishop read his letter to the congregation in sacrament meeting. What was it about THE PLAN that Riley didn't like? He wanted to get married, didn't he? After all, that was the only way you could have sex.

Two years earlier the executive secretary had dismissed the young men from a priesthood meeting so the stake president could talk to the adults. They closed the giant accordion-like partition at the back of the chapel but forgot about Paris Carter, who remained on the organ bench. Paris told Riley the stake president announced that Brother Hansen, Julie's dad, had been excommunicated for marital infidelity. "What exactly does that mean, do you think?" Riley asked his friend. "What did Brother Hansen do?"

"I could tell you some amazing things," Paris said. "They don't know the half of what goes on." His comment just annoyed Riley because he knew his friend was exaggerating.

Suddenly, Riley's whistle flew out of his hand, the centrif-ugal force carrying it across the jouncy water to narrowly miss the head of a girl bobbing up and down. Riley apologized and wondered if there was something wrong with him, to be so lost in thought that he could harm someone he was supposed to be protecting. It wouldn't happen again, he said to himself.

21 | VESPERS

"You're making this harder than it is," Lucy was saying. "You're the one with three notebooks full of words."

"Words like *insouciant* that don't help me write a speech."

"I'm not a writer either, you know. Your mom would be a better tutor here," Lucy said while doing the dishes one-handed and bouncing number three on her hip as if in time to a metronome. Leslie had taken the two oldest children out with him on errands. "What's the talk supposed to be about?"

"Gifts," he said. "This is the last chance I'll have to really say something. To shake things up."

"Like what?" she asked, tossing the limp dishcloth into the sink and sitting down in the same beat. The baby pawed at the air.

"Well, ... for example the priesthood thing, which I had thought of mentioning." The prophet had recently received a revelation allowing black men to be ordained to the priesthood. Gus had taken it in stride, as if it had been a change in the weather. Lucy wanted to know why it took so long and how it squared with earlier edicts prohibiting it.

"Well, that's why people need to have their own commitment to the truth," she said. "Otherwise, you can't live with all the unanswered questions."

"That whole thing makes me furious," Riley said. "The Brethren say we're supposed to be obedient, then they say we were all wrong—not that they were wrong, of course."

Lucy didn't say anything for a moment. "Sounds to me like your objective here is to stir up some trouble at vespers, not to give a heart-felt opinion. Is that true?"

The truth was, Riley had no opinions of his own. Instead, in high school he had gone from collecting words to collecting opinions. His fix was still the same. They were not his, anymore than the lists of words in his notebooks were his.

"High school has been a disappointment, hasn't it?" Lucy said as she moved the baby to its crib.

"I feel like I've been competing with everyone, and for no good reason. We're supposed to win awards, to become the most popular, to be the most spiritual …"

"The most spiritual?" Lucy laughed. "Only in Utah! Listen, I'm sorry you didn't get the Sterling Scholar," she said matter-of-factly. "I know that was disappointing."

"I lost at everything I did," he said.

"What about your speech on democracy?"

"Second place."

"Second place isn't bad."

"Two years in a row?"

They watched the baby play with its toes. "Riley you don't have to be like your dad."

Riley was startled by that declaration. "I don't want to be," he said a little too quickly.

"What I mean is you don't have to convince anyone of anything, especially not in your vespers talk."

"Then what's the point?" he asked. "Why am I giving a speech at all?"

"To inspire people?"

As far as Riley was concerned, there was a language he had learned as a child that only Mormons used. Words like *righteousness*, *repentance*, THE GOSPEL with a capital G. They were words designed to manipulate people, fill them with guilt. But then there were the other words, a whole universe of luminous pin points that gave voice to a greater creation, expanding wildly beyond a life happening on Golan Drive. He had read about *logos*, a term from the Stoics. *Logos* meant not only "the word," but reason, ideas. It was about the things that words were tethered to, a place where speaking meant more than just parroting something back verbatim, ultimately to form an identity of one's own.

Joan ended up dictating to Riley a short sermon on the evils of narcissism that made Riley and his fellow competitors crave recognition. Riley contributed some additional material he collected from Ayn Rand's *The Virtue of Selfishness*, which he knew would be an objectionable title, even before he quoted from it.

"From the Greeks we read the myth of a young man named Narcissus," he reported to his class and their parents while standing in his suit in the auditorium. He looked like a missionary except that he had long hair curling onto his ears and over his back collar. Lucy was sitting near the front with Leslie and Dryden, who was nearly four. "As Narcissus bent over a pool, he saw himself reflected in the water," Riley read, explaining how the young man fell in love with himself "because he was handsome and undoubtedly selfish."

He had practiced this many times, and when he said *selfish* he looked up with the same condemning gaze his father used. The truth was, Riley thought of himself when he spoke of the handsomeness of Narcissus. To his dismay, he couldn't get comfortable in front of people. He stood as straight as a tin soldier, his necktie knotted so big it got in his way when he looked down at his notes. He was flushed with adrenaline and discretely pulled at his crotch behind the lectern where his new suit pinched him. Was he getting aroused?

"Today society is producing many Narcissists." He looked up at Alan Winthrop, the class president who won the Sterling Scholar and relegated Riley to second place for eternity. Alan had played the lead in *Our Town* and had been accepted to BYU but chose to attend Dartmouth instead. He would be the valedictorian speaker the following day.

"Although this philosophy of putting oneself first, at the expense of others, can be effective for an individual, people who find true fulfillment in life claim the opposite, that doing good turns for other people is what is the most satisfying to them," he said. He noticed that Alan flinched.

The audience clapped politely. Riley had to get back to his seat without revealing what was going on with his crotch, so he carried his crumpled notes in front of him, which was awkward. He nevertheless thought about the power of *logos* and how he had created a new reality by his spoken words. He even used one of the selections from his notebook, *perspicacious*, meaning "to have keen judgment."

People came up to congratulate him, including Alan. "Good job, Riley. A lot better than I could've done," he said easily if still somewhat competitively. "I think you should give the commencement address," he added, smiling.

Shortly after Riley's graduation, Lucy and her family moved to California, where Leslie had gotten a job testing soil samples for the Bureau of Land Management out of Fresno. They would return to Utah on visits, wrinkled and tired from the long drive across the desert and always with a new little one in tow. Lucy became the Relief Society president of her ward. Shortly after their arrival in Fresno, she wrote to Riley that

> Latter-day Saints are a little more relaxed out here. They eat out on the Sabbath, for instance. The girls wear two-piecers at the beach. My new bishop knows about your dad. Heck, everyone does, and everyone thinks he's going to be called to be a general authority soon. When things get crazy, I ask myself what your parents would do. I still think the church is the only thing in the world that makes any sense.

Of course, Riley could not comprehend a world without his faith. Everyone told him to be grateful because he had been selected to be born into a forever family out of all the spirits waiting in the pre-existence for their chance to get a mortal body. What lay outside of THE GOSPEL was unimaginable. How did people get through their lives without knowing they were in the true church?

22 | THE QUESTION THAT WAS GUS

Gus was Riley's backstage pass around BYU, where the freshman with the recognizable surname got a lot of mileage with professors and bookstore cashiers. The priorities at BYU were spirituality, good looks, and money. With two out of the three in one's dad, whose rousing sermons could be heard every Sunday night on the radio, Riley was treated like royalty.

Sometimes admiring students visited Gus in his office at the foot of the hill below campus. The office was decorated with huge sepia-toned photographs of his family and lined with bookshelves with titles like *We Can Become Perfect*. Most fascinating to Riley was the twenty-six-volume *Journal of Discourses*, which was most often quoted by anti-Mormons for its toe-curling statements by Brigham Young and others about race, theology, and the evils of reading novels. The mere presence of the tomes spoke to Gus's fearlessness in the pursuit of spiritual knowledge. Riley wasn't motivated to go so far as to crack one of them open to see its contents, but to gaze upon them in the bookshelf was to see tangible evidence of his father's scholarship. The Brethren didn't want people reading old speeches, Gus told Riley, which led members to "delve into the mysteries" and become confused. And yet, there were the books on his father's shelf. Riley noticed that there was barely any indication in the office that Gus sold life insurance. Everything spoke to religious interests.

That was because Gus's real life existed far outside the brick-faced office building. The insurance he sold wasn't a guarantee of security in mortality. The only reason he didn't join the BYU faculty was because he lacked the academic credentials. To compensate for that, he was installed as a campus stake president over several university wards. It was there that he thrived. The students loved him because he was upbeat and in touch with their concerns. He was well known for his vigorous handshake. He liked to slap-grab a student's hand, pull the unsuspecting victim toward himself, and put one hand on the student's elbow as if he were about to devour him or her (he subjected both men and women to his rough handling). When he did that, you could feel the warmth of his broad chest and see his prominent chin below the Irish eyes. It was the disarming embrace of a lover. After his talks, there were always students hovering about to be counseled on private concerns ranging from their relationship with Jesus Christ to the propriety of married couples giving each other oral sex.

One day after class, Riley stopped by Gus's office to hitch a ride home and could hear through the office door the low murmur of Gus's voice, a bark-like sound in his throat when he cleared it, and the higher-pitched voice of a woman. Riley sat down in front of Juanita's desk to study, the secretary having left for the day. Repeatedly he was distracted by the woman's voice rising and falling, spiked with hysteria. There was a sob, a groan, and suddenly he heard a chair slide and topple, then urgent footsteps. The door opened. There stood Gus, an arm half supporting a rag-doll of a woman.

"Riley!" he said like a frightened child. "She just … kind of collapsed!" Riley stood up and rushed over. Gus had a hand under the woman's left armpit so her blouse was pulled up almost over her breasts, and he was trying to get the blouse back down over her bra. The woman's hair had fallen onto her face.

"What happened?" Riley asked as they lowered the woman to the floor and tried to fix her skirt so it wouldn't be hiked up to her panties. Gus grabbed a throw pillow and placed it under her head.

"I was about to give her a blessing. She was … crying about … I think I'd better call an ambulance." He dashed out the door toward Juanita's desk.

Kneeling next to the woman, Riley straightened one of her arms and looked at her face. She was in her late twenties, a little heavy, and kept her hair in place with a barrette. She had deep acne marks across her cheeks. Her blouse was white. Her skirt was beginning to fray at the edge. Her sandals were square and had clunky heels. She smelled like hair spray.

Riley listened for sounds from his father down the hall. The woman looked worn and frightened, like so many of Gus's female admirers who remained single beyond the time most Mormon women had children. She was probably getting a masters degree in something like childhood education.

Suddenly the woman opened her eyes and tried to sneak a look at him, then closed them tightly, realizing she had given herself away. Riley kept quiet and let the EMTs treat her for heat exhaustion. The next Sunday she came to the house for dinner, and before long Sandy Greenwood had become a family regular who dined with them and drew strength from some domestic ideal she saw in the Hartleys. Joan set out dishes like American chop suey for dinner while the young woman enjoyed watching Gus tumble with the kids in the living room. Joan took Sandy's adoration of her husband in stride.

It turned out that Sandy wasn't a BYU student, although she had been. She left school mid-semester to return to Mesa to recuperate from a mysterious illness. While she was there, a friend sent her Gus's book. She read it in one sitting. Her experience was often repeated by young people who wrote letters and phoned from around the country. They liked the perfected narrative of Gus's life, which he had improved on through his many tellings of it at firesides. In addition to that, he told people they were as much entitled to revelation as the prophet himself, and people liked that message. Gus came to that realization growing up on the family farm and wrestling with the meaning of life, the meaning of religion, and the meaning of Gus. Reading the book, you could smell the hay being brought in from the fields and hear the wind blowing through Lombardy poplars as Gus engaged in "mighty prayer" between planting cotton and milking cows. The book contained every intimate detail of Gus's spiritual life. Sandy Greenwood was seduced by it.

Joan looked incredulously at her husband one day while she was stirring spaghetti forms into a pan of boiling water. "You told her to come here and model her swimming suit?" she gasped.

Gus fidgeted, his face turning red, his smile goofy. "She was so happy she found a suit she liked. She's lost weight. I was just thinking …"

"You weren't thinking, Nelson. You say whatever *poops* into your head." She stopped short, a wooden spoon held in the air, and realized she had just used a bathroom word. "I mean *pops* into your head, you know, pops," she corrected herself. Susan, now six, laughed out loud and covered her mouth.

"She knew I wasn't serious," Gus said. "That's not what she meant when she said she'd be back in a minute."

"Nelson, this is a woman who six months ago moved here and rented Sister Sullivan's apartment a half block away because she read your book!" She turned back toward the stove and slammed the lid down on the pot. "Yes dear, I think she just might show up here any minute in her bathing suit."

Ancient though I was, I could not imagine Sandy in a swimming suit, whether now or later. But she did have a sweetness about her. Just not the kind you wanted to see swathed in a lycra-blend suit.

"Sandy is lonely," said Gus.

"Exactly," said Mom. She sighed and thought of Bruce, a student who had shown up one night and stayed for two weeks. He was the kind of guy who knew there were people who wouldn't ever ask you to leave. And now here was Sandy, who told Gus she received a revelation in which Satan himself appeared to her to try to rape her. At the moment of violation, she was saved by an angel. The winged savior told her she would marry a man who already had ten children. That was the sum total of the revelation.

23 | THE TEST

When Joan insisted that Sandy stay away from her husband, the young woman went to her bishop and confessed that she had had an affair with Gus. Since Gus was a stake president, he had to be cleared by one of the Brethren in the Church Administration Building before the young woman's claim could be dismissed. That was when Joan's colitis started up again. Gus was shaken. He hadn't done anything wrong, but he felt humiliated. He explained that when Sandy fainted in his office, that was the first time he had ever seen her, that she just appeared out of nowhere from Arizona, her car still packed.

When things did not move fast enough for Sandy, she went to the press, and for a while the scandal lit a fire under Gus's book sales. Soon enough, though, the *Herald* found a professor who said, albeit anonymously, that Gus's theory about everyone being free to importune the Lord over personal issues was "wearying to the Lord," if not also to the Brethren. Sandy Greenwood was an example of what happens when people are told they can get personal revelation, the professor implied.

And so it was that the scene was set for Elder J. Rufus Gray to come to campus and hold a knife over Gus's body. Ironically, it was the apostle Gus had quoted more than any other in his book. That proved to be no barrier at all for the tall, raw-boned, onetime lawyer from Alberta who lambasted Riley's dad for preaching personal revelation. Elder Gray quoted offending passages from the book, then summarized: "As the church carries the gospel to the children of the Almighty everywhere, we cannot, as those who have been called by inspiration and authority, allow the continuing public fallout of misdirected zeal."

The speech had the effect of being a violent squall occurring in a campus greenhouse, the sealed-off environment having recently withstood criticism from outside Baptists who accused the religion faculty of promoting "deviant teachings." Now there was criticism from within campus. Gus's book was soon pulled by his publisher and its claims retracted in a press release. "No one need rely on anything more than the church's counsel," the publisher wrote. Gus's insurance clients dropped in half during the following months. Joan had to add two new classes to the Tutu school.

One day the phone rang from someone in Ely, Nevada, asking if it were true that Brother Hartley had been excommunicated. "I mean *the* Brother Hartley," he said. Joan assured the caller that no Brother Hartley she knew of had been excommunicated.

Gus tried to keep calm amid the cyclone of disapprobation, but at home he let his feelings vent. Every conversation in the house spiraled toward Sandy Greenwood and the talk by Elder Gray, even after Sandy retracted her accusations. None of the other Brethren came to Gus's defense, even those who privately subscribed to what Gus had taught. Even Grandpa Chaz indulged in obsessive commentary on Elder Gray's remarks. "You're the apostle's hobby horse," he liked to say. "Anyone can see it's just jealousy. Elder Gray didn't like that you were outselling his dry old books."

He was right, of course, as were the other die-hard disciples who sat in the living room and voiced their disgust. It was as if, for a minute, all of them—Gus, Joan, students, and neighbors—collectively cleared their throat like they might say something, but then reconsidered and decided not to stick their necks out. No one dared go on record in Gus's defense except Gary Stringham, who wrote a scathing opinion piece and was therefore called into his bishop's office and threatened with his membership if he didn't toe the line.

24 | I, ZEDEKIAH

I keep telling Verus that I'm not back in New York because of the theater. I gave up that obsession nearly a hundred years ago. He doesn't believe me. These days when I excuse myself from time to time, he gives me that look and says something like, "Give my best to Belle and the Beast," or, "Say hello to Joe and Harper Pitt," referring to two of the characters in *Angels in America*, which he knows gets me all *verklempt*. He knows I'm off to see Riley.

On the streets of the Big Apple, there are Mormon missionaries in white shirts, back packs, short hair, looking like they're fresh out of boot camp, which of course they are. Last week Riley allowed two of them to stop him on 5th Avenue and 23rd Street in Sunset Park, where they addressed him in Spanish until he replied in English. After telling them he was from Utah, their eyes grew wide and the color in their young necks got pinker. Riley waited almost with as much anticipation as they did to resolve the inevitable question, "Are you Mormon?"

He knows what it's like for missionaries on the streets of New York because a decade earlier he was at the swimming pool putting life guard trunks over his Speedo when his mother called to say that his mission call had arrived in the mail, that he should hurry home. He felt like his feet were in concrete, knowing this would signal the end of his carefree summer. Other people he knew were already on their way to their missions. Alan had finished a year at Dartmouth and was called to Japan. Other acquaintances were in Melbourne, Munich, Sao Paulo, as if the flood gates had opened and every young man in the valley had been sucked into some culvert and randomly sprayed out like fertilizer into what the church called the mission field. Would Riley ever know if he really wanted this? What did he really believe? Was he just afraid of the consequences if he didn't go? He needed more than a borrowed opinion at this point. He needed "to know."

He turned into the gravel driveway and parked. The door of the car felt heavy as he pushed it shut. The ground was too uneven for his flip flops. Noticing an unfamiliar station wagon out front, he assumed it was another of Gus's fans. The sprinklers were on, and two of Riley's sisters ran through them, their tiny tanned bodies dancing through the spray that shimmered when it landed on the trees. He would soon leave them behind, their dress-ups, their laughs when Gus tickled them, the smell of their sound sleep when he walked into the nursery to wake them up for church.

As he entered the front hall, he could hear Lucy's voice. She was here? She smiled so that her eyes became black slits as she pointed to Joan standing in her slippers, her hair smooshed, an envelope in her hand. Riley looked back at Lucy talking on the phone. "Go on," she whispered, then she narrated out loud for Leslie's benefit the drama unfolding before her.

"Joan is holding the envelope," she said. "Riley is in his shorts and T-shirt, looking tanned. Looking good, Rile!" she added as an aside. "Riley's walking to his mom. Joan is handing him the envelope. Rile is sitting in the captain's chair in the living room. He's tearing it open like a crazy man. There's a pause. He's reading …"

"New York City!" Riley announced.

"New York City," repeated Lucy. "Riley's crying, Joan is hugging him. Riley is going to the heart of Babylon!"

I determined at that point that it was time for me to make my appearance, so I opened the ceiling and let light stream into the living room. I could hear Lucy on the phone, but she sounded far away. Starting from atop Squaw Peak, I descended in a white robe, open in the front, and swept through the pillar of light. I screamed through a hooked beak and hovered three feet above the floor as a voice crackled from above saying, "This is my servant." My beak plunged upward into the light. I screamed again, pulling the boy to me, the feathers of my head hard against his cheek, my beak lowering to his ear. I lifted him off the floor in my arms, my face twisted in agony. He dropped the letter. Under my robe, my body roiled with his own spasms and the beating of my wings. He went limp and fell to the floor, and I left through a fissure. In a blink of light, I was gone. There was wetness all around and the smell of musk.

It was kind of daring—more drama than had been asked for. Verus called me on it. "Scenery-chewing stuff," he said afterward, "but I confess it gave me chills. The wings and everything! Nice job." His remark made me blush. I was doing what I was called to, wasn't I? In any case, it's what the kid wanted.

25 | NAMES UNSPOKEN

At Riley's mission farewell, Gus spoke, as was customary for a new missionary's parents. Anticipating that fact, the chapel was so full they had to open the accordion doors to the cultural hall and seat people on the stage at the other end of the hall. Gus could have given the obligatory, five-minute, proud-of-my-son address, but he chose to speak for twenty minutes, his feet planted apart, his shoulders squared. It was as if he were proclaiming Jesus's second coming. He looked out at the audience with his trademark melancholy smile. If he were standing before the Lord himself, he said, he would not be able to say with more conviction that Latter-day Saints were God's standard bearers. He unequivocally supported the Brethren, he added, although without mentioning Elder Gray specifically.

His performance was so convincing that Continuing Education signed him up again as a Know Your Religion circuit speaker. He got a contract for a Deseret Recordings audiotape. In the eyes of the public, he was back on track, his baptism by fire having burned itself out, his hair turning a more thorough gray in the process and making him look more wise. Riley realized that he was part of the anonymous admiring crowd at his own missionary farewell, sitting in a pew to be wowed by a famous preacher-orator whose enthusiasm increased as he stepped to the lectern and faded when he sat down, the SPIRIT there for a moment and then gone until the next cue to perform. That was all Riley could ever be for his father, he realized: a member of the audience.

"When Jody received her endowment, she was moved to tears," said Joan. His mother was in the front seat of the family car, trying to put on her mascara. Gus was driving and was in a hurry. "Jody kept saying over and over again, 'It's beautiful. It's just so beautiful!'" Joan held the tiny round brush over an eyelash, her face looking long, like a collie's muzzle, while Gus accelerated the pace. She dabbed at her eyelash between bumps and swerves so expertly you would have thought she had two pair of eyes.

The three of them were due at the temple for Riley's endowment, the apogee of the faith. Since the ordinance is secret, except in anti-Mormon literature, Riley was clueless about what to expect. He felt like his life would probably be an open book to the officiators, who would certainly be able to perceive his level of worthiness, the way Jesus in the Book of Mormon told his American disciples, "Behold, I know your thoughts." Back in that day, it created a mixed sense of excitement and trepidation for us to stand in the presence of the Lord, and it certainly did now for Riley as he headed for the House of the Lord. Even if the temple wasn't a pentecostal feast, ever since that moment in his flip flops in the living room, with the letter signed by the prophet lying at his feet, Riley had been able to pronounce with conviction his gratitude and certainty of the truth. The way I looked at it, he had just needed a hook to hang his doubts on, in order to proceed with his life.

After attending the temple, Riley would be required to wear

the special undergarments some of the boys at school had taken to calling Jesus jammies. Lucy complained that on her wedding night the garments blunted her sexiness, but beyond that she wore them all the time, even under her sweats when she played racquetball.

As they entered the grounds, the other patrons, carrying their change of clothing in little flowered suitcases, seemed like a scene from Shangri-La. What secrets lay in the way they walked silently toward the door? he wondered.

"Do they wash your private parts?" he had asked Gus the day before. He was envisioning how embarrassing that would be.

"It's done modestly," Gus said. He pulled his son in close to him with a mighty arm and said, "You'll see." The last time Riley had been to the temple grounds was when Jody got married to her quiet-spoken husband, a recent divorcee. There was a reception at the dream house for them, and that's where Riley met Warren's two children for the first time. Riley would be able to attend other people's temple weddings after this and wouldn't have to wait outside.

Gus asked Riley if he had his recommend.

"Yes," he said, pulling the small card that was required for entry out of his front pocket and showing it to him. Suddenly Gus started patting his own pockets.

"Nelson!" Joan cried. "You didn't?"

"Just kidding," he said, smiling broadly, then followed with, "Give me a kiss," to which she replied that she wouldn't, "not after that stunt. Anyway, you need to behave," she said. "We're at the temple."

When they exited the car, they linked arms with Riley and walked together to the glass doors that whisked open like at a department store. Riley was taller than his parents but more slender. The three of them were smartly dressed and felt confident. Riley imagined that this was what it was like to be an only child.

The temple had the smell of sanitized air. In the dressing room, three different men stopped Gus to say hello. Gus couldn't remember people's names, so he would say, after shaking someone's hand in his meaningful way, "It's Jim, right?" Or for females, "It's Susan, right?" It never was, and they would gently correct him and he would feign to remember. "This is my son, Riley," he said to each man, his big flat hand to Riley's back. "He's here for the first time, leaving on his mission to New York City in a month." Riley shook their hands as heartily as his father.

In the dressing room, Gus and Riley stripped. Gus helped his son put his head through the hole in a sheet they called the shield, which hung to his knees. To Riley's surprise, Arnie Chambers from school was also there with his dad. Riley could see Arnie's flanks through the open sides of his shield, the white skin looking like a baby's butt. Riley held his shield closed as best he could. A question mark sat painfully in Arnie's face as they laughed nervously.

They walked to a marble-walled room with washing and anointing stations. From there, Gus said, Riley was on his own. A temple worker directed him inside a cubicle, fronted by a white curtain, where the officiator motioned for him to sit on a small stool. The elderly man touched different parts of his body and head while dipping his fingers in a tiny silver sink in a symbolic washing, his lips murmuring the words of the anointing by rote, as susurrant as a distant brook. Then the officiator began anointing him with the same tender touches, his fingers dipping into a silver bowl into which olive oil dripped from the ornate spigot. He told Riley, through the liturgy, that he was being anointed to be a spiritual priest and king.

Riley shivered from the man's first touch, but simultaneously thought of King David's anointing and felt connected to all his hoary ancestors whose tiny oval pictures his mother had lovingly pasted into their family pedigree chart. This was his link to Grandpa Riley, to Moses, Abraham, and everyone all the way back to Adam.

The officiator was breathing hard. It was hard work for him, bent over Riley as he was, his hands respectfully entering through the sides of the shield and lightly touching Riley's chest, shoulders, legs and feet, and crown of his head, all the while whispering the ritual prayer. When the officiator touched the small of Riley's back, he called it his "loins" and blessed him "that you may be fruitful in propagating a good seed." A tide of cant ebbed from the adjacent cubicles, behind curtains, opaque and shifting in the astringent air. Everywhere in the room was the sound of the liturgy, interrupted by deep sighs, the exhaling of weariness everywhere as if the eternal work of God was suddenly all present like a painting that was begun and completed in a second and could be viewed in a single moment in its totality. The water and oil flowed everywhere, dripping into the little cauldrons and producing an echo, pooling in their glistening tarn of loss and hope. Riley quietly wept.

He was not likely to remember what the officiator looked like who dressed him in the garment of the holy priesthood, but when he leaned heavily with a sniffle into the curtained side and grasped for support, the officiator seemed concerned. The man placed a veined hand behind Riley's neck, pulled him toward him, and spontaneously kissed him on the cheek.

Waiting outside the cubicle was Arnie, who stood next to his father and appeared shell-shocked, his face turned blank. Back in the dressing room, it was clear that Arnie was not having the same transcendent experience Riley was. "Just try to focus on the feeling of it," Riley said as they dressed in prescribed clothing and shoes, all white. "You have to remember that lots of other people have done this before."

In another booth, Riley and Arnie each received a new name—just as Lucy had explained would happen. Then they were guided upstairs to where the women briefly joined them from their own quarters and then sat across the aisle on the women's side. The ceremony began with instructions on how to don the apron that represented the fig leaves worn by Adam and Eve, tied around the waist on top of the men's white slacks and the women's white dresses. Gus carefully unfolded Grandpa Riley's antique silk embroidery featuring seven large, intricately patterned leaves. Joan had kept the fragile heirloom wrapped in tissue paper in a box on her closet shelf. Gus helped his son tie the apron, to nods of approval from the other men standing nearby. Now Riley was ready to take the oaths of righteousness and learn the handshakes of fellowship.

After a prayer circle around an altar, they were led to a VEIL, the floor-to-ceiling white curtain where they spoke the lines they had rehearsed during the ritual, which were required for entrance to the other side where the Celestial Room awaited them, a chandeliered palace salon with pillowed seats representing heaven. It was in this room where Riley and those in his entourage met again and he could greet his three older sisters and brothers-in-law.

Everyone kept smiling their approval. Riley looked down at Grandpa Riley's apron, falling nearly to his knees. The embroidery was intricate. Everything in his ensemble was white except for the patch of natural green over his groin. He sat down exhausted, next to a giant vase of purple and pink flowers. This is what they meant when they talked about families being forever, sealed to God in the highest kingdom of heaven, he thought. Now he had been endowed with the knowledge he needed to meet with the sentinel angels after death. Would he slip up and forget the lines or default by divulging his secret name? He hoped not.

In the parking lot, he fought the recurring mental image of cutting his throat, disemboweling and castration of himself, which the participants had been prompted to mime at one point in the ceremony to metaphorically depict the punishment awaiting the unrighteous. He thought about his name, Mosiah from the Book of Mormon, and the new words he had learned that were incomprehensible, strung together from the Adamic language, he was told. There was now another form of notation, another language, that perhaps signified who he really was inside. Intoned together, the three words pointed to God's approbation and were said to be a key to unlocking the mysteries of God, perhaps even the mystery of Riley himself.

Back to work the following week, he told Brad McKinley, who was going to France on his mission, that he had just been to the temple, to which Brad said, "What did you think?"

"It was okay," said Riley, giving the perfect noncommittal response.

"I'll tell you, at first I thought I was in the wrong place, different church. All that rigmarole … scared the shit out of me."

"You know you can't swear like that on a mission," Riley said, then walked to his chair, his whistle bumping at his chest. They both knew what the symbols stitched over the breast, the navel, and the right knee meant on temple garments. It was a serious commitment, this religion thing.

A half a dozen people lounged in the indoor pool. School had started, and there were only adults and small children now. He thought of the prescription to wear the garment day and night. That was hardly possible for a lifeguard. Since he was saving money for his mission, he rationalized, it was okay.

One of the other guards, Janie, blew her whistle and yelled "Everybody out!" at the end of their shift and the water became still when the swimmers left, their voices echoing in the locker rooms. Janie climbed off her chair, did some side twists and yawned, then waved goodbye. "You going to turn off the lights?" she asked.

He nodded. "I'll be out in a minute," he said. The pool, left to itself, mirrored its surroundings. Though the water was always a distortion of what was there, it was an efficiently diluting body, not unlike the world Riley now found himself in. He could almost forget where his fingertips, lips and toes were, where his jelly fish hair ended and the amniotic fluid of his destined life began when he was swimming laps. The temple was emblematic of all that.

What if a fish had a name for the water it swam in? The water is everything to a fish. It knows it to be the embodiment of buoyancy and risk. Would the fish know anything more if it had a name for it? If anything, it would be more limited in its understanding of what water was. As with me. I saw immortality as a calling, then as a sentence. When I realized I had changed the definition, I knew I was in trouble. The same thing was happening to Riley. His definitions were changing, and that was a problem for him.

26 | DRESSED FOR SUCCESS

The first of Riley's seven missionary companions was Elder Pinter, known for his silver buckle that looked like a small pie tin with gold lettering. His belt brought to mind his pre-mission life at the wheel of a dusty Dodge in Montpelier, Idaho. All the elders wore the same Swedish-knit suits in conservative colors, as recommended in *Dress for Success*, the secular scripture for missionaries.

"It couldn't be colder," said Elder Pinter, the construction he often employed. ("I couldn't be hungrier," "This couldn't be harder.") He had probably picked it up from the country-western radio jockeys he admired. The four missionaries flew to New York together and spent their first night in the attic dormitory of the mission home on West 67th Street, a brownstone with a decorative cornice around a gabled roof. They were met at the airport by President Anderson and the office staff, all of whom sported knowing smiles and firm handshakes. They loaded the luggage into a station wagon and left two of the staff to accompany the greenies on the subway, which they said would give them a good opportunity to practice talking to people about the gospel. One moment Riley was being served a chicken dinner by a stewardess on United Airlines, the next moment he was nervously fingering a paperback Book of Mormon on a subway car and talking to a black man who had strangely clumped hair.

"Why don't you put your pajamas on if you're cold, elder?" said Riley to Elder Pinter, who was in his nylon-mesh temple garments, standing under the room's sloping ceiling. He'd been assigned as Riley's companion in Provo, and Riley was already in the mood to divorce him. Of course, none of them wore pajamas. They were all getting used to the garments that hung in the damp air like crepe paper in a rained-on parade.

Elder Pinter sank into his bed. Riley hated everything about this person whom the little white handbook said he was supposed to love more than anyone else in the world. Back at the Missionary Training Center, Elder Pinter's favorite sport was to lie down on the bunk and plant his feet on Riley's mattress above him so he could bounce Riley up and down like a cowboy in a rodeo. One day Elder Pinter tried to do it in his suit pants and split the seat out. He was already putting on weight.

"If I'm not here tomorrow morning, Elder Hartley, you'll understand, won't you?" Elder Pinter said. He was homesick and feigning dissatisfaction with New York.

Elder Woskowski was silently pining for the girl who saw him off at the airport. "I'm thinking," panted Elder Woskowski, his chest rising and falling below the scoop of his garment top, "that my asthma might not do very well in this climate. Has anyone seen my inhaler?" he said, coughing.

Riley confessed to his journal that he would like to be tied to Elder Woskowski's companion, Elder Chandler, a tall, thick-necked boy with a fierce faith, whose cheeks burned when he bore his testimony. He had been high school student body president and the football captain. Ever since one of the Brethren spoke to them about how the scriptures were the journal entries of former missionaries, he had kept a journal, and Riley assumed that if anyone's daily entries were destined to become the word of God it was Elder Chandler's. Both of them had been saddled with losers, a pot-bellied cowboy and a whiny asthmatic, neither of whom really wanted to be there.

"You guys are going to be great," Elder Chandler said cheerily to his disconsolate brethren. He was lying in bed, writing in his journal. "Tomorrow you'll be with your first real companions."

"I've heard a lot of horror stories," said Elder Pinter, "This guy from Salmon was telling me they tricked him into drinkin' wine while they were all drinkin' grape juice. They were saying to him the whole time, Hey Elder, this is Paris, man. Even Mormons drink wine here. Just about gave him a cor'nary," Elder Pinter concluded as he scratched his balls and slid off the bed to his knees to pray. Elder Woskowski sat cross-legged on his bed, sucking on his inhaler, his eyes squeezed shut. Outside a siren climbed several registers. It even *sounded* like Babylon out there.

"How do you spell *millennium*?" whispered Elder Chandler, deferring to Elder Pinter's praying. They were forbidden to call each other by first names. Riley liked it when Elder Chandler asked him something. His idol had read Gus's book and said he "really dug it," and he told Riley he admired the fact that Riley was not only spiritual but smart. He must have taken a cue from the high-octane vocabulary Riley liked to drop in conversation. You wouldn't know it to read Riley's journal entries, though, which were just notes, written in spare unemotional language.

"Two *l*s and two *n*s," Riley whispered, pawing through his stuff, looking for something. When he found it, he crawled into bed. Before long his companion had finished praying. "Aren't you going to say your prayers, Apostle Fart?" Elder Pinter said.

Riley chose not to answer. "He's so perfect he doesn't fart on the toilet," his companion had said at the MTC, thus the pseud-onym only Elder Pinter used.

"Leave your companion alone," said Elder Chandler. Riley looked at Elder Chandler and rolled his eyes. Elder Chandler smiled back.

Riley looked at Lucy's letter, hand-delivered that morning by his mother at the airport. Most everyone had been there, and it was emotional since he hadn't seen his older sisters for some time. Jody's hair was short. His two little sisters held butcher paper that read, "Take Manhattan, Elder Hartley!" Candace stood nearby cradling number two. She and Sam had been sealed in the tem-ple. His sister still radiated sensuality, despite having a tiny baby sleeping against her effulgent breasts. She was all but falling out of her snug dress, decorated with tiny white pompoms.

Then there was Cade, a senior in high school and the swim team's most valuable sprinter. He had won every 50-yard freestyle race he had entered. Never before had Cade and Riley had more in common, but they looked at each other like they had blown in sideways from different ends of the universe. Here was Riley, starched and uncomfortable in his suit and black mailman shoes, and there was Cade, tall and tan, his carved torso pressed into his thin T-shirt. He was Riley a year earlier, swinging a whistle at the pool, and Riley had become something else.

On the other hand, Riley was going to New York City, which seemed pretty cool. What wasn't cool was having to wear a black plastic name tag, which Elder Pinter derisively called "a bill-board." The tag said "Elder Hartley," along with the church's logo.

"Good luck, Riley," his brother whispered as they more-or-less embraced in a false start of inept grappling, Cade's poky ear hard against his brother's cheek. "Give 'em hell," he said, and smiled. Riley gave him a thumbs up and wondered if it was in keeping with the quiet dignity they had been told to project.

"You're looking strong, Cade," he said. "You can probably beat Dad in an arm wrestle." At that, Cade grinned. The thought of beating Gus at anything seemed like some kind of unachievable sacrilege, like questioning THE GOSPEL, and the idea of it met with his approval.

There were tears at the airport farewell. First it was Gus, his thick shoulders shaking, then Jody and Candace, then Winnie, who at fifteen was attracting goo-goo eyes from the phalanx of missionary groups waiting for their flights. Riley looked around. Muriel, the oldest, wasn't there. She and Scott had moved to California where Scott was going to go to graduate school.

"See you in two years," Riley said, hugging Gus, who was himself wearing a dark suit and white shirt—the uniform.

"Work hard," Gus said.

"I'll send that other pair of pants out with Brother Williams," Joan said as Riley reached to embrace her. She stiffened, opting for practical things. "Doris says he gets out to New York every month." She took in a quick breath. "Maybe he can drop it off at the mission home. I love you, honey," she said.

Riley walked away, gave his ticket to the agent, and turned in time to see a tissue pressed to his mother's nose. Poor Mom, still taking care of everyone. It was Joan who explained how he would receive his monthly allowance. She was the one who picked up an extra white shirt and kneaded it into Riley's over-stuffed suitcase at the airport. She was the one who thought to bring him Lucy's letter, which was now spread out before him on blue stationary, all the way from the west coast.

Dear Rile,

Hope you got the overcoat we sent. Your mom said you'd need a size 38. I hear it rains a lot in Babylon, so there you are.

Last week a returned missionary said his companion slipped and hit his head on a cobblestone and was knocked out. He wanted to give him a blessing but didn't have any consecrated oil, but he saw a man standing next to him holding olive oil in some kind of ancient-looking bottle.

The elder takes the bottle, and after the blessing turns around, but the man is gone. There's no one on the street. It was one of the three Nephites looking out for the missionaries.

Sometimes I wish I could serve a mission like the elders who converted me. Your mom says I need to raise a good family, and that's my mission, so I'm doing my best. Did I tell you that I'm expecting twins?

You're like a brother to me, Rile. Do well out there. I know you will.

Love, Lucy

Elder Pinter looked like a child who wanted to be tucked in by mom. He was snoring. Riley stuffed Lucy's letter back into its envelope and slid it into one of his shoes on the floor. Elder Chandler had gotten down onto his knees and was leaning into his covers, his face in his hands. Elder Woskowski lay on his bed with his arms behind his head, focused on his breathing. There were still sirens outside. Would it ever quiet down?

I liked that Riley was reading anecdotes about my two colleagues and me. If you were to ask him, he would say it was all nonsense, but on the other hand he might admit to you that he sensed something in the room that he couldn't see. In any case, people expected great things of him, as even the bishop said. "You're the son of Nelson Hartley, so everyone wants to know where you're going on your mission," the man had said, beaming at him. Well, what if the Lord didn't bless Riley with baptisms? It had put a lot of pressure on him.

Riley pulled the covers up over his head and closed his eyes as a loud sharp voice came in off the street through the window. In twelve hours he would be stopping men in suits on the street as they hurried through the Wall Street district. "Hello, I'm Elder Hartley," he would say, "and this is Elder So-and-So. We're missionaries for the Mormon Church. Have you heard of Mormons?"

Maybe he could find one heroin-sick hippie to baptize, and it would be worth having to put up with companions like Elder Pinter. Someone as wonderful and stalwart as Lucy was bound to come along, someone who would forever thank him for bringing THE GOSPEL to her, the gift of eternal life. He rolled over in bed.

Elder Chandler got off his knees and switched off the lamp next to his bed. "Good night, elders," he said.

27 | DEPOSITION

For a missionary, bad news from the family is an open wound in search of a balm. That was how the death of Lucy's baby sat with Riley. He remembered it every morning he got up, and there was nothing he could do to stop thinking about little Riley, one of the newborn twins, his own namesake, gone from the world through SIDS.

He had knocked on doors for almost two years, recited memorized lines to potential converts, and had been regularly driven off porches. One tenth of his life, a full tithe, had slipped away with nothing to show for it. He fantasized about being hit by a car and put out of his misery, then at least he would get his name in the newspaper. But in fact, he would not die in White Plains, New York, an area smitten not with evangelical Christianity, the bane of missionaries, but with lapsed Catholics and polite Rotarians.

At the funeral for little Riley, Leslie carried the tiny casket himself on one shoulder to the front of the chapel. Lucy walked slowly behind it with a tired look on her face. In her arms, elbows out, was the surviving twin, a sort of talisman in bunting that everyone expressed their pity for. The rest of the children followed: four-year-old Sam; his sister Sylvia, who was a year younger; and five-year-old Dryden in his slicked-down hair with a few unruly spikes sticking up.

The children sang "I Am a Child of God." It was supposed to comfort them, but it instilled more dread than awe. The bishop said the deceased was in heaven. He had been taken for a purpose and would receive his body again, good as new, in the resurrection.

Lucy managed not to cry when she eulogized her son and guaranteed her fellow Latter-day Saints regarding the strength of her beliefs. She wore a colored dress. To reassure others in the face of hardship was the *sine qua non* of Zion. Here was a reformed hippie from San Jose doing it with such polish that even Joan Hartley, firm-lipped to show her own resolve, paled beside this woman's performance in bidding her little son goodbye. Standing in the podium lights, Lucy was bathed in a soft corona that looked like it had been beamed in from an empyrean world.

The organist accompanied the congregation to sing

> Oh my Father …
> In my first primeval childhood
> Was I nurtured near thy side? …

Afterward, Leslie came forward and picked up the tiny casket again, and the family went out the side door to the hearse. The caravan crawled through the streets to the edge of Selma, the town where Lucy and Leslie had made their home. The hole to the grave was tiny, like an attic window looking up and padded with artificial turf. The bishop said a few words and then the procession trailed away, arm-in-arm, restless for something to eat. Lucy shepherded the children to the car. If the hymn was still reverberating in Lucy's mind, it did not comfort her, but only reinforced the task at hand.

When I leave this frail existence,
When I lay this mortal by,
Father, Mother, may I meet you
In your royal courts on high?

What reassurance she did feel came from a tribal understanding that even in her baby's death, there was assurance that they were on the right course. *Thank God for that!* she thought.

Riley felt defeated as he turned his filmstrips and pamphlets over to Elder Leavitt, his junior companion fresh off the bus. How ironic that Elder Pinter had been the most successful missionary, even with his big silver belt buckles and his reputation in Nassau County for having slept in till noon every day. "Good luck, Elder Leavitt," Riley said to his green companion. "If I had twenty months to go like you do, I'd slit my wrists with a rusty spoon." It was a standard missionary saying.

Riley packed his extra pair of mailman shoes, his white shirts, now badly yellowed, his scriptures, and his box of letters and left on the Metro North line for the mission home in Manhattan. President Anderson and his wife had planned dinner for the three departing missionaries who had trundled in together two years earlier. Only one of that group of four had failed to "return with honor" from his proselyting duties. Somewhere in the Bronx, halfway through his mission, Elder Chandler fell in love with a Chinese student and disappeared. When he resurfaced three weeks later, he was married to her. President Anderson held a disciplinary court and apparently disfellowshipped him, according to the grapevine.

Despite that turn of events, Riley had no doubt that if anyone's journal deserved to be canonized, it was still Elder Chandler's. Now all that would remain on file would be the mission communication to Elder Chandler's bishop informing him that the missionary had failed to complete his tour of duty. Riley, by contrast, would be honorably released but had not baptised a soul.

In the attic again, Elder Pinter, Elder Woskowski and Riley prepared to turn in so they could make their seven o'clock flight the next morning. They had gathered briefly after dinner in the parlor with their mission parents. As they reminisced, Riley felt at home in the warmth of their utter fusion to the cause they had pursued, the sense of belonging to something greater than himself. The GOSPEL was the most important thing ever, but it was either incomprehensible or consciously rejected by the majority of people in the country's most populated city.

Elder Pinter was taking off his silver belt buckle for the night but seemed chastened by the evening's conversation. "I liked it better when it was all about baptisms," he said, trying on a new pair of boots his father had sent for his homecoming. Sitting on the bed, he struggled with them, lifting his right leg high in the air. "All of the sudden, the talk is about whether people are *truly converted*, whatever that means." He had a disgusted look on his face. There was a *thunk* as his heel dropped into the boot. He stood up and inspected it, looking fey in the dim light in his under garments, his belly showing slightly and the brand-new boots stealing all the light in the room. "You get 'em in the water, that's our duty," he said and bent over as he spoke, as if he were dunking someone. "It's the people in the ward who'll keep them active in the faith. We're specialists. We teach, we don't fellowship. Anyone can fellowship."

Apparently new converts weren't being properly assimilated into wards, though. Riley had heard from Eric Whitworth in Kyoto that only twenty percent of the converts there stayed in the church. In New York it was twice that many, but still not even half.

"You know what Elder Cline told me?" said Elder Woskowski. He was trying to decide whether to pack his missionary flip chart or chuck it. "Elder Cline told me his uncle who works in Washington heard that President Reagan met with the missionaries and is going to join the church as soon as he leaves office."

Elder Pinter looked at him with contempt. "Just throw the flippin' flip chart away, elder! What are you going to do with it, take it on dates?"

Elder Woskowski looked wounded. "I like the pictures."

"Throw it away!" Elder Pinter yelled, at which Elder Woskowski jettisoned the large black binder into the waste basket. "There's a new rumor every day," Elder Pinter exclaimed with contempt. "I had a member in the Bronx tell me the Indians' skin was turning white like in the Book of Mormon. For heck's sake!"

When Elder Pinter finished letting off some steam, he looked at Riley and shook his head. "The church is like any other institution, you know? It's about advertising. It comes down to how you sell it. If not, they wouldn't have told us to read *The World's Greatest Salesman*. Why did they take time at the MTC to show us how to get our foot in the door when we were out tracting?" He went squeaking in his boots past Riley's bed, looking like an antique stripper.

"Whaddya think elders?" Elder Pinter said, meaning his boots. "Pretty good shit-kickers, aren't they?"

"I hope the president doesn't hear you talking like that," Riley said. Elder Pinter stopped in his tracks and studied him.

"You know what's wrong with you?" he said. He was standing almost directly in front of Riley, his arm on a hip. "You never get real."

"You look ridiculous in those," Riley shot back and laughed, then turned around to stuff his suitcase with socks and garments and his Christmas scarf.

"I don't think there's any real part of you," Pinter continued. "You're like one of those do-dads where you look in one end and twist the other and you think you're seeing the universe or something."

"A kaleidoscope," offered Elder Woskowski.

"But when you take your eye away, there's nothing there. It's as flat as a pancake at the end, a buncha broken glass in there, that's all."

"What's your point?"

"I'm not so sure you've got anything under that pretty Utah picture you carry around in your head, just a bunch of wacky reflections of light. Is there anything in those pants of yours anyway? Is there a penis somewhere in there?"

Riley turned back around and faced him. Elder Pinter stood taller, as if he were daring him to say something.

"Hey cool it, you guys. Remember who we are," said Elder Woskowski.

Elder Pinter had a point. Who were they exactly? Twenty-one-year-olds. When they weren't getting indifferent refusals from Catholics, they were being chased down and scolded by Baptist ministers. What did they know about anything? Maybe he was right and they were just point men for a slick advertising campaign. Riley felt like he was some kind of equal and opposite force pushing back at something that fundamentally resisted him. He was the counterpoint to the Jehovah's Witnesses, to society, to Elder Pinter, to God.

It was a shame he never learned to keep his thumb outside his fist when striking someone. He doubled up his fist and connected with Elder Pinter, who collapsed to the floor in a spray of blood.

"Shit, shit, shit," Elder Pinter bellowed. He pulled his knees up to his chest, looking even more ridiculous in his garments and boots.

Riley's hand stung, but the pain felt holy and utterly clarifying. There was no question now about what was real, there was blood to show for it. As my charge had suspected, Pinter wasn't much of a cowboy.

"We've seen people fall before," my cranky-old friend Verus said. It was true. We had, but usually not literally like Elder Pinter did. At home he told people he was hit by a born-again Christian after quoting the "faith without works is dead" passage in the Bible. Riley's thumb was broken, but it would heal up without any lasting scars, not on the outside anyway. He got it bandaged up to keep it in place for the flight home.

From his window seat, he thought of his ancestors crisscrossing the continent to the Great Basin and back again on missions, then home again. What could Riley see from this high up? What remained of all the wending ways of his forefathers? Which scrubby Iowa town below was Mt. Pisgah, he wondered, to which a woman had staggered, carrying her infant who had been dead for three weeks, hoping to get a proper trail-side dedication by a Mormon bishop? Could that low-lying hump be Independence Rock below, where 10,000 pioneer names are etched into its rock wall? Could one make out Devil's Gate or does everything crumble into nothing on the high plains from this far up? What could a young man see of the remembered tales and unheard-of stories that characterized a place and his life in it like a scent? What words, O God, could he conjure to tag the uncanny necessity of claiming it as his own and being revealed, not just to strangers on their stoops, but to himself as well?

The old family portrait in the house had been taken down in anticipation of Elder Hartley's return and a new group photo. There was new carpeting, forest green couches. The maple Postum table with the polyurethane top was gone. In its place was a perfectly square glass-topped mahogany table with a ceramic vase of dried flowers on top, indicating that there were no more toddlers at home.

Riley wanted to see his former acquaintances before he started back to school at BYU. With nothing better to do, he inquired about Paris, who he had heard had AIDS. He wrote to him once from his mission but hadn't heard back. He was at the Utah Valley Medical Center, his mother said.

"I'm here to see Paris Carter," he told the young woman behind the counter.

"Do you have a cold?" she asked.

"What? No, I don't," Riley replied.

"Are you comfortable without a mask?"

He froze. Had he thought this through? "I don't need a mask," he said. At that, they walked past a hand-written sign taped to a door jamb that read, *Please see nurse before entering.*

"There you go," the nurse said.

"Riley?" Paris said immediately. "You look good!"

"You're in good spirits for a sick guy," Riley said.

"For someone who's dying," Paris retorted.

There was a pause. "I hear they're working on a cure," Riley said.

"That's what they say." Paris turned to look at the *I Love Lucy* rerun playing on the television. He looked as old as Grandpa Chaz but still had the voice of a teenager.

"Are you going to sit down? Right over there." Riley sat. "What happened to your hand?" said Paris, still looking away.

"Caught it in the subway door." Riley shifted his weight in his chair so he could see the IV above the bed. "The doctor says it will be fine. Broken thumb. How's the food here?" He didn't know what to say.

"I always wanted to break a bone," Paris responded to Riley's injury. Paris lay in his bed, his bald head on two pillows. He sounded different without his teeth. "My cousin broke his leg up at Sundance. Remember that? Fifth grade. Everyone signed his cast and brought him presents. Lucky guy. Look at me." He rolled his eyes in that way Riley remembered and raised his arms as if presenting himself to the world, then dropped them to the bed. "No one brings me presents."

They were silent until Riley said, "Paris, I want you to know that a long time ago when we, you know …"

Paris looked at him without an expression, the lower jackets of his eyes red and elongated, several strands of hair plastered to his head like cracks in his skull, unnoticed. He coughed deeply and reached for water.

Riley half-stood to collect the tumbler for him. Paris took it as if it were breakable, gently lifting it to his lips, and handed it back. His fingers touched Riley's hand. Would that mean he would get sick? Riley wondered. The moment converged like it did long ago in the attic. Riley tried to smooth it over by deliberately taking Paris by the hand.

"That feels nice. My mother is the only one who touches

me like that now," he said. "Do you want to see something?" He pulled back the sheet with some difficulty. "This one is my favorite mark," Paris said, touching one of four black lesions festering on his right leg. There was a smell of lotion and flesh.

"Are there more?" Riley asked, not sure how to proceed. His stomach was turning.

"Every week the nurse counts them. I've got some on my back too. I think this one looks like Australia," he said, poking at it, "so I call him Aussie. Hi, Aussie baby. How ya doin, honey? It's a nickname for Australians."

"What's that?" Riley asked, indicating a large patch of moldy-looking flesh on his left ankle.

"Gangrene," he said. "From shooting up."

"Drugs?"

Paris looked at him, then laughed weakly. The room brightened and eased.

"Sometimes I wish I was like you," said Paris and then promptly vaulted into another coughing fit. "Speed," he said finally, catching his breath. "I sold it for a while and made $60,000 one month, more than I ever made with music."

"I read somewhere that you get this from needles."

"No." He breathed in heavily, and Riley could hear hollow sounds of pneumonia in his lungs. "Did you hear about the two addicts who shared needles until someone told them they were going to get AIDS? They said, no we're not, we're both wearing condoms!"

Riley blushed. Paris didn't laugh either, or even smile. Everywhere it seemed these days, there was talk of the risk of infection, the need to use rubbers, to not share needles. Riley's brain had to process visual clues that this was even Paris. He could see evidence of his former friend in the eyes, the way he rolled them and shook his head like the burden of the world was knocking at his door, which it was.

"Everyone thinks it must be so hard to have lost my looks," said Paris. "But do you know what?"

Riley smiled. "Tell me."

"Now I look as bad as I feel. When I look in the hand mirror, what I see makes sense. Remember when I was in LA and getting work playing the keyboard at parties? Everyone thought I was handsome, but I didn't feel handsome. Now I look the way I feel."

"Did you get my letter?" Riley asked.

"Yeah, you know, I never got a letter in California. Everyone was mad at me or something."

The nurse entered and said, "I think that's enough for today. We allow a few minutes, is all. How ya doin' Paris?" she asked.

"About as good as Clark Gable. I know, he's dead." He turned toward Riley to add, "I said Cary Grant last time."

"Is he dead too?" Riley asked.

"He's a fag like me. He and Randolph Scott. Give us a few more minutes, would you, Susie? Pretty please with sugar on top?"

"Two minutes," she said and left.

"Susie doesn't like me to use bad language like *faggot*. Well, faggot, faggot, faggot! I love her anyway. Some nurses won't work here."

Riley turned around in his chair, thinking someone was standing there, but he saw nothing. "She seems nice," he said.

"Well, she's paid to be," said Paris. "I think she likes me." He looked back at the television to see Lucy crying in her bellowing way. Ricky was patting her and rolling his eyes. "You know, some-thing, Riley. They were right."

"Who?"

"If you break a commandment, it's easier to break another one, then you're ruined. You just say fuck the whole thing, I don't need it. It's like someone turns off the lights and you have to find your way in the dark, you don't have a clue anymore what's okay and what's not."

"Falling into vice, you mean?" Riley offered, the profanity still hanging in the air.

"No, I mean doing things that turn out to be wrong for you. I don't mean in a cosmic way, just in general. There was a guy in LA from Australia who liked Mormon boys because, he said, everything was new to them and so they were up for anything. That was my mistake."

"Do you still like guys?"

"I love guys. I loved you, Riley. Does that bother you? I had to swear off sex, and for that I got my family back. My mom, bless her, I missed her so much." He looked away. "One thing I regret is that I'll probably never play the organ in church again."

Riley wasn't sure why he'd asked the question about Paris's erotic preferences. It didn't matter. And it didn't matter that his friend had once been in love with him either. There was something otherworldly about Paris as he lay there, gaunt and coughing, making his way slowly to the other side of the VEIL. Riley admired that at least his friend knew where he stood.

"I miss the profanity," Paris said.

"What?"

"That was definitely better than I thought it would be."

177

"What do you mean?"

"You know, *fuck* and *goddammit*. I used to put a whole string of 'em together because I liked the way it felt on my tongue. It made my head hum. *Goddamn mother-fuckin' jism-sucking asshole of a cunt*. See what I mean? Fabulous."

"Well," Riley didn't know what to say. "I better go." He stood up, feeling extremely uncomfortable.

"I'm sorry," Paris said. "It's not your thing, I know. Well, thanks for coming by. It was good to see you."

"Sure …"

"And remember, you can get friends in high places, but it's better to get high in friends' places." He cackled, and Riley smiled at the banality of it.

Turning to go, Riley stopped and said, "You know my thumb?" He lifted his bandaged hand. "What I told you was a lie."

"I know," Paris said.

"I hit a missionary and broke his nose."

"Good for you!"

Riley felt relieved to speak the truth about himself. Instantly he felt like he had acquired a kind of warm confidence.

"Was he cute?" Paris wanted to know.

"Definitely not! I mean, I don't know … maybe you'd think so."

Paris grinned. "Will you come and visit me again?" he said.

Riley nodded in the affirmative.

29 | VENGEANCE IS OURS

The power of the word is two-edged. It can constrain you, Riley learned. A kind of reverse logos. Back home he was struck by how religion seemed to be spoken into a wide-mouthed canning jar and quickly sealed, but the most amazing permutation of toxins began in that sterile environment. *Morality* turned into moralism. *Courage* became obedience. *Values* were edicts. *Self-discipline* became mental subjugation. The WORD became simply an act of preservation, of enduring toward some kind of end.

You could argue that's exactly what we immortals have done—locked ourselves into a story entombed in obscure scripture, constricted ourselves so that we're not open to new experiences. We justify waiting for Christ's return, wandering from place to place instead of changing how we think. Riley is the same. Wander as he may, he can't liberate himself to make room for his soul.

"Could be worse," Verus says of our situation. "People make up stories about you, saying you appeared to them, but you don't have people claiming you're married to Miriam and that you were Pilate's butler."

"Fair enough," I say.

Despite the efforts of the former Miss Utah to tastefully

redecorate the living room, it was around the kitchen table that the Hartleys liked to congregate. One late Sunday afternoon, Joan, Gus, and Riley were seated at the table talking, and the house was uncannily quiet except for the dishwasher humming away in the background. The next day would be Paris's funeral. Riley felt out of sorts. He could see that everyone else in the family had a purpose in life but him. The mission president had glossed over his violence to a fellow missionary and granted him an honorable release. It didn't matter because Riley didn't know who he was anymore in his post-Babylonian environment. Maybe he should have been disfellowshipped like Elder Chandler whom Riley never saw again. He had to consider marriage, of course, followed by children. He would get a job somewhere, although he didn't know who would hire a returned missionary with a facility for collecting words and not much more to show for himself. His father was recording bizarre video pitches for a food storage company that helped Latter-day Saints sock away a year's worth of food in preparation for the end times. Even Cade, who had refused a mission, seemed to have found some gainful hobby, turning from swimming to bodybuilding. As for Riley, he had no armor like his brother's muscles, only the approval of his parents who now sat before him like a moated castle, defended.

"They're good people," Gus said, referring to Paris's mom and dad. "I've known Garth for a long time, and it's tragic to see them going through this. At least Paris is at peace now."

Riley said he went to the hospital to see Paris, but he didn't tell his parents what Paris had said. The way he saw it, Paris spoke in judgment of more than just the local community. The whole world received a bad review in that hospital room. How could Riley convey that to his parents?

The phone rang. Gus leaped up from the table and took the call in the other room. It was about Riley's sister who had acute anemia and wasn't eating. People had started calling her Skinny Winnie, but without knowing she had a psychological problem.

"I got a call from Leslie the other day," said Joan, moving to a different subject, picking her words carefully. Riley's mother had changed clothes and was sitting at the table in a house dress and slippers, her earrings still pinned to her ears like they were forgotten Christmas decorations. "He says Lucy isn't doing too well."

"What's wrong?" Riley asked.

"She has a drinking problem," Joan said matter-of-factly and pressed her finger into a crumb on the table to pick it up and deposit it in a tissue.

Riley didn't know what to say. Why was he finding out about this only now, and through his parents? Why hadn't Lucy confided in him? They had written each other and she had said nothing about this.

"How's the new baby? Hasn't that helped?" Riley asked. Lucy had recently delivered number seven, a girl. He couldn't remember the child's name.

"It's been hard," said his mom. "She lies in bed. They've had the Relief Society come in and take care of the child. I don't know, Riley. I feel sorry for Leslie."

"Leslie? He isn't the *easiest* guy himself," Riley countered. "She makes all the decisions in the family because he's so passive. He's a dork." Riley was breathing hard when Gus, having heard the outburst, returned.

"You're talking about Lucy," Gus said. "That situation is a heartbreaker. We pray for her every day."

"Muriel told me Lucy was concerned that Cade turned nineteen and wasn't going on a mission," Riley offered. "She wanted to know how you and Dad were taking it."

"Why would that be her business?" Joan asked.

"Because she thought we were the perfect family," Riley said.

"The perfect family?" cried Joan. "We never suggested that our family doesn't have its challenges."

"We act like it's what we're about," he fumed. "Even to ourselves." He stood and walked to the sink, where he emptied a half-empty glass of water before returning to the table. "Muriel told Lucy everything was fine, that you and Dad let your children make their own decisions. She said it was a revelation to Lucy that we could be like other people."

"Lucy is a troubled girl," said Gus. He was standing against the wall, his arms folded across his chest, his green eyes on guard.

"What's going on here, Riley?" his mother said sternly. "Spit it out! What is it you want to say and haven't?" Her directness startled him. She was this way once before when he was sixteen and was expected to baptize Jessica, just turned eight, the next day. It was late at night. Gus was in bed. Riley had alluded to his mother that he didn't feel worthy to perform the ordinance.

"You know what you have to do," she blurted out, standing there in her nightgown while Riley was doubled over on the couch. "If you're not straight with the Lord, then get down on your knees, Riley, and make it right. Stop putting it off. Just do it!" She turned, flipped off the lights, and went to bed.

"Not everyone thinks the same way Dad does," Riley finally said. "Even my religion professors don't talk like that."

"So there we have it. You think your father is a fanatic," she said, still in direct mode.

"I'm saying there's a bigger world out there, and it has to be connected to the gospel in some way. We can't live in our own little universe doing things our way and making up whatever stories we think will support our way of life." He avoided looking at Gus, who remained quiet but was breathing deeply. Riley thought about a letter his father had sent him on his mission expressing his belief that, if the church wasn't sending young men out to spread the gospel, there wouldn't be a nation on earth with any semblance of stability.

"Your dad's opinions are based on the scriptures," said Joan, "and the teachings of the Brethren."

"Apparently not," Riley argued, the specter of Elder Gray suddenly in the room. "What if I disagree with the Brethren anyway?" Riley said. "Doesn't that mean, according to Dad, that I'm hiding some kind of sexual sin?" Gus scowled to realize he was being talked about in third-person.

"It might mean that," said his mom. "It could also mean that you're intellectually off-base, which happens to young people when they go to school and learn new things before they can process it all. But the Brethren speak and …"

"And the thinking stops, right? As Joseph Fielding Smith said. What about when Dad speaks. What then?"

Joan shifted in her chair. "When we lived in Los Angeles," she said, "your dad was getting a lot of pressure from people like Clyde Sanders, you remember him? We were driving to conference one day with him and Francine and they asked your dad if he believed Heavenly Father didn't want blacks to have the priesthood. When your dad said yes, they laughed right in the car." Riley couldn't tell where his mother was going with that thread.

"I questioned your dad that night when we got home," she went on, "not about blacks and supporting the Brethren, but his emphasis on other things."

"On personal revelation," Riley interrupted.

"Yes, that," said Joan. Each Latter-day Saint was supposed to receive revelation, but Gus's take on it was that the SPIRIT wouldn't allow you to sin once you began getting revelations. It was that, not so much Sandy Greenwood's accusation, that spurred Elder Gray to caution people against it. "Your father told me point blank," she continued, "that I had to get a confirmation of the doctrine myself," so she prayed and decided there was no free agency when it came to truth. There weren't options, just obedience. "We're the ones with the truth," she insisted. "It wasn't easy. I had questions that were at least as hard as the kinds of things Lucy asked. The women's movement was underway, and I was a stay-at-home mom with five children. How do you think that looked? But after I got my witness of the truth, I didn't care anymore, and I have never questioned what your dad is doing since then."

Her hands were folded in front of her, white and rigid, the blue veins shining through. She licked her lips. I could sense that Riley was sinking into a place that was dangerous because it was becoming so obvious. I could have interceded, but the former Miss Utah was not someone to tangle with haphazardly.

"Now I don't know what kind of ideas you were exposed to

in New York," she said in a softer voice. "I prayed every day for your safety. Now it's up to you to get right with the gospel."

"Which gospel?"

"*The* gospel," she said sharply and slapped her hand on the table. Gus looked on with a startled expression.

"I want to go to California," Riley said abruptly, turning over his chair as he stood.

"I'm sure Lucy would love to see you, but now isn't the best time," said Joan, steeling herself.

"I'll go after Paris's funeral," he said. "She's not a hard case, like you guys say. She's not unable to see things because she's a convert. She's not hopeless." He turned to put his chair in place.

"We don't think she's hopeless, Riley," said Mom. "We haven't told you everything."

"You told me. She's an alcoholic."

"She's seeing another man," Gus said, his eyes fixed on the floor. "She feels that they connect on the deeper meaning of the gospel which has led from one thing to another."

Finally, Riley thought. *She's found someone else who shares her love for living the questions.*

"She has some kind of hokey pokey interpretation of the scriptures to justify it," Gus added. "She thinks she's bringing God into the relationship, if you can imagine that." Gus's jaw was ratcheting down tight. All that could be heard was the dishwasher rotating into the rinse cycle, spinning and spinning.

30 | NUTCRACKER

The wig that Paris was given seemed too big for his gaunt face. There was no white clothing, no pleated robe over the right shoulder, no bright-green apron of silk fig leaves around the waist. He was dressed in a suit. His family wanted him to go to the temple before he died so he would learn the signs and tokens to give the sentinel angels at the gates of heaven and would be dressed like every other good Mormon when he was placed in the casket. Considering the circumstances, the bishop thought it best to wait and have Paris's temple ordinances performed by proxy after his death.

To Joan Hartley, the temple was a big-top tent where everyone shed their earthly personae, along with their garb, and came to the VEIL repenting, and that was what made it so spiritual. She went as often as she could. Usually in the afternoon before school was out, she would break away to drive down the hill alone. After the endowment, she liked to spend a few moments in the resplendent Celestial Room, the one place where she could envision her life along a continuum that extended from her urban childhood in Salt Lake and early married years in Los Angeles to her present circumstances on Golan Drive.

Occasionally she would recall with unresolved grief the time she spent in Atlantic City with her mother twenty-eight years earlier. The expectation was that she might actually win the title of Miss America that year, which makes her shake her head in embarrassment now. She remembered chatting excitedly with other girls from around the country, all of whom seemed infinitely more sophisticated. For the swim suit competition, they rubbed Vaseline on their legs to make them shine. Miss Ohio, a bubbly brunette from Columbus, confirmed how fabulous Joan's legs looked with the sheen. When Joan's mother entered the dressing area, she grimaced at the girls, including her own, greasing up like strong men in some voyeuristic enterprise. She didn't say anything but didn't have to, and Joan carried her mother's look of disapproval the rest of her life like a stone in her chest. It would never occur to Joan that her mother, beautiful but scarred by her experience with the Great Depression, was envious of her daughter about to be seen nationwide on television.

In the Celestial Room, Joan found a kind of nostalgia in these recollections, a preamble to the continuing longing she had now for her children. How she loved them! In that holy place, she could pray silently, sometimes kneeling at the arm of a chair for her daughter who was starving herself to death, for her son who was grotesquely muscled and smelled of cigarettes, for the daughter who had been in fundamentalism, and for the daughter who had become pregnant before marriage.

In that most beautiful place where eternity made contact with the finite world, and wherein humanity would one day be linked together by ordinance into a giant family, her thoughts turned to Riley, her oldest son, who was angrier and more confused than most young men his age, especially since return-ing from his mission.

At the same moment Joan was basking in the peacefulness of the temple, Riley was driving down the hill thinking of his mother. He didn't know where he was going, just not anywhere religious. At the pulpit the day before, at Paris's funeral, the bishop had expounded on the deceased's talents, his musician-ship, and his service to other people, but neglected to say why Paris had died a few days before his twenty-second birthday. There was no mention of why a boy of seventeen would leave home for a place where no one knew him. Maybe Riley was fleeing too, turning right on Center Street and driving toward the freeway. What did it matter that he was a returned mission-ary? What difference was it that he was a son of Nelson Hartley and had knocked on doors for two years? Who cared that he had been chaste for two years and suffered the indignity of waking up in the middle of the night to wet dreams, all for the sake of not having masturbated? Still tender from having hit Elder Pinter, his hand was throbbing. He had homework to do. He should call Muriel … no, Lucy. Maybe his parents were mistaken about her drinking and getting involved with another man.

Downtown Provo was like a ghost town. He drove past a department store, J C Penny, that was hanging onto a last gasp where there had been a thriving business district. It was like a balloon had deflated when the new mall was built in the next town over. There were a few small shops. A used bookstore, a fabric store, a Walgreen's, and a Jimba's. The city fathers had installed new sidewalks with planters. There was a fire sale at an antique store. At the west end of the street was a new eight-story hotel, lured there in an effort to reclaim the area. Its brown-brick exterior seemed out of place with the smart-looking glass atrium that stood behind the angled entryway.

Riley pulled over and parked on the street. A doorman, about his age, stood in front of the revolving door, looking like a nut-cracker in his green outfit with gold buttons and top hat. The temperature was cold, even though the winter sun was warm. There were piles of snow crusted along the sides of the street where it had turned brown as passing cars added sludge to the piles.

The hotel took advantage of the view to the east, which was something Riley rarely saw since they lived there, more or less on the mountain itself. The most impressive thing about the foot-hills, from the perspective of the Hartley house, was Squaw Peak. From the hotel, it looked puny in front of the broadly scalloped and frosted mountain that served as its backdrop. Riley remem-bered his vision of Squaw Peak and the winged creature that had come crashing down from the ledge of the peak, the pain in his chest as the thing gnawed at his organs. Now that seemed far away and irrelevant, more tawdry than seminal, a testament to the kind of psychological tricks the mind plays and the pressure he had been under.

The nutcracker blushed as he tipped his hat to Riley. Inside the revolving door, past the whoosh of air, Riley stood at the foot of a giant red-and-orange painting of Bryce Canyon. The carpet smelled new. A harp was being played somewhere. There was a free-standing black felt board announcing an Amway convention scheduled to begin the next day.

He stood in his parka and wondered if he looked silly. At the reception desk, a uniformed woman with feathered hair was studying something on the counter. She smiled when she looked up. "May I help you?" she said. Riley thought she looked like Stevie Nicks. He shifted his weight.

"Just looking around," he said. Then suddenly, Riley knew what he had to do. "How much are the rooms?" he asked.

"Well," she said, pausing. "We have suites that go for as much as $500 a night. The Governor's Suite is gorgeous," she said while noticing his soiled parka. "It has a Jacuzzi. Are you interested in just one night?"

"Sort of. What about regular rooms?"

The woman looked down at a book, turned a few pages. "We have a standard room for $69," she said, "and if you have a promotional discount, it's even less."

"I'm with Amway," he said without hesitation.

She smiled. "Amway makes your dreams come true!" she sang while she placed a registration form on the counter.

On the walls near the bank of elevators were some grainy pictures of old settlers standing ankle-deep in mud and looking depressed, flanked by droopy headed horses. One of them showed a man with a shovel-head brow and long unruly beard hiding his mouth. Riley's great-great-grandfather hadn't lived in Provo, so this couldn't be him presiding over the vacant lobby and the returned missionary whose pocket was weighted down with a room key.

Then again, it could have been him. It could have been any of thousands of early settlers who sported the same vexed look, hardened by the desert sun. The settlers were the bedrock of the local culture. What did it matter if it were Grandpa Riley pictured on the wall or some other poor refugee from the east, co-opted here for the civic good by the local chapter of the Daughters of the Utah Pioneers? They were all fanatics, closed off from the rest of the world like his mother with her tight-lipped look of disapproval and Gus's narcissistic flights of fancy.

"You had it easy," Riley muttered out loud to the portrait. "Marrying three wives, knocking out twenty-four kids, taking your youngest wife and hightailing it to Mexico. At least you had someplace to go. You had the feds chasing you down, someone you could shoot at. What do I have?"

In room 416, Riley took off his outer clothes and his garments and made love to himself for several long minutes. He thought about how Paris locked the door to his bedroom several years back. He thought about the hookers and sex shops he witnessed on West 42nd Street. And he thought about Lucy whom he fantasized embracing him to rock away his fear. He wept soundlessly for a long time.

Afterwards, sleeping in the sheets smelling like bleach, I held Riley in my arms. And there he dreamt of seeing the Green Loaf screech to a halt at the street curb where he is sitting with his father, his mother at the wheel. She pulls a revolver on her husband who draws his own gun in response and shoots her in the head. One of his sisters places a coat over their mother's head. He wants to see her one more time and removes the coat to find her skin has shriveled up like on a cadaver. As Riley lifts the leathery skull, he hears her sob. Then he sees a knife blade appear at his throat. He thinks it's Gus, but when he gets up the nerve to look, it's his mother holding the knife. Gus is nowhere to be seen.

31 | THE GLORY OF GOD IS INTELLIGENCE

Today, while he is out picking up the *New York Times*, Riley sees one of his sisters, or what could have been one of his sisters. She's on the opposite side of the street waiting to cross, and when she lifts her hand to her hair, the way a self-conscious woman places an errant strand behind an ear, she is Muriel for a split second. The newspaper feels limp in his hand and that familiar feeling of sweet mourning swims the butterfly through his heart.

The problem is not that he has actually seen his sister in that particular woman standing at the street corner but that he sees all of his sisters all of the time in New York. It is the agony of having eight of them at home, none of whom really look alike, all of whom are beautiful, sad, and distantly his. In high school Riley wrote a two-lined poem titled "Eight Sisters."

> My sister died today.
> That's okay, I have seven more.

All of the girls have married in the temple. Like their mother, they are keeping the commandment to multiply and replenish. Even Winnie, who was hospitalized for bulimia, delivered a pree-mie that survived, no doubt the first of many children.

Lucy? Riley doesn't see her in the crowds. His brain has

consigned her to the status of an outsider, so he doesn't notice her form when he sees strangers. He didn't visit her in California after Paris's funeral, as he had threatened to do. Instead, he had just imagined her with her lover, a young man, maybe in college like Riley, narrating their love making with fragrant and crackling words ascending into the air like handfuls of diamonds.

Lucy didn't directly contact him either. It was as though she knew that whatever she was doing out there in California was, if not iniquitous, at least not appropriate to relate to the family she once lived with in Zion.

What Riley was reminded of repeatedly at BYU was that it was time for him to get married. Good thing he was at the Lord's University because it was arguably the best place to be for that kind of quest. It was also the right place for Dina Papanikolas, who was in the same honors seminar he had signed up for. The class met in the granite building, gutted by its nine-story atrium, that Riley thought looked like the box the Salt Lake Temple came in, a monstrosity of financial excess. When he attended his campus ward that Sunday, she was there too. He learned she was a geology major and only had one semester left. He noticed how smartly she dressed, not with the typically patterned froufrou or wrap-around skirt that BYU coeds were known for, but in a blazer with a turtleneck and sensible skirt that had pockets. When Riley's friend Brad saw her, he said, "My friend, I think the bakery just got busy and made you a cupcake." She exuded an urbane flair that Riley liked. But how would he ever conjure enough courage to ask her out?

She was always with her roommate, whose sensibilities reminded Riley of Sandy Greenwood's forced femininity, in contrast to which the gray-eyed Dina, with her short dark hair and nonchalance, was like nectar to a bee. He learned that she had converted to the church in Michigan. That might be why she seemed different, too new to the game to be a caricature of local womanhood. In any case, her intensity was striking, her questions in class pointed and sometimes confrontational, making Riley wince. Their professor, Roland Derringer, was unfazed. But he was not a typical professor either. He had a moustache and never wore a tie—this at a school where going without socks could land you in the office of University Standards. He was divorced. Recently Elder Gray had come to campus and hammered away about the necessity for single men to find a mate, quoting Brigham Young's aphorism that unmarried males were "a menace to society." Professor Derringer didn't seem to have noticed and was in no hurry to rectify his status. He told his students to call him Roland.

Riley was too intimidated by Dina to have a conversation with her. Once on his way out of class, he saw her stop and talk to Jeremy, a guy who was majoring in math and wore muscle shirts. She didn't give Riley a passing glance. It wasn't until Roland arranged a class excursion to Arches National Park over a weekend, saying it would be to discuss *Zen and the Art of Motorcycle Maintenance,* that Riley got to know Dina better.

The last time he had visited the park, he was a little boy. Gus had taken the family to Moab to see some people who were devoted to his ideas. When they arrived, their hosts loaded them into an old school bus and showed them around the most famous panoramas of old Hollywood westerns. Returning to the same location was *déjà vu* for Riley, this time with twelve students and a professor in place of Gus in a university van.

Before they headed out from Provo, Roland offered a brief prayer. Riley and Dina sat next to each other, so Riley was able to hear about her misadventures in Australia as a sister missionary, as well as her current interest in plate tectonics. Her leg rubbed up against his when she turned to speak to someone behind them. It was easy to become so preoccupied with school that the real world erased itself—the fragrant world of farms and canyons, abandoned mines, herds of cattle, and miles of barbed-wire fences that lay beyond campus as they drove farther south.

In Sanpete County they passed by the limestone walls of the Manti temple with its metallic-topped steeples shimmering like old twin lighthouses in the fog. The van grew quiet except for Jeremy, who Riley had decided was a nominal Mormon. Dina leaned over Riley to get a better look, leaving the faintest hint of perfume and the thrill of her hand on his leg. He could see the curved inner conch of her ear, a silver ring on her earlobe, as she strained to see the edifice through the window.

"It's so beautiful," she said, and Riley turned himself from her ear to the building which by then was partly hidden by pine trees. "Have you been inside it?" she asked, leaning back against the seat.

"No, I'd like to," he said. She looked directly into his eyes but didn't say anything. "It has a famous spiral staircase," he said. Pause. "I've seen pictures of it."

"Oh?"

"My parents used to come down here before they built the one in Provo."

"Are you a son of Nelson Hartley?"

Riley stiffened. He didn't know by the question if she might be friend or foe. What side of the fence would a smart, beautiful honors student from Michigan fall on? He felt the familiar toxic mix of exhilaration and defensiveness rise in him.

"I used to listen to his tapes on my mission," she said and smiled. "He's great. I'd love to meet him some day."

"I could arrange that." Riley felt relieved, the tension turning from toxic to thrilling.

Clouds began trundling in overhead when they got to the park after dark. The plan had been to pitch two tents, one for the women and one for the guys, but by the time they got the first one up there was heavy rain and everyone dashed inside and lay there giggling. Roland was always talking about "useful criteria" for analyzing ideas, theories, paradigms. The world seemed to him to be a vast puzzle with temporary solutions that worked "in context" but didn't provide universal answers. Ambiguity was beautiful, he liked to say, and ultimately what underscored his faith. In the tent he spoke of pursuing questions rather than relying on preset answers. As they talked, the rain pocked the canvas of the tent as its sides blew in and out. Riley listened closely to him, alternately gripped by his compelling arguments, the way they made his head buzz in ascendancy, and horrified by his professor's relativism. How could this man be a Latter-day Saint? And yet, of course, he was. Riley had seen the scooped neck of his garments beneath his shirt and knew that he had served a mission to North Carolina.

Suddenly there was Dina's voice in the dark, speaking in limpid tones, unencumbered by institutional assumptions and gloriously oblivious to the fact that some questions are less appropriate than others. "Do you even believe in God?" she was asking.

Everyone seemed to hold their breath, and even the tent stopped sighing for a moment. "By definition I'm someone who believes. I'm Mormon. Don't Mormons believe in God?"

"You say it's *useful* to believe certain things, but that's not the same as believing something in the absence of evidence."

Another pause. "I'm more Mormon than you think," he said. "The model I like is utilitarian, and in fact, that's just like what we hear in church. In our pre-existent state, we were intelligences before God experimented to see what would become of us as spirits and then human beings. He—or she, or they—could have done it differently, but this was what was decided on, we are told. It was a committee. Joseph Smith said that *god* was the title of someone who held the chief office, like a political leader or, let's say, a scientist."

"You can get away with believing that?" Dina asked.

Roland laughed. "I can get away with believing anything," he said. "Well, okay, whether I can get away with expressing it publicly remains to be seen, but here's the point. It ultimately depends on whether or not my heresy exceeds my usefulness to the church."

It seemed to Riley that heresy was just another word for apostasy. Is that why Roland had taken them to the desert, to lure them away from the standard trail and initiate them into a path of apostasy? Was this the face of betrayal?

Roland quoted scripture. "'For this is my work and my glory, to bring to pass the immortality and eternal life of man.' Or woman, I might add." He was talking about Heavenly Father, and it was unnerving. The professor had a penchant for quoting scripture and then questioning every assumption about it from the ground up. The week before he had suggested that the Book of Mormon's warnings about pride and wickedness were directed not to outsiders, as it was commonly interpreted, but toward the church's own members in the future when they would find themselves in a state of prosperity. It was directed toward the church's powerful leaders.

"You sound like an existentialist," said Jeremy. Riley could imagine him saying this while lying on his sleeping bag, his eyes squinting because his glasses were tucked away in his tennis shoes. "I agree with Dina. Mormon existentialism is contradictory."

"Kierkegaard was a Christian existentialist," Riley said. He could play that game too, and he imagined Dina smiling to herself to hear him join the banter.

"Is that you, Riley?" said Roland. "I thought you were asleep." In this darkness, to speak was to create yourself. "I think if it was good enough for Kierkegaard, it's worth taking a look at," Roland continued. "He was impressive."

It was predictable. Everything for Roland was an *option*, not a definitive answer. "I don't believe God knows everything," Riley said, practicing his own dissent.

"That's an interesting point," said Roland, "and in keeping with the idea that godhood is an office. So, the question becomes what qualifies God to hold that position?"

Riley smiled while he answered that "maybe God learned how to manage ambiguity. He solves things—or she does."

"Exactly," said Roland, taking it seriously. "In the temple we're all anointed to the office of king or queen, after we've proved ourselves worthy." If that was not what Riley had intended, it should have been, as elegant as it sounded, and Dina had been a witness to it. He felt closer to her, as if they were lost in the narrative of some future scripture. "(1) And she did cleave unto the teachings of the prophets in a place called Michigan," it might read, "and did find herself in the waters of baptism, yeah, even in the Kingdom of God where she did flourish. (2) And it came to pass that she did seek after greater learning in Zion and was in due time led by the Spirit unto the place in which she would find her eternal mate, even to one named Riley, born of goodly parents."

Dina was raised Greek Orthodox. In Mormon circles, that meant she had been foreordained to find her way to Zion. Having traveled so far, physically and spiritually, marked her as one of the chosen ones. Not only that, Riley thought, she was unusually attractive for someone who had abandoned her previous life for an altogether new one. He fantasized about her full lips and low-riding jeans, which he saw in person the next day as she hiked in front of him to the towering, free-standing Delicate Arch, her light cotton blouse riding up in front and swinging back and forth below her breasts like a dare. She was two years older than Riley but still seemed impish and youthful, especially when she smiled in an over-the-top way. For some reason it embarrassed him to see her expose her left front tooth, the way it was tilted slightly to one side.

He worried that Gus would think her substandard for being a convert to the faith. He shouldn't have, because when he finally brought Dina over to meet his parents, all he detected from his father was a stolen glance at her breasts. On top of that, Dina was such a fan of his book that he had to approve of her. That was really all Gus needed to know about a potential daughter-in-law. Riley could almost hear the *cha-ching* in the cash register of his father's approval.

32 | THE EDSEL

Riley was dreaming more and more about Dina. She was the perfect match for someone who wanted it both ways, a wife who believed in THE GOSPEL enough to satisfy his parents and who thought enough about things that didn't have to do with religion to satisfy him. She would probably even be game for the sixty different sexual positions he had read about. All it would take was a couple hours in the temple and they'd be married and he could begin a lifetime of uninhibited sex.

That summer, after Dina graduated, she and Riley took another trip to southern Utah, this time alone. Their friend Brad had inherited three Edsels, and Riley talked him into letting them borrow one.

"You really like that girl, don't you?" Brad said. He had just made the shocking confession that he had slept with two of the four coeds he visited for the church once a month. Riley shook his head to think of all of what went on that he didn't know about. "Do you like her?" Brad said, wanting confirmation to his suspicion.

"She's pretty okay," Riley said, apprehensive about saying too much around his predatory friend.

"Well, the car's a guzzler," he said, turning his attention to the Edsel and handing Riley the keys.

"Are you sure you don't mind?"

"Just don't do anything I wouldn't in the back seat," he said and laughed. "And take lots of money for gas."

The Edsel was freakish in a fabulous way—huge, like a boat, but with whitewall tires as if it were wearing a valet's gloves. Its two-toned paint job and scalloped design somehow made it seem both clunky and aerodynamic at the same time. When Riley pulled up in front of Dina's apartment, she was standing there with a large, old-styled suitcase she had purchased at a thrift store for the occasion. She had put on an airy blouse, tied at the waist, and high-water pants, high heels, and a straw hat with a magenta scarf to tie it down around her chin. She wore cat-eye sunglasses and carried a white vinyl purse.

"You're kidding." Riley said, noticing a beauty mark the size of a dime next to her mouth.

"Hey sailor," she said, leaning in through the car window. "Thought I'd dress to match the occasion," she said, and thumped the car's roof. Riley got out to get her suitcase.

"Geez, we could put a couple of bodies in here," she said, peering into the trunk. "Did you bring beer?"

"On tap," Riley said, playing along with her. He closed the trunk with a thud.

She smirked, the beauty mark ludicrously scrunching up to her cheek. "Lips that touch liquor shall never touch mine," she said.

"You're a real Zoobie then, after all," he said, using the local moniker for BYU students.

As he opened her door, she said, "Why thank you, sir. You've passed the first test." They both smiled.

In Fillmore, where they stopped for gas, Dina picked her way across the asphalt toward the bathroom in her heels, then gave up and walked barefoot, her shoes and purse dangling from one hand. Back in the car, they talked about their missions and future plans.

As the miles wore on and they passed rangeland and irrigated fields, they drifted into silence. Riley could see himself married to Dina, driving around, if not in an Edsel, then cruising about in their own ironic way, telling jokes. She would like sex, he could tell, because she talked about it candidly, venturing an off-color joke now and again as they got farther from home.

She laughed at his two-liner: "What did Adam say to Eve the first time they had sex?"

"What?" Dina said with a laugh.

"Stand back, Eve. We don't know how big this thing's gonna get!"

He decided to ask what she looked for in a guy. She sat thinking for a moment, her dark hair blowing wildly from the open window.

"Has to make me laugh," she said.

"Really? In what way? Do you think I'm funny?"

"Not especially," she said and turned back to face forward, knowing her answer would irritate him. "And you're too short," she said. "What do you look for in a girl?" she continued play-fully. "Besides an impeccable taste in sunglasses?"

"She has to be smart," he said.

"And looks?"

"Even more important," he said, realizing his compliment might sound like an inadvertent admission.

"What do you mean exactly? Are you saying I'm smart?"

"Not especially!" he said, and they both laughed.

Brad was right about the Edsel because it didn't go far without needing a fill-up. It slowed down the pace of their drive enough that they had to stop in Cedar City for the night. They found a motel off the main road and rented adjacent rooms. Dina changed into blue jeans and sandals. Riley liked that people assumed they were married, how Dina made the waitress laugh when they went to eat. They heard about an outdoor staging of *Twelfth Night* and decided to get tickets.

Settling into their seats, Dina took Riley's hand in hers and whispered, "You know what I look for in a guy? What I like is someone who drives five hours in an Edsel to see Shakespeare."

"Then I'm your guy," he said.

The next morning they drove up a nearby canyon of sculpted red rock. Halfway up they had to let the Edsel cool down after plumes of steam poured out from under the hood. People stopped to look at the car and marvel at how large the steering wheel was and the fact that it had buttons for shifting gears. Its imposing dashboard with its art-deco design and the broad fins made it look like something alien. One admirer had extra coolant, which they felt fortunate to be able to help themselves to. Dina chatted merrily with the guy while they filled their radiator.

After that, they continued over the mountain and got out and hiked, then drove down the other side. Exhausted and sun burned, they talked intermittently. "What made you convert?" Riley asked as they headed north and settled into a long stretch of the old highway.

"The missionaries were so cute!" she said.

"I'll bet they were."

"I used to wonder why we didn't have people anymore like

Moses or Paul, the great prophets and missionaries of the Bible. When the missionaries told me they did, I was intrigued."

"Our family has a friend who converted," Riley said, referring to Lucy. "She told me once, she converted because it answered all her questions about life."

"All of them!"

"Well, she'd say that, then she'd spend all her time asking more questions. Sometimes I wondered what questions she thought *had* been answered."

"I like the feeling of community. I needed that when I left home."

"What about your parents? Are they okay with you being here?" Dina turned away. She seemed tiny with her elbow propped up on the sill, as if she were a little girl.

"I didn't really care what they thought about it," she said. "The way I saw it, it was my life. Do you know what I mean?"

"More or less," he said.

She took off her glasses. "I like you, Riley. Maybe it's time for you to meet Pap."

"Pap?"

"That's my dad."

"Is this a proposal?"

"Protocol demands that you be the one to suggest it."

"Okay. When can I meet Pap to see if he approves of us getting serious?"

"He'll probably say something like, Why bother asking me? If you become an item, you're the one who's going to have to live with her, not me."

He smiled. Even though he figured she was joking about the

whole marriage thing, as they approached Provo he imagined that people were looking at them more than at the car. She looked Greek. He was sunburned. They dressed like they were from California. If they did get married, they were going to redefine what it meant to be Latter-day Saints, he thought. Neither Gus nor Elder Gray nor any of the Brethren (or sisters) would have anything to say about it.

33 | THE WAILING WALL

Dina may have excelled at irony, but she was not a joker, at least not about marriage. They were to marry, and because Dina's parents would not be able to witness the ceremony anyway, Riley never did ask Pap for his daughter's hand.

Brad shook his head when Riley announced his engagement. "I knew I should've never let you borrow that Edsel, Riley. Are you sure about this?" He was sure. And they planned to marry in the old pioneer temple in Manti.

Before the ceremony a gray-haired temple worker escorted Riley to the Celestial Room, which was convenient because the antique chandeliers provided a perfect perch for me. Riley sat alone on a sofa near the TEMPLE VEIL that was billowing and shuddering like the patterns in a vertical-wave tank. Riley was dressed in the robe, apron, sash, and baker-style hat he would be buried in. Dina would soon approach THE VEIL from the other side. He thought of how she would look, dressed in her white robe, a wedding veil pinned to her hair. He wondered about the course of events that had brought him to that destination and decided he had to face a simple truth, that all his decisions in life had involved some flying leap of faith, some grand gesture that forced doubt aside. Now there would be someone else involved.

How could he risk telling Dina to hold his hand and jump into the void with him?

There was a rustling behind THE VEIL, and as he heard his fiancé's hesitant whispering voice, his escort reappeared and walked him to it. There were three knocks of a mallet from the side Dina was on. Riley was prompted to part the VEIL slightly and initiate the practiced exchange with Dina. An officiator on the other side spoke first on behalf of her client, requesting that "Eve" be allowed to converse "with the Lord through the VEIL." This was when Riley would learn Dina's new name, given to her during her own endowment. In the role Riley was now playing, he wasn't Adam seeking light and knowledge, he was God's representative who was supposed to determine whether or not the petitioner would be admitted into heaven.

A disembodied hand appeared through the VEIL. Riley grasped her hand and noticed that it was covered in a hint of sweat. The escort prompted him to recite the liturgy, again whispered through the VEIL. He leaned in, turning his ear to the airy curtain through which Dina whispered the name she'd been given. "Rebecca," she said in a breathy voice

"Did you get that?" the escort whispered off-script. Riley nodded.

The ceremony continued through the rest of the scripted part to the stylized embrace, touching in five places through the VEIL as if they were going to begin a ballroom dance, fitting their two hands together, putting another hand on their partner's back, aligning the inside of one foot against the inside of the other's foot, right knees touching, and their mouths pressed against each other's ears. As the curtain bunched and draped between them,

Riley felt his spirit leave his body and rise to the top of the room, like he was aiming right at me on the chandelier. But instead he hovered there and watched his physical self collapsed against the VEIL as if it were a kind of stone wall. As he and Dina recited their promise of an eternal future together, he rocked slightly, as if in adulation to God. Perhaps it was only from this height, up next to the dimmed lights hiding several strands of dusty cobweb, that Riley was able to understand the meaning of what he was saying, like hearing one's voice for the first time played back on a tape recorder.

Still unseen to each other, Riley disentangled himself from Dina through the VEIL. At the sound of three more mallet knocks, Dina asked that Eve be allowed to pass through to the other side, at which Riley parted the floor-to-ceiling opening and pulled his beloved through by the hand into the presence of God. On seeing her, he gasped at her lithe form, swathed in white, her dark hair backed by the folds of her own veil.

I confess I was romanced by it all too, and for a moment I thought to myself that maybe everything would work out okay between them. I wasn't given that much information, just told to observe and be on guard.

34 | IN MY FATHER'S HOUSE

"How are you doing?" Riley asked. They were sitting on the edge of a four-poster bed at the Manti Inn where they were staying, each rubbing their feet after a long day of standing in the temple.

"Tired."

"We can wait till tomorrow."

Dina limped to the bureau and faced the mirror, gazing through her begowned image to another place where Riley was not allowed. Coitus loomed over them as the next expectation in THE PROGRAM, the life path Riley had been taught since birth. It was the thing they were supposed to do now to meet every station on the road to eternal life.

What had happened to their plan to be different and to buck the stereotype? Riley thought they should have had sex right before the wedding to spite the officious busybodies.

"Remember I said that when I was growing up, a friend got pregnant?" asked Dina. "She was fifteen; her parents sent her away to Chicago and I never saw her after that. I guess after the baby was born, she stayed there." She breathed in slowly, her breast moving under the tight bodice of her gown. "I'm not ready to have children, Riley. I know what the prophet says, but I ... I

210

want to have a baby because *we* want to have one, not for someone else. Is that okay?"

It was a thrilling thought. "I like that idea," he said.

"I got fitted with a diaphragm."

"Okay."

"I need to take a shower."

"Right," he said and smiled. "I'll be here."

When she came out of the bathroom, she was in a thick robe, loosely tied at the waist, her hair wet and shiny. She blushed. "Your turn," she said.

Riley allowed himself to meld with the hot water. Everyone from the family had been at the wedding in the small side room at the temple, the Sealing Room, they called it. Riley's brother, Cade, now twenty years old, stood with Gus as one of the formal witnesses. Three months earlier Cade had announced that he had experienced a conversion and wanted to serve a mission. The younger girls had waited outside the temple. Only Lucy was entirely AWOL. She had sent a gift that Riley and Dina would soon discover, among the bath towels and silverware, was strange and wonderful—a compact, two-volume version of the *Oxford English Dictionary*. It came complete with a magnifying glass for its tiny print. In the front cover, she had inscribed,

> To Riley and Dina, I can't find the words to express the joy I felt at hearing of your nuptials. Maybe you can find a few words yourselves in the OED. Like they say, Bright is the ring of words when the right man rings them. —Love, Lucy, Les, and the little terrors.

In the shower, Riley was full of anticipation and could barely wash himself. He laughed at the sight of himself in the mirror. Even though he could hardly see through the steamed surface, beaded with water drops, he thought he looked absurd in his aroused state. It caused him to feel a sudden nervousness that rolled over him in waves. When he emerged, Dina was lying on her side but was still dressed in her robe, the toes of one foot curled around the other. He lay down next to her. She moved into him and they kissed, leaving short wet strands of her hair matted against his face.

"I love you, Riley," she said. They began to shyly touch each other, as if they thought something might break if they touched too hard.

"I am so in love with you," Riley responded.

"Are you going to stay for this?" asked Verus. He was standing behind me, unannounced. It startled me.

I turned to look at him. "He needs me," I said.

"He needs *her*," Versus insisted.

"Look at me, Zed." I turned back to him, my eyes welling with tears. "You're just jealous, aren't you? You wish *you* were that beautiful."

Verus took me by the arm. He was right.

Dina and Riley delayed their trip to Michigan until Dina had gotten squared away at the University of Utah where they had taken an apartment nearby. Dina was more than happy to put off her visit home. Since leaving six years earlier, she had never really looked back, rarely returning until she had found another life and now another family.

Driving to Michigan, Dina began to shut down. Near Chicago she awoke in the middle of the night sweating. She had confided to Riley during their short courtship that she and her parents didn't get along very well. Now she told him that if he imagined a welcoming party, he would be disappointed. In fact, when they arrived, no one was even home. They sat outside in front of the wooden mailbox announcing the PAPANIKOLAS FAMILY. The house was a large Tudor-style structure, surrounded by natural landscape that spoke of money and moral superiority. It reminded Riley of the homes on Golan Drive.

When the Papanikolases arrived, Riley was immediately drawn to Dina's brothers, Nick and Bobby, who had the same good looks as their sister and the kind of coiled-spring athleticism that bespoke the contact sport they loved and at which they apparently excelled. They ate dinner like it was a football scrimmage. They liked Riley too, probably because he asked about their high school mascot, the Fordson Tractor; the nearby Detroit Pistons; and the Madonna concert they were taking dates to.

They talked through a traditional meal of lamb, rice, and dolmades. There was fruit for dessert, but Dina excused herself from the table, saying she did not feel well. Dina's mother, who reminded Riley of the secretary on the *Perry Mason* reruns his mom had liked to watch, went in search of an antacid. Riley pretended not to notice Dina's grimace as she glanced at her father on the way out. Strangely enough, Pap had only said five words during dinner. He was more content to munch on leftover grape leaves and later the *koulourakia* cookies than to have to engage in small talk. His coffee was darker than anything Riley had ever seen, and served with a side of water.

Seeing Riley notice his coffee, Pap said matter-of-factly that "otherwise you're courting bad luck"—those were his five words.

As soon as Dina left the room, however, Pap wanted to know how his "little Konstantina is doing anyway?"

His wife looked at him sharply, then collapsed her gaze back to the table. "Bobby, there's more fruit," she said.

Pap sighed, pushing his plate away and pulling out a pack of cigarettes. He bit a smoke directly out of the pack, then reached for one of the candles to light it. All of them watched, holding their breath as he pulled air through the cylinder.

"Dina's a little tired from the drive," Riley said.

Pap looked at him, expressionless, and Riley realized the man was not happy to have had his daughter stolen away.

Mrs. Papanikolas began clearing the dishes. "Boys," she said, "homework?"

"It's Friday," said Bobby. "*Miami Vice* is on."

"Are you talking back?" asked Pap, smoke pouring out of his nose.

"No, sir," the boy said.

Nick, the older one, looked at Riley and gave his eyes a conspiratorial roll.

His father noticed. "Do you have something to say to me?" he demanded.

"No sir," the boy said and slid out of his chair as inconspicuously as possible.

"They seem like good kids, Mr. Papanikolas," Riley said, addressing Dina's father directly for the first time.

"Everyone calls me Pap," he said and tapped the ash from his cigarette. "What do you plan on doing after graduation? Going to teach?"

Riley hadn't told anyone he was considering education, but

people assumed that was what English majors did. "Or more school, sir," he said. "I haven't decided which."

"What do you want to teach?" Pap asked.

"Law," Riley replied. He actually had no intention of going to law school, but it sounded good.

"Wish I had a better opinion of lawyers. Might as well be up-front about that," Pap said. He moved the ashtray to the edge of the table.

"What do you call fifty lawyers on the bottom of the ocean?" Riley asked. "A good start."

Pap didn't react. "Someone told me you have sex on the altar in front of everyone in your temple," he said.

Riley looked at him, shocked, and felt a sudden resentment toward this blocky, crew-cut Greek who was so abrupt.

"If that were true, I'd be going to a whole lot more weddings," Riley said.

Pap looked at him, his eyes widening slightly before he burst into a hoarse cackle, wagging his reddening head back and forth and slapping the table.

Riley felt embarrassed and took a sip of water. "Your daughter's doing fine, Pap." Riley said, feeling bolder.

"Still on meds for depression?" Pap fired back.

Riley looked perplexed but recovered quickly. "She's a little worried about graduate school."

Pap leaned back and looked at his guest again, this time as if he had just stumbled onto some modern art he didn't know what to make of. "There's a lot I admire about your people," he said. "They're patriotic, they're hard working, they're clean. Never saw such a clean city as Salt Lake, and those wide streets and all that."

"I didn't know you'd been there."

"But I have something to tell you, Riley." He thumped his chair back down on all fours. "You're hiding something out there. It's like being in Ireland. Something's going on they're not telling you about, but you can't put your finger on it because it's a secret. And I don't mean just those weddings of yours no one can go to. In Dublin, the jolly Irishman act is just a cover for something, and I'll bet the clean-cut Mormon thing is the same."

"I'm sorry you feel that way, that you didn't feel welcome."

"Oh, I felt welcome. Never saw such nice people, in fact. I saw Mormons in the army too, and they were always smiling and polite, but it makes you wonder what the hell they're hiding. You put two of 'em in a room together and suddenly it's like the Irish carrying on about the IRA or something, 'the troubles,' they call it. I'm not sure what happened to Dina, but she came back from Chicago different than she had been, and then she went to Australia on that church mission of yours, and now here she is sitting at my table with someone she tells me is her husband!"

Chicago? Riley was taken back. "If you'll excuse me, I think I'll check on Dina, sir," Riley said.

Pap placed his hard ruddy hand on Riley's arm. Riley was close enough to smell the man's aftershave. "Don't get me wrong, I'm not saying you're lying about anything to me. I'm saying sometimes people lie to themselves. That's their problem until you find yourself in a foxhole with one of them, and then you have no idea if you can trust them."

When Riley got to Dina's room, she was asleep. The hall light banded across her face so it seemed grainy, cinematic. What was it Pap suspected him of? What was he saying exactly? In the mirror above the bureau, Riley caught a darkening reflection of himself, the married man at twenty-three, far from home, with a woman he hardly knew and her family whom he barely understood.

"Riley?"

"I'm here, Dina." He sat on the side of the bed next to her sleeping warmth.

"It's my period, you know? I always get nauseated." It seemed that she fell apart when she got her period, all tears and frightening talk about how she was unworthy to be with Riley. "What did you guys talk about?" She was lying on her side.

"Just stuff. Your brothers are doing their homework or watching *Miami Vice*, I'm not sure. I need to tell your parents goodnight, but I wanted to check on you first." They could hear Pap downstairs clearing his throat, the low notes making him seem a few footsteps away.

"What did my dad tell you?" she asked. There was a pause as Riley processed the information about Dina having disappeared to Chicago long ago.

"Military stuff," he said.

She sighed and rolled onto her back, her left arm over her white forehead, a tear in the corner of one eye. "I always forget why I had to leave home. I always thought it would be nice to have a close family … and a sister, for instance. To think you had eight of them! That's a real family." She paused for a moment and drew her arms around her chest. "I always felt lonely here. Do you know what I mean? Do you see why I had to leave?"

"I guess so."

"It was awful."

In the weeks leading up to their marriage, Dina had seemed

to lose her confidence, her verve. Now as she lay in the dim room that used to be hers, she could have passed for fourteen. She placed her hand between Riley's legs and gently rubbed against his jeans. "Do you want to do something?" she asked.

"Here? In your parents' house?" he gasped. "I thought it was your period."

"It was over two days ago."

He was puzzled. "You're okay then?"

"There's a window of opportunity, Riley."

He got up to close the door.

"Leave it open."

"But your parents."

"We'll be quiet," she said, and there was a look of shy satisfaction in her face as she slowly slipped her nightgown and garment top over her head in one larcenous move.

35 | THREE MARYS

Where was Riley supposed to file the report in his mind on Lucy's adultery? Was she an eccentric or a criminal, an independent-minded person versus someone on the lunatic fringe? It was an important question because Riley and Dina saw themselves as modern-day Mormons who were smart and urban, not members of a cult like Pap had suggested. Riley thought the fact that he worked Sundays at the recreation center proved he wasn't a fanatic, and Dina being in graduate school and on birth control confirmed that she was just as level-headed. To her father, though, she had been duped.

There were warning signs, though. Dina's love of animals hinted at a lack of ordered priorities. If she saw Ethiopians starving on television, it didn't move her quite as much as a segment about neglected retrievers at a puppy farm. The puppy story would produce tears and insomnia. It didn't make sense because a geologist was supposed to be interested in non-living things, but they were almost eighteen months into the marriage and there had been a steady stream of pets crawling, hopping, slithering, bounding, and flying through the front door. None of them was quite so adored as Chauncey, the African Grey that sat in a cage the size of a small refrigerator box and steadfastly refused to talk.

The bird's reticence didn't keep Dina from fawning on the monochromatic creature that had the shockingly yellow eyes. She took him on walks in their neighborhood up by the university, the parrot hunched over her shoulder, head cocked to one side, occasionally preening the hair behind Dina's ear with a black beak so Dina would feel compelled to shrug and say, "Now Chauncey, go chew on your own ear!" Once when the two of them were in front of the apartment, a pre-school class came by, six pairs of kids holding hands, and squealed in mock horror as Dina gently placed the bird on the shoulder of each one. She smiled heartily, showing her crooked tooth, her eyes ablaze with delight.

Their post-honeymoon life together had turned tense almost immediately after they moved in together because of the attachment to a third entity. "It doesn't have to be another African Grey," she said, angling one weekend for yet another bird. Riley's exasperation with her pets had become evident, and he responded with a grunt.

"I take good care of these guys," she said. "I'd do the same for another one."

"There's shit everywhere," he said. His mom would shudder if she heard him talk like that. "It's everywhere, all over your clothes." Riley flicked a crusted dropping, half green, half white, off her shirt sleeve while Chauncey eyed him suspiciously.

"I can design a cape for that," she said and disappeared into the kitchen. When she returned, she had made a crude sketch of what looked like a royal mantle with a wire lining at the bottom.

"You're not wearing that around here," Riley said, handing the sketch back to her with disgust.

She looked at the sketch again, tipped her head to the side and, bumping Chauncey so that he squawked loudly, said, "Maybe if I made it a little wider here?"

When she wasn't fixated on her pets, she was depressed. Sometimes she became obsessed with a homemaking project and would put up 200 quarts of tomatoes, rather than the customary 24 like the other women in the ward, then fall into a lethargy so acute she would skip classes. Sex was vigorous, if also edged with hostility, beginning that night in Michigan where Riley had to quiet her because the bed springs were creaking so loudly her parents would have heard them, and she dug her fingernails so far into his chest it caused him pain.

They got another bird, a great green-and-red Amazon parrot named Buckshot. Riley tried to be supportive and got his wife a subscription to *Bird Talk* for Christmas. He wasn't entirely indifferent.

At the annual family Christmas party, everyone except Cade, who was now in Mexico on his mission, gathered at the dream house like the holy family returning to Bethlehem. There was a letter from Cade, who said they had so many baptisms he looked like a prune from the waist down. Dina had wanted to bring the birds to the party, she said, but Riley put his foot down.

"The kids would love them," she insisted. "I embarrass you, don't I?" she said, changing tack. She was decked out in a flowered dress with mutton sleeves, a far cry from the preppy look of her college days. She had also grown out her hair into a feathered mane like Riley's sisters and every other young woman in Provo.

On the way, Dina kept turning down the volume on the stereo because it unsettled her. Riley was so happy to hear Jody's offer to whisk Dina off to the kitchen, he all but pushed Dina in that direction. His wife launched into a geology theme. His father gushed as usual, pulling Dina into one of his famous bear hugs, his voice turning squeaky high. "Hey little lady," he said, "don't you look sensational tonight! How is that handsome son of mine?"

Joan, heavier by the year but still sporting queenly legs, tried hard to appear more than perfunctory in her affection to the in-laws, her arm hooked through Dina's. The daughter-in-law responded by spending most of her time straightening out the lower half of her tight sleeves. Joan's face beamed like a TV advertisement. "A uh, a uh, … really?" she said in response to Dina's patter.

Riley nodded to Sam, that year's Santa, and got a loud response. "Hey, when you gonna have us up to watch the Jazz with you?" Sam shouted. Riley's sister Candace, buxom and handsome as ever and cradling one of the twins she had recently delivered, smiled at Riley and blushed on behalf of everyone present at her husband's outburst. Since her gunshot wedding, a perpetual little cloud of cosmic disapproval seemed to follow her around.

Riley smiled back at Candace. At the bottom of the stairs, a cacophony of sounds from children at play spewed forth where tumbles, fake fart sounds, and screams were the norm. Some forced hebephrenic laughter came from a child Riley thought must be Clay, the oldest of the grandchildren. Then he saw a tiny form dressed in white, a loop of tinsel fallen half over her face, standing nearby at the bottom of the stairs. She would be one of the angelic hosts in the nativity scene being assembled downstairs. Clay was roped into being Joseph, or maybe the donkey Mary would get to ride, and not happy about it. Riley had himself served such roles for the benefit of the younger children in his time.

He leaned over the wrought-iron railing and looked into the dim light. "Amanda, is that you?" he called. She was Jody's second child, a three-year-old, and at that moment pulling at her cotton gown as if it were stuck in her panties. There was a piercing shriek from one of Riley's youngest sisters, Jessica, who was kneeling on the floor with bobby pins in her mouth. A shepherd's shawl floated in front of her, half-pinned to a child's pate.

"I'm an angel," Amanda said, as if her uncle would not believe her.

"I see that. Are you going to get to visit the baby Jesus tonight?"

She stared at him for a moment, processing the question, then held up her hand to show him something, a doll. "It's the baby Je-e-esus," she said with a smile, her eyes catching the light from the hall lamp. Then she was gone in a single jump, back into the gumbo, the door closing behind her.

Riley was surprised Gus deferred to Grandpa Chaz to offer the blessing on the holiday ham, hard rolls, and ubiquitous Jell-O salad as everyone crowded festively at the kitchen table. Grandpa and Grandma were notoriously affectionate with each other in public—holding hands, sneaking smooches from each other when the sacrament was being passed at church. It embarrassed Joan but impressed Riley. He walked over to Dina and put his arm around her. She smiled but tensed up. They bowed their heads in prayer.

The house seemed small that night with the flocked Christmas tree in one corner and clusters of family members and relatives digging into Gram's banana cream pie, everyone's favorite. Chums, now seventeen and starting her first year at BYU, sat next to a dark-skinned defensive back from Tonga. The boy's most interesting feature, Riley thought, was that he talked freely about his love for the Lord but admitted he didn't want to serve a mission. Riley wondered how his thin blonde sister could be in college—and whether she felt like her future had been sketched out for her on graph paper like Riley's had been years ago. He remembered what it was like to sit in the lifeguard chair and consider his future prospects through his parents' eyes.

Maybe his sister didn't care. Maybe she was working THE PROGRAM to her advantage, thinking a "Lamanite convert" was enough variation to bring something original to THE PLAN but still be within acceptable boundaries. All that was left for her to do was marry this Polynesian boy with the short hair and seemingly no neck and issue forth enough children to start a baseball team and she would be accepted.

"Shistle" came a familiar voice. He felt a poke to the ribs. It was Muriel.

"Pit," he said back with as much larceny as he could muster.

"Shistle"

"Pit"

"Shistle"

"Pit," he said, turning and taking her in a hug. "When did you get here?"

"Last night," she said. "We're staying at Gram's." In Riley's arms, Muriel looked as tiny as Chums standing next to her boyfriend and seemed even more exotic, as if her time in California had given her a burnished gloss of sea breeze and avocados. They stood there, Muriel holding both his hands tightly.

"Where's Dina?" she said, looking around. "I haven't seen her since the wedding."

"In the kitchen, I think, with Jody. How's Lucy doing?"

His sister's face darkened. "For a while we were talking every day," she said and pulled him toward the front hall for privacy. "She's about two hundred miles from us, so we can't see her often. Met her at a restaurant in Fresno once. It was weird."

"Yeah?"

"I don't know just … she stopped seeing that guy."

"Did they hold a court for her?" he said directly.

"Yeah, she was disfellowshipped."

"I guess it could've been worse. How's she taking it?"

Muriel sighed. "You know how intense she is."

"Yeah," he said, bringing her image to mind.

"She fires questions at you like a gun and wanted to know about Winnie's bulimia, why Cade was cutting his arms, and how this could happen to our family. Ever since Jody got involved with that Alvin guy, she's been like that. It's like she's determined to … "

"At least she's brave enough to ask about it," he interrupted with a spike of hostility. Joan and Gus referred to their children's struggles as though they were minor speed bumps that they had negotiated with the SPIRIT and laid to rest. Such things could only be discussed when they were no longer a problem, solved by the miraculous calculus of THE GOSPEL.

Muriel took Riley's arm, this time as the oldest child of the Hartley family. "I worry about our parents, Rile, and I try to be the child they don't have to worry about."

Riley looked at her for a long time, her message sinking in like a stone hurled into a lake.

"Now, what do I have to do to find my only sister-in-law?" she asked and turned away.

The family was gathering in the living room for the nativity scene. Agnes sat at the piano waiting to play carols at intervals during the reading from the Gospel of Luke. The younger people sat on folding chairs or sprawled out on the floor. There were babies everywhere, and they were passed around like sandbags. Dina sat next to Riley on the couch and looked as breakable as the glass-topped Postum table in front of them. Gus was circulating. He didn't sit at the center of the family but orbited it.

This year they had three Marys because of an abundance of little girls. They stood side-by-side, holding hands, one with a thumb in her mouth, next to Clay. "And so it was, that while they were there, the days were accomplished that she should be delivered," Jody read.

When the Marys, "being great with child," arrived with Joseph at the crowded inn, the pageant ground to a halt. Fifteen-year-old Jessica realized she had forgotten to cast the inn keeper. "Oh my heck!" she whispered, darting glances around at the grownups.

"Get up there!" Jody whispered to Riley. He heard Sam snicker, and before he could think, Dina, who had been holding one of the sand bags, passed off her bundle of a sleeping child and stood up, straightened her dress, and marched to the front of the room. With the verisimilitude of an impatient clerk at a Motel 6, she announced, "There is *no* room in the *inn*!" She smiled. The family smiled back as she sat down, small beads of sweat on her upper lip.

Suddenly the three Marys were holding three holy bundles

of babies, each girl partially veiled by a white shawl, the Mormon color for Mary as opposed to the Catholic blue. They knelt. Clay stood behind them with a look of contempt. "And she brought forth her firstborn son, and wrapped him in swaddling clothes, and laid him in a manger," reported Jody, her face screwing up. She cried in the same place every year.

Shepherds appeared with brooms in their hands and every kind of dish towel arranged with haste on their small heads. There were more tears from Jody as she struggled through the angel's recitation, "Fear not: for behold, I bring you good tidings of great joy, which shall be to all people."

When the wise men appeared, they were decked out in Afghans, tin-foil crowns, and brightly colored headbands. This year they traipsed in with a selection of Joan's old beauty pageant mementos. One of them held a sculpted brass vase with the words "Miss Congeniality" engraved on it. As Agnes plinked out the piano accompaniment, the forever family launched into "We Three Kings" and Gus began with vigor, but he collapsed into vigorous humming when he became uncertain of the lyrics.

"Silent Night" signaled the end of the scene. While they waited for the kids to shed their biblical garb and for Sam to secretly change into the Santa suit and a beard made with cotton balls, Dina excused herself to go to the bathroom.

"Are you feeling okay?" Riley asked as solicitously as possible. She appeared pale and carried the pained expression that he had grown to dread.

"Fine," she said, and turned, trying to shake the wrinkles out of her skirt.

Riley watched her navigate her way, her smile having taken

on the strain of molded plastic, like an expression his mother might have. As usual there was too much to process at the family gathering. Despite all the role-playing, the structure seemed to lack any true color, the exceptions being the children, who were boisterous and naughty, and of course Sam, whose only gear was relaxed. As an adult, Sam was dismissible in this setting, especially by his wife, Candace, who seemed in her sad, frustrated way never to have quite fallen out of love with her own father.

What would Cade be doing tonight in Mexico? Riley wondered. Would he be eating tamales with church members? Did his companion wonder why he had marks on his arms and left ankle? Riley felt sorry for his brother. Maybe Elder Hartley would find a hotel room somewhere in the jumble of Mexico City where he could escape and wrestle with his thoughts in a safe place the way Riley had.

On the way home, Dina and Riley quarreled. She said his family looked at her critically. "What have you been telling them?" she wanted to know. She meant, had Riley told them she went to Chicago as a teenager to deliver a baby, something she had subsequently confided to him, or that she had smoked pot at a high school party and hitched a ride home with the wrong guy? All she could remember, she had told Riley through tears, were the maple leaves clinging to the wet windshield of the car.

"I haven't told them anything," Riley lied to her. He had, in fact, divulged to Jody at Thanksgiving that Dina had experienced bouts of depression, probably having to do with her past.

"What past?" his sister had asked, and he said she had gone through a wild phase in high school.

"It's the way you look at me too," Dina said, rubbing a small porthole in the fogged-up car window. "I sense contempt, like …" She peered through the hole, into the night.

"Like what?" Riley asked. "Like I'm your father? I'm not."

"No you're not," she said, turning to him. "Unlike my father, everyone likes you. He even likes you now, although I don't know why."

"But you think I'm …"

"I think you're just as screwed up as me sometimes."

"I never said I was perfect."

"Then why do you act like somehow you are? Why do you look at me like, 'if it weren't for you …'"

They were silent the rest of the way home. At the apartment, Dina sprang from the car, her winter coat over her arm, her dress appearing as if it might go in an opposite direction. Riley gathered the leftover pie Gram had insisted they take home. Dina could get so out of control. Only a week earlier she had shrieked when he changed out of his sweats on the new sofa. Earlier she had started crying when he said her necklaces sporting a key design gave her away as Greek-American.

"You're so critical," she had cried, her eyes wild with tears. "First I'm too religious, then I'm too Greek. And my birds, you can't stand them …"

"They're noisy and they poop everywhere," he'd said calmly, the perfect stinging antidote to her hysterics.

Inside the apartment Dina was changing out of her dress and into blue jeans and a shirt.

"Where are you going?"

"I have to go to the university."

"On Christmas Eve?"

"I need to pick up my mail," she said and grabbed her backpack. "You know what I could never figure out about your family?" She seemed calm now, her eyes red but no longer teary. "They're terrified of everything that goes on outside of their house. The real show tonight wasn't the nativity scene."

"What do you mean?"

"That right there! What you said just now, as if I can't have an opinion about anything without martialing evidence to back it up."

"Proof of what?" He too was calm, but the direction of her remarks made him shiver. Dina paused. She seemed defeated. "What do you want me to say when you're trashing my family?" Riley demanded.

"That's not what I'm doing."

"Then what?" He folded his arms across his chest and shifted his weight.

Dina hoisted the pack to her shoulder and looked at him for a long time. "I'm wondering when we're going to start being a married couple and not worry about your clan and what they think of us at their Christmas party."

The door quietly closed behind her. Riley stood until the cold turned to rage. Chauncey and Buckshot had been put to bed, the cover to their cage carefully positioned by Dina before she left. Chauncey squawked while Riley paced the living room. He wasn't afraid of what people thought. He had his own opinions and expressed them, something he had learned from Lucy. He had stood up to Gus, adopted Roland's views on theology, registered as a Democrat! Where did Dina get off calling his forever family a *clan*? He wasn't beholden to them. He had even stood up to her dad's own cutting remarks about her mental health. He had been patient with her need to have hobbies. Hadn't he been patient with her damn birds? Hadn't he … married her, for God's sake?

The birds were playing off of each other in an ecstasy of loud piercing shrieks. "Shut-up!" he yelled at them. He noticed the *Oxford English Dictionary* Lucy had given them on the floor next to the stereo, two bird droppings on it, one of them dripping down the side like dried mucous except a shade of light green.

There was an old cast-iron frying pan in the kitchen. Riley walked deliberately there, as if moving too fast might make something fall out of his head. He picked up the pan with both hands, like a broad sword, and returned to the living room to beat the top and sides of the shrouded bird cage with mighty whacks, the smell of bird talc and feathers filling the room, the vibration of the pan hurting his wrists as the clanging sound rang out like a cathedral bell. He kept at it until the cage bent in on itself and looked like a civic sculpture under wraps, awaiting some absurd ribbon-cutting event, the sound of the birds completely silenced.

36 | A HIGHER LAW

Lucy contemplated Brigham Young's statement that if you could glimpse the spirit world, you would commit suicide to get there. Brigham liked to say stuff like that, Lucy knew, because she was reading the *Journal of Discourses*. Once in a while she would call up Gus or Joan and ask how they could justify polygamy or executions in old Utah based on "blood atonement" or whatever she had stumbled on. Brigham used frontier metaphors, even sayings tied to drinking. "My blood was as clear as a West India rum," he said, and he was "filled with the Holy Ghost, so he felt like he could jump up and holler." Other times he "felt as if the grave was better for him than anything." Lucy found that, in an odd way, she could relate to such mood swings.

Chauncey and Buckshot survived the Christmas Eve incident. Riley had mixed feelings about that. Dina straightened the cage as best she could, using a crow bar, but the birds kept to themselves and then began picking their feathers until, finally, Chauncey died. They took him to Emigration Canyon where they found a quiet turn-off behind some large boulders and dug a small hole in the hard soil. "Should we dedicate it?" Dina asked, kneeling next to the open grave. They put Chauncey in the bottom of the hole, wrapped in paper towels.

"Dear Heavenly Father," Riley offered, "I'm sorry that Chauncey died. Maybe it was for the best because he seemed to be suffering a lot."

He expected a protest until he noticed that Dina was crying. "The little guy loved us," she said in an impromptu eulogy. "He was good, and I loved him too. He meant more to me than ... I can't explain it." She wiped her nose with the back of her hand and returned her hand to the pocket of her parka. She stood. "Can you say a real prayer?" she asked Riley. "And make it good."

"By the holy Melchizedek priesthood which I hold, I dedicate this grave for ... Chauncey, the African Grey, that he may rest in peace here until the morning of the first resurrection. In the name of Jesus Christ, Amen." He wasn't sure if pets came forth in the first resurrection, but he figured it would not hurt to say it.

Dina took the trowel and covered the bird quickly. On the way back, she said, "The pet store at Cottonwood Mall has a bulletin board for people to post notices for pets they can't take care of anymore. There's a one-year-old African Grey for sale. Get this. His name is Chauncey."

While he nodded his assent, Riley was thinking he needed to get away. Brad was going to California to pick up an Edsel, and he wanted someone to spot him driving. Riley called Lucy to see if they could spend a couple nights with her and Leslie.

"It's really you?" she said when he called. "I can't believe it! Do you use that *OED* we gave you?" she asked abruptly.

"All the time," he answered. Actually, the dictionary sat in the living room looking impenetrable and joyless. He preferred *Webster's* rather than having to wade through the overkill of what a word has meant through history. The OED had four pages alone on the word *love*.

"Language grounds us, Riley, and elevates our minds, our souls. It's what you'd call a paradox."

He listened to her familiar voice, the inquisitive tone mixed with salty outrage. *She* was what had grounded Riley when he was growing up, not the words she coaxed him with. She was the pinpoint of articulated desire and joyful seeking that had continued to elude him at twenty-four years of age. She was his conscience.

"You can sleep together on the futon," she said, "if that's all right. Leslie will be out of town on BLM business studying the dirt. They've got a lot of dirt at the BLM, you know. It never ends. Guess what?"

"You're expecting?"

"No, thank goodness! Dryden got baptized last week."

"Dryden? He's eight?"

"Yes sir. Our little missionary-in-embryo. We'll see you when we see you," she said, and hung up.

The men headed south on I-15, the winter sky lowering over the mountains. Brad played a cassette tape with George Strait songs on it. "Every time you throw dirt on her, you lose a little ground," went one of them.

Occasionally, Riley wore cowboy boots and listened to KSOP Country FM to blend in with his friend. One time at Jackson Hole, he and Brad were hiking along the back side of the Grand Teton with the smell of pine sharp in the air and he could see his friend's backpack bulging behind his stout neck, and Riley's heart melted for his redneck college buddy. In fact, the warp and woof of Country Western meant nothing to him if it hadn't been connected to his friend. Sometimes he felt like his own identity was fused to Brad's, as if only together they made a complete man.

To cross into Nevada from Utah, the friends had to drop from the high plains to the low desert, accompanied by enough rise in temperature that you wouldn't know it was February. Outside of the many spiny Joshua trees, named after the biblical troops that had stormed Jericho, there were several casinos to draw Jack Mormons and non-members across the state line into their mirrored money halls. Despite this, Nevada–the Silver State–was still part of the Mormon Corridor, the occasional settlement conspicuously anchored by the local ward house, identifiable by its low-slung, dull-colored brick and the satellite dish to bring news from Salt Lake City

In California the church's influence wanes. By the time you reach dusty Bakersfield, you sense that, if the landscape hasn't changed, the ambiance has. It is already more affluent than Nevada. Past Barstow, on the way to Los Angeles, you feel the growing influence of corporate earnings rather than gambling money, the electronically gated driveways and tennis courts and boats visible up the sides of hilly suburbs. There's the intangible but ever-present scent of Hollywood money, rich farmland, and technology.

It was late when they pulled into Selma, turned into the driveway, and quieted the car's hot engine. The porch light was on. Everywhere along the walk were high bushes with fragrant honeysuckle. In the middle of the front yard was a stout palm tree.

"Riley, is that you?" came a voice from an open bedroom window. "Just a minute."

Brad stood behind Riley and stared bleary-eyed, his T-shirt pulled out in the back. Riley looked at him and smiled. "You'll like Lucy," he said. "She's cool."

"I just need to sleep," Brad responded, yawning.

A light came on and the door opened and there was Lucy in silhouette, night-gowned and imposing as ever, her signature bushy hair shorter now but still sticking out crazily. "I can't believe it!" she said and let out a little shriek as she jumped at Riley. They embraced and teetered back and forth like a child standing on a skateboard. Riley looked over at Brad, who raised his eyebrows. Lucy hugged him too.

The next morning Riley awoke to the faces of two small children staring at him, inches away. "Mommy says we have to be quiet," one of the girls said. The other, about one year old, leaned against the bed, her tongue periodically darting up to a stream of snot. Riley tried to sit up, his garment top twisted almost backward. He saw that Brad was still fast asleep on the floor.

All the glamour of worldly California dissolved back into the drab milieu of Riley's childhood, as if they had stepped through the magic wardrobe into Narnia. There was a green-faced television screen smeared with greasy handprints, a bowl spilling soggy Cheerios on top of the TV. The floor around Brad was strewn with mashed crayons, Matchbox cars, and a child's pajamas lying inside out. The drapes opposite them had been partially ripped from the top down. The book case was filled with religious titles, some of them crammed into the shelves sideways. Riley thought he caught a glimpse of Gus's own out-of-print book, worn down, its slip cover half ripped.

Riley smiled at the two children and lay back down on the futon. There was something else in the air he could not make out, some essence that felt familiar. When he finally stumbled into the shower, hunted down a towel, and got dressed, he found Lucy on the phone in the kitchen.

"I'll have to call you back," she said and hung up. "We do cold cereal," she said distractedly. "Dryden" she called out. "The bus will be here in ten minutes."

"I can't believe Dryden's eight," said Riley.

"Eight going on eighteen. Your toast is still waiting for you!" Lucy shouted again.

Riley thought Lucy looked older, her skin less clear, her chin doubling over like his mother's. She took Riley's face in her hands and gave him a big kiss. She smelled like grapes.

"The plan is that Brad's going to look at the Edsel," Riley said. "If he decides to buy it, which I think he will, then we'll pick it up this evening."

"So it's just me and you, kid," she said and smiled, "and the kids."

"And the kids," he repeated, noticing the one-year-old in a high chair trying to spoon dry Cheerios into her mouth.

Dryden appeared, a dark-haired boy in a Huey Lewis T-shirt, Levis, and athletic shoes. He was dumping what looked like half a jar of jelly onto his toast.

"Dryden, come and say hello." The boy didn't look up. "He doesn't like me today," said Lucy.

"I never said that," said Dryden.

"Well, what is it, Eeyore?"

Dryden remained silent.

"He's a handsome kid," Riley said *sotto voce*.

She looked at him with a tired smile, then turned back toward her son. "Do you know who this is?" she tried again. "He's one of the Hartley family."

Dryden suddenly looked at Riley like he was an alien dropped in from the Milky Way, but without saying anything.

"I lived with them when I was in college. His parents are two of the greatest people I know."

The boy turned away and bit into his toast.

"What grade are you in?" Riley asked with high hopes. The boy ignored him, except to point to his full mouth.

"He's being a real drag today," said Lucy and sighed. She plopped down into a kitchen chair, her arm over the back. For a moment she looked like she was back in the dream house in Provo formulating a question for Gus. "How's Cade?"

"He's doing okay. Muriel said she saw you."

"Just once," said Lucy. "Everything's fine here, although I kind of lost my equilibrium after the baby died." She paused. "I haven't been to his grave since the funeral, which has been four and a half years. He'd be the same age as his sister, of course. Sometimes I see him in her, and it …" Her voice cracked. Thankfully, Dryden was suddenly banging dishes into the sink and Lucy exhaled, then looked at Dryden for a minute with longing while the boy walked to the table and picked up his sack lunch.

"Nice to meet you," he said to Riley.

"You gonna give your Mom a kiss, Eeyore?"

Dryden looked at Lucy in a way that belied his age, indicating disdain for everything having to do with the adult world.

He loped out the door while pulling at his un-tucked oversized T-shirt. There was the sound of the screen door slamming.

Lucy got up and wiped jelly and toast crumbs off the counter. "His baptism didn't go so well either," she said finally. "His knee kept coming up out of the water, so we had to do it three times. It may have been on purpose, we weren't sure. Leslie was pretty annoyed."

She said she was still seeing Warren even though she was on probation with the church and had told her bishop she had forsaken her sin. Warren was ten years younger. They met between the time he returned home from his mission to South Africa and when he began attending classes at the local college. He was bored and found her attractive. He told her about his adventures in Johannesburg, how despite the fact that blacks could now have the priesthood, the missionaries were supposed to only proselytize among the white Boers.

"You know, I never really got that revelation to marry Leslie," she said to Riley. She scratched her scalp slowly, trying to remember something. "At the end of the court, I was disfellowshipped, but Warren was excommunicated because he's a guy. Leslie didn't say a word about it. Have you ever had that feeling, Riley, that even though you're doing the wrong thing, it's really the right thing on some other level?"

"That sounds screwed up," Riley offered.

"Well, I decided I would continue to see him on one condition, which was that we would bring God into our relationship, to sanctify it."

"What does that mean?"

"I told Warren he'd have to marry me."

"You'd get a divorce?"

"No, I don't mean a civil marriage. I mean a temple sealing."

"I can't believe I'm hearing this," Riley said. "We shouldn't even be talking about it."

"Suit yourself."

"Did Leslie go along with it?"

"He doesn't know," she said as she walked to the sink with a couple of plates.

Riley's heart was pounding. It sounded like Lucy was reinventing polygamy, this time in reverse so that one woman could have several husbands. "You need to talk to my parents," he said. "This is way over my head."

Lucy laughed. She knew her spell on Riley had dissipated. "I broke the prayer barrier, like your father said we needed to do, and got my own revelation. There are precedents, you know, in celestial marriage."

"You're saying you're going to have two husbands, then?" Riley asked.

"When Joseph married other women, he did it secretly, you know? Emma didn't know about it. Some of the women he married had living husbands. Do you know what that means?"

"What, exactly?"

"The woman, in those instances, had two husbands."

"Wow. You went to a fundamentalist to get married, didn't you? Except that I don't think even *they* would go *that* far."

"We did it ourselves, by the authority we received in the temple. What good is it to be ordained a priestess if it's just pretend, if I don't exercise the authority I was given?"

Riley shook his head. "And how do you know God has given you this permission, Lucy? I mean … did you have a vision or something about this Warren guy?"

Lucy walked to where Riley was sitting. She picked up his hand and placed it over her heart. She was warm. "You feel that, Riley? There's a heart in there. That's where God speaks to us."

His hand was frozen on her breast, and he could, in fact, feel the faint thumping of her heart under her cotton shirt. She looked into his eyes and fell silent for a moment, then she placed his hand over his own heart.

"Life is a conversation, Rile. A conversation between your heart and your mind, your soul and your senses. God gave it all to us to reach the truth with. It's about having a conversation with yourself … and with the divine." She slowly let go of his hand. Riley kept his hand on his chest where his own heart was thumping harder and harder. Lucy sat back down at the table. "The church isn't ready to live THE GOSPEL in its fullness," she said, "but the Lord has appointed some of us to preserve his word."

"Lucy, have you talked to a counselor about this?"

"They wouldn't understand. This is about revelation. They don't deal with that. The world lives under the Law of Moses, you know, so people aren't prepared for it."

"A counselor could help you see the consequences of what you're doing."

"I know what I'm doing, Riley" she said, this time with a hint of frustration. "They gave me sleeping pills after the baby died, but I don't want to skew my dreams. That's where the Lord talks to me, just like in ancient days with Father Lehi."

"Maybe you should talk to Mom and Dad," he said as meekly as possible.

Lucy nodded slowly, her jaw tensed. "It would have to be in person," she said. "I don't need their approval, though, Riley. I can't rely on your parents' faith. I have my own."

After lunch, Brad appeared, all smiles, and said the sale went through and the owner had saved them a trip by following Brad back with the prize. Riley made him promise to let him drive the Edsel halfway home.

"I just hope it will make it," he said.

"You'll stay close behind me, then, won't you?"

"Yeah, but I'm driving first to be sure it's okay."

Later they were standing in the driveway, thinking how perfectly the car went with Lucy's house. They were anxious to get started and decided they wouldn't stay another night. "Lucy's different, isn't she?" said Brad.

"What do you mean?"

"I mean, I can't see her at BYU, for instance."

Riley wondered what vibes he was picking up, but after a moment's thought decided not to tell him anything. "She is kind of tomboyish," he conceded.

They went inside and announced their new plans. Lucy prepared something for them to eat on the way and gave them two cans of ginger ale. "Be careful out there," she said.

Riley gave one of the kids a playful noogie and extended his hand to Dryden, who responded with an indifferent handshake. Lucy seemed normal again, the same Lucy that Riley had known in Provo, with the same imperfect angular look and, like his parents said, some big problems to overcome.

"Thanks for thinking of us, Riley," she said and began to cry. Brad picked up their bags to put them in the cars.

"Everything will be all right," Riley said to her. She nodded through her tears, hugging herself.

"I know you're trying to stand on your own testimony," he said to her. "At the same time, we can all use a second opinion once in a while. Give my folks a call, will you?"

She nodded. The two embraced. He was close enough to feel again her heart beating.

"All I ever wanted was to be a worthy vessel of the Lord," she said through more tears. "Like your folks. But things just haven't worked out that way, and now …"

I saw Riley momentarily pull away, not just from Lucy but from himself, and ascend up for a few seconds, above the house and lights of the neighborhood, away in the wind blowing east, then back again.

"You better get on your way, Riley Hartley. It's getting late." She walked him to the door, then out to the front porch.

Brad was already in the Edsel, illuminated by the yellowish hue the Spanish-styled porch light cast on the yard, creating shadows under Lucy's wet eyes. Riley got inside the car and stared through the windshield at the car in front of him, where Brad was scrutinizing the dashboard. There was a guttural sound as the mammoth engine started.

"Don't forget to call Mom and Dad," Riley said to her as he moved his foot to the accelerator.

Unknown to Riley, Lucy left for Provo one day later. I watched her cross the desert, the red shine of her taillights sometimes the only thing visible for miles, the little Toyota Celica backlit by a sky flecked with stars. As she skirted the southern tip of Death Valley, the mile markers streamed by like immovable sentinels. Above her, the greased concentric orbs of the universe swirled oblivious to human concern, the far-off chawing of their gears almost audible. And unknown to Lucy, I was in the passenger seat next to her as we passed an alliterative string of small towns—Boron, Barstow, Baker—and stopped for gas at a truck stop in Sloan. The gaudy lights of Las Vegas came and went, followed by low-rising peaks that looked two-dimensional on the horizon. Another alliterative string of names—Muddy, Mormon, Mt. Bang—as we zoomed along like a June bug, the line of the freeway so true, we sometimes seemed to be standing still, wheels spinning below and jack rabbits leaping through the high beams into sagebrush.

At two in the morning we could see the St. George temple's soft white glow, like one would expect from Florentine alabaster. It seemed to comfort Lucy. The edifice stared dolefully over the dark streets of the town, away toward the interstate, until it turned off its lights in an expressionless sigh. Lucy shifted into fifth gear and sang

> Beautiful Zion for me
> Down in the valley reclining,
> Memories sacred to thee,
> Close round my heart are entwining,
> Clasped in the mountain's embrace,
> Safe from the spoiler forever.

By three o'clock she was back on the high plateau where the Hurricane Cliffs bleed red toward the quiet college town of Cedar City. She gassed up and bought a Dr. Pepper from a pimple-faced boy who looked at her suspiciously, her strong shoulders long since defeated by the steering wheel.

Back outside, the cold air revived her. The half moon above Lone Tree Peak was beautiful. She thought she could make out the outline of needled trees on the peak's clime, her vision remaining excellent. She turned back toward the car and was startled to see me standing there, gray-haired, holding her infant in my arms, the head resting against the dingy yellow of my travel-worn corduroy jacket. She held her breath when I lifted the infant up as if I were showing it to the congregation after being named and blessed. The gown that served for its blessing and burial fell like a filmy waterfall down to the ground around my feet. The baby's eyes were closed. Its lips were red, its eyelashes dark and long. At the funeral home after the child died, Lucy had tried to rub off the lipstick because, she said, his lips had never looked that red.

"There you are," she said in a stupor. "I didn't visit your grave because I thought it would mean you hadn't gone to the celestial kingdom. Here you are," she said, and motioned toward the still baby whose gown was coiling upward into a colorful, gravity-defying waterfall, falling up into a pulsating stream in the sky. "You haven't gone there yet?" Her hands trembled, her can of soda lay fizzing on the ground. She was thinking of Philadelphia, where she had left her first baby. She grabbed her stomach and bent over. *They've come for me*, she thought.

Instead, I carried the infant up along the cascading northern lights, climbing to that astral point where they vanish, the baby's head like a violin between my chin and collar. The tires of an eighteen-wheeler burned down I-15 past the gas station. Lucy's breath pounded at the cold air. Slowly she re-entered her car and drove past Parowan and Paragonah, then Beaver, Fillmore, Nephi, the mountains rising in earnest to nearly twelve thousand feet, daylight misting up from the orchards. She hummed another tune.

> The morning breaks
> The shadows flee;
> Lo Zion's standard is unfurled!

When she turned on the radio to stay awake, she laughed to hear them play "In a Gadda Da Vida." Beyond the valley, the mountains were blue, the frozen lake opposite Provo inflamed with orange. She was struck with the fact that, for the first time in over twelve years, this was not her home. It was no longer where she belonged. Too late now for that, even though she still saw Golan Drive as her last hope, the place where she intended to plant her ensign, tattered as it was, and receive "further light and knowledge," like the temple gods promised in the endowment ceremony.

Exiting off the freeway on University Avenue, she approached the mouth of Rock Canyon, turned right into the foothills, and prayed to herself in the Adamic language, as she was taught in the temple. There were three holy words that were said to be useful in conjuring messengers from heaven and creating life from out of the void. She turned a corner to park outside the dream house and spoke the words again, this time in translation: *Oh God, hear the words of my mouth.* It was seven in the morning.

38 | OUR DAILY STONES

Lucy arrived at the house on bread day when Joan was in the middle of kneading whole-wheat dough scaled down to a mere four loaves from her peak of eight. Gus was working from home promoting a multi-level-marketing fruit juice from Samoa that was said to spike one's red blood-cell count. He was simultaneously the chief endorser and motivational speaker for a series of other products. These side jobs brought in enough extra cash that Joan didn't have to bake bread, but it had become a habit. She carefully rolled the dough into four loaves and imprinted them sideways with light karate-chops, just like her mother had taught her.

"I never thought my faith would get me into so much trouble," Lucy began, sitting on a stool at the kitchen counter. When Gus walked in, Lucy pulled him into a huge locked embrace and let out a couple of sobs. Everything was going to be okay now, she thought. They moved to the living room and sat around the cluttered Postum table to the smell of baking bread.

Lucy thought Joan and Gus had always been there for her, but the truth was that they could never adapt to her strong personality. Gus instinctively moved back when Lucy leaned forward on the couch. She presented herself as one of their products, someone who had followed their charge to live THE GOSPEL to the fullest, remaining a type and shadow of them, as scripture would phrase it. "Most of the time," Joan later explained, "Lucy talked on and on and we couldn't tell what her real concerns were." It is a story that Riley still attempts now to piece together.

Lucy folds her arms, her eyes weary and red. She crosses one leg over the other and bounces it slightly, her dingy athletic shoes looking like growths at the ends of her legs. Gus listens with pursed lips, his chin up, eyes cast down at the floor. Joan has carefully folded her apron, splotched with flour, and placed it on her lap. She listens closely, her hand repeatedly reaching up with forefinger and thumb to rub out the lipstick in the corners of her mouth.

"The Lord doesn't tell us every little thing, I've learned," Lucy says, paraphrasing the Doctrine and Covenants. "We're supposed to be anxiously engaged in finding answers of our own accord."

Gus laughs nervously. "But obedience is still important, Lucy," he says. "It's the first law of heaven."

She shakes her head, muttering. "I know … but I don't really accept that anymore. I mean, what are you saying exactly? Obedience to what? You can't just say obey and not have an object to the verb. Obey what? What are the parameters? It's not ethical to just obey, and … it's disingenuous to say so, I think."

"I don't think that's what I said, Lucy. I'm not talking about blind obedience here."

"Then what? It seems like … oh gosh!" She puts her head in her hands and rubs her eyes for a few seconds. "It seems like when you say these things, they sound so … reasonable, so pleasing, but to go out and live it, … it doesn't come together, it doesn't coalesce with seven kids and only so much time and expectations and obligations …"

"Maybe, Lucy … you're asking *to whom* we should be obedient," says Gus.

"Exactly!" she exclaims and claps her hands together once. "Obedience should be to God, right?"

More nervous laughs from Gus, followed by a monstrous clearing of his throat. "In my estimation—the way it's been explained to me—the Brethren are the Lord's servants, so they're the ones we need to follow, right down to the ward bishop."

"The bishop?" says Lucy in horror. "My bishop has undocumented immigrants harvesting almonds for less than minimum wage. Their children don't go to school because they move so often." That was as much as she could think of to paint a picture of how compromised her bishop was.

"It sounds to me like you have a personal issue with him," Joan says. "Is that what this is about?"

Lucy looks at Joan for a long time. The imploring girl begins to morph into a confident debater, leaning forward and sighing. "You can't be expected to be obedient," she says, "without being told what you should be obedient to. There has to be a principle or doctrine you're committed to. You can't give leaders *carte blanche* to say or do anything they want, which would just be a way to prey on people's ignorance."

"Do you think the prophet preys on people's ignorance?" asks Joan in a shocked tone.

"Well, he's not infallible," Lucy says.

"In my estimation," Gus ventures, "he's infallible about the things that matter. The Lord has said he would never let him lead the church astray."

"Who actually said that?"

"The prophet."

"So it's circular!" says Lucy, emitting a half giggle. "The *prophet* says the *prophet* is never wrong. Well, isn't that convenient?"

"It's not like the pope," interjects Joan, "it's only about important things."

"Like chastity," Gus says.

"Okay," says Lucy. "Okay." She decides to take him on. "Joseph Smith took some forty wives Emma didn't know about. The church didn't know about it."

"He was protecting the weak members of the church from the hard truths," Gus says, leaning back, his hands behind his head. This is more familiar ground for him, like lecturing at a Know Your Religion venue or hyping Silver Rain bacteriostatic soap to a roomful of potential distributors.

"Exactly," Lucy says excitedly, "and it's the same for us. When we get a revelation to do something, no one else knows, but that's what we have to do to be obedient to God. What I'm saying is … Heavenly Father has given me greater understanding about certain things. *Higher laws*, like he did to Joseph Smith."

Gus is silent, except for his shallow breathing. He looks at Joan. By now she has rubbed the lipstick out of the corners of her mouth completely.

"Nelson has never told you to go against the Lord's anointed," Joan says. "If this … revelation … authorized you to have relations with that boy, it goes against every principle of THE GOSPEL."

"It goes against tradition, is what it goes against, and so did giving the priesthood to the blacks, and so did polygamy, and so did …"

"Don't you say that!" says Joan, not so calmly now, putting a finger in the air for emphasis. "Polygamy was then, and this is now. You can't conflate the two."

"They said polygamy would never be taken from the earth," Lucy interrupted. "They said it would be the sign of a fallen church if they repudiated it."

Joan stares at Lucy. The younger woman has never interrupted her like that. Joan shifts into another gear, raising her voice to a more forceful level. "You can't claim to be getting revelations that re-write church doctrine!"

Lucy abruptly stands, begins to pace, fighting the swelling feeling of a sob. "I'm not arguing for polygamy," she says. "It's just an example …"

"Of what, Lucy? Tell us what you're getting at," Joan says with renewed patience in her voice.

"I've always loved you, Joan." Lucy swallows hard, trying to catch her breath. "However, I don't think revelation is supposed to apply to things that don't matter, like whether I should decorate my house in early American or French Provincial. It's not who I am!" She stares out the windows at the blanket of crusted snow.

Gus clears his throat. "As it's been explained to me," he begins, "a conflict with the Brethren is the result of one of two things."

"Intellectual pride," says Lucy. "I've heard that before."

"That's one," says Gus. "The other is sexual sin."

Lucy is still for a moment, her breathing arrested, one hand atop her short spiky hair, the other across her breasts. She begins to swoon.

Gus leaps up, stops short, and stands by not sure whether to embrace or tackle her. "Oh, Lucy, dear, I'm sorry." He turns to his wife, who reaches for his hand. Then just as suddenly, Lucy stops crying.

"It wasn't like that," she says. She sits and rocks for a moment, muttering something about "surviving … the sense of …" Gus's face is etched with pity and judgment. "Isn't there the remotest possibility that the system is what's deficient and not me?" she says.

Gus looks to Joan. He musters some control, a sort of *ersatz* humility he uses in his lectures that magically makes him sound shaken and solemn at the same time. "I don't really think so, Lucy. Not if you have a testimony of the truth," he says.

"Lucy, honey," chimes Joan, "There are scriptural figures who've done what you've done and they've repented. Remember Corianton in the Book of Mormon?" She looks at Lucy to see if she's pushed her too far. It would never occur to Riley's mother to tell Lucy she understood and respected her choices, as different as they may be from what Joan might do. "You need to repent," she says finally.

"We all need to repent," Lucy agrees. "But I never imagined I was expected to lose my agency. I'm not supposed to have a voice, am I?" She walks toward the windows. "Gee, what happened to the trees?" she asks out of the blue. She sounds calmer now.

"Trees?" Gus says with some relief. He looks out the windows.

"The poplars."

"Got cut down."

"I can see that," she says. "Why?"

"The city cut the tops off." Gus returns to his seat carefully,

253

as if any wrong move will give him away somehow, although over what, he is not sure.

"I'd say they did more than that. They look like porcupines." Lucy laughs, her shoulders shaking once again.

"They said the trees were interfering with the power lines," says Joan.

"I loved those guys," says Lucy. "I remember when you planted them, Nelson. It was right after I moved in with the family." She returns to the couch and sinks deep into the cushions, although retaining her posture as if she's balancing something on her head. "All I ever wanted was to be like you two. It doesn't seem to be working, does it? I've buried a baby …" she continues.

"Now Lucy," Gus interrupts.

"Let her talk," Joan says. She rubs her husband's knee as if trying to grind out the edgy tone of her last remark.

"My husband is out of town all the time. My parents and I haven't spoken in a year. Dryden's uncontrollable and he's only eight! How did you do it? It seems like even when Candace had to get married, and Jody ran off with Alvin, when Cade was cutting himself, when Winnie had bulimia, you were able to find your way through it."

Joan stands, places her apron on the Postum table, and moves next to Lucy. She puts a hand on Lucy's shoulder, who leans into her. Lucy cries again, this time full on. Joan pats her. "We had to be strong as well as compassionate," she will tell a nodding Gus weeks later. "The truth can't be swayed into compromise because of a girl's hysterics. We need to love the sinner, not the sin."

"Can you understand how this feels?" says Lucy finally, through sniffles. Gus gets up and hands her a tissue.

"Lucy, we want you to know," Gus says plaintively, choking back his own tears. Joan shushes him. He sits back down obediently.

"I'm not expecting you to say you agree with me," Lucy says tentatively, almost scrubbing her eyes with the tissue, "just that you concede the possibility that I could be right and that my revelations are the foundation of my testimony. God gave them to *me*, like he gave me my children. Remember in the Book of Mormon where Nephi was told to kill Laban? What would you do in that situation? Don't you think that sometimes you have to sin to do the right thing?"

Riley's parents were perplexed. They had no answers for such questions. None. "You couldn't expect us to justify adultery, just because she was distraught, could you?" his mother would later ask her son, deep in retelling the story of that fateful day.

But as Riley retells the story to himself, he can hear his own questions reverberate through that intimate but strikingly cool scene that must have felt like the dark mahogany of a legal chamber to Lucy. Sometimes the questions discharge in his mind in the form of a half-scream. "Couldn't you have admitted to her that you have had doubts too?" "Couldn't you have intimated that the system *is* sometimes flawed, that it's not always one's own inadequacy, one's lack of faith?" Riley asks himself the question Eve asks in the temple during the Garden of Eden re-enactment. After Lucifer has given her the fruit to eat so that she will be "as the gods, knowing good and evil," she asks him, "Is there no other way?"

When Joan puts her hand on Lucy's shoulder, Riley imagines that it must feel like a granite block, perfectly immovable. The connection to the forever family has come to an end. What Lucy gains from her conversation is a clear view of what her future holds. She will make one last lunge at the wall looming before her.

"When Elder Gray came down on you guys, I remember how devastated you were," Lucy says. "And furious. Weren't you disobeying the Brethren by expressing your disagreement with him? Just because you were careful in doing so in private doesn't mean you weren't out of harmony."

"She was trying to suggest," Joan would report to the rest of the family, "that expressing our sadness over being treated poorly was the same as her sleeping with a recently returned missionary."

"Lucy," Joan says, deciding to pull the plug on the conversation, "think of your children. How can you be this kind of mother for your children?"

It was a good question. What kind of person would the ideal mother be?

Gus asserts himself by asking Lucy if she would like him to give her a blessing. He squeezes consecrated oil onto her head from the plastic vial he always carries with him and places his hands on her head. "Lucy Barclay Clark, I hereby seal the anointing with oil and give you a blessing …"

"Your father blessed Lucy," Joan would explain, "that she would understand the gravity of her situation and return to the true and living church. She was told that she was loved. That we loved her."

On the porch Gus gives Lucy a vigorous bear hug, but he is distracted now that the scene is over for him. He is looking at the mountain above the street, his view boomeranging back down on his own stalwart self, where he is the humble but able servant in a stirring scene of tragic proportions. For Gus, there is only one way to stand out, and that is to be a bigger and better Mormon than anyone else.

Joan is there, and unlike Gus she is aware of what is at stake, a fracture in the collective. She doesn't care as much about Lucy's indiscretion as she does about the grand scheme of things and has already forgotten that Lucy came to them for reassurance of the type that falls neither to the side of judgment nor absolution. Lucy had come to them for that fine and human thing, the spiritual tissue that connects the daughters of Eve and sons of Adam to each other, however far apart they may be.

And Lucy? She is holding a loaf of Joan's homemade bread. "Thank you for talking to me," she says. She can feel the warmth of the bread against her palm, and she hears Lucifer, the devil, screaming back at Eve, who has the fruit still dangling in her hand in the temple scene, telling her in a cruel way, meant to be ironic, THERE IS NO OTHER WAY!

The official cause of Lucy's death was an overdose of sleeping pills after driving back home and sleeping for two days, then confessing to the bishop about her continued dalliance with Warren. On a Saturday three weeks after her return she was up early to make everyone a hearty breakfast of pancakes and sausage. Then Lucy took twenty-five Secobarbital and lay down, never to wake again and without leaving a note. In the end there were no words. It was ten o'clock in the morning.

At the same time in Utah, Dina was talking about going off the pill. She didn't want to finish graduate school, she told Riley, and felt that they were disobeying the prophet's counsel by delaying their family. A fight started with all the low-grade sticking points. Dina's new obsession with a national animal rights group, whose local chapter had just set 1,500 turkeys loose in Juab County (Riley's opener), was countered with a question about where Riley was last Tuesday for three hours after he got off work while she was waiting at home (her opener). That she had inexplicably stopped taking her anti-depressant (his turn), was responded to with a remark that Riley was judgmental and too harsh: "You've never admitted to what happened to the birds' cage last Christmas" (hers).

Dina decided to bring out the heavy artillery. She told Riley she thought he was more in love with Brad than with her. Riley picked up the phone book and sent it sailing across the room, hitting the sides of the Levelors and bending them. "Your father was right, you're crazy," said Riley.

"He never said that!"

"He told me he felt sorry for me and that it would never work out," Riley shouted. It was a lie.

Dina staggered, dropped to her knees, and let out a soft wail Riley had never heard before.

Riley really did love Brad, but not that way. "I could *never* have a child with you in good conscience," he said to Dina as his parting line.

He pulled into the driveway of the Hartley house about the time Leslie Clark was kneeling at Lucy's side taking her pulse, watching the cosmos re-configure over his head in a cocktail of fear and relief. In the next room was the oddly comforting sound of Dryden cranking up his stereo. Back in Zion, Riley's parents sat with him on the couch, his mom patting his back. She kept saying exactly what Riley hoped she would, that "Dina doesn't understand how important family is and the commitment it takes." Maybe it was because she was a convert to the church, his mother said. "It isn't her fault."

"I haven't been unfaithful," Riley said through flushed cheeks.

"Well, that's the important thing," his mother agreed.

There was something patently false about the kind of technical truth Riley was indulging in, as with Gus's denials of impropriety with Sandy Greenwood. He left for his uncertain plans in Salt Lake City as Lucy's body lay in the county morgue for her autopsy.

Leslie called the bishop, who activated the Relief Society women, who were at the house within minutes in full grieving mode, arranging for everything in their warm way.

Dina took the birds with her in their carrying cage. In their place she left a note stating where she would be staying, with a friend from the university. She didn't mention that her father had called and she told him she couldn't stay with a man who didn't want to have children. Nor did she mention that she went to the temple and prayed in the Celestial Room, where she received a revelation to leave her husband. She would call an attorney in the morning.

Riley sat on the floor next to the empty bird cage in the quiet apartment, listening to the occasional police car or fire engine wail by. He undressed in the bathroom, filled the tub with warm water, and sat down in it. There was a razor on the sink. He leaned back and submerged his head in the water. It gave him a familiar feeling from his swimming days when everything would go silent and he was aware of nothing beyond his efforts to propel himself through that alternate world.

When his lungs burned, he surfaced and picked up the razor, then ran it along one of his legs like he used to do before swimming finals, like Cade did during his bodybuilding days. Then the next leg. When the razor became dull, he got another. He took it to his chest, leaving a clear trail of bare flesh behind the razor like the path of a harvester in a field of alfalfa. How simple it was to look that different, to emerge another man. How clean and young he looked, the outline of his muscles so pronounced. There would be no air bubbles trapped in his hair when he coursed through water.

He continued shaving his stomach and armpits and then his arms and pubic hair, refilling the tub to rinse himself and look at himself in the mirror, at the freakish apparition he had become. He could only catch a distorted view of himself through the steamed surface, but it looked like a boy the size of a man or a grown man in the body of a boy. He laughed at the absurdity of it. Everything looked different, the way his abs moved when he breathed and how the muscles in his forearms rippled like cords. His cock looked like it did when Paris gripped it way back when. When the phone rang later that evening, he was still lying naked on the floor of the living room. The apartment smelled faintly of Sulphur. It was nearly twelve thirty. Soon he would have something else, other than a fleeting regret for having shaved his body, to attach his grief to.

40 | JACK MORMON

Few passages in the Book of Mormon record the day-to-day agony of my people the way a verse in the thin book of Jacob explains how we *felt*.

> And it came to pass that I began to be old, wherefore I conclude this record, declaring that I have written according to the best of my knowledge, by saying that the time passed away with us, and also our lives passed away like as it were unto us a dream, we being a lonesome and a solemn people, wanderers ... wherefore, we did mourn out our days.

Riley imagined that he too was beginning to grow old and lonesome. It wasn't just because of Lucy's death or because of his wife's decision to leave him. Something else had attached itself to him. The attempt Dina and Riley had made, to lightly tether themselves to THE GOSPEL, had proven unworkable. There was too much personal responsibility to own and not enough certainty to hold one upright. And now, between the station stops of marriage and children, which were the major life events in THE PLAN the church had sketched out for him, Riley had seen a widening aperture he couldn't negotiate, a trap door that placed a stigma on male members of his tribe to indicate that they were damaged goods. They were considered unable to achieve a place in heaven without a wife. Still, Riley was the son of Nelson and Joan, and despite the way the family scripture got written—Dina and Riley split because she would not take her Prozac—he was justified to refuse children who under the circumstances would only be victim to their parents' intractable problems.

In early Utah there was a lot of divorce, especially among the polygamists. Despite the fact that marriage was designed for eternity, there was still an experimental aspect to it. If things didn't work out, there were other men and women waiting in the wings. Women could choose a new husband from among the men of higher rank, and the men could claim the wife of someone of lower rank. The protocol was different in the modern era. Riley was supposed to keep his head down until he remarried, at which time he would be accepted again by the collective, good as new.

The cynicism and homogeneity weren't all that bothered him. There was something else lingering nearby like a low pressure system, too subtle to notice at first … until the moment when suddenly the explanation sat down hard before him. It was the realization of what a forever family was and what they might be capable of. His parents were oblivious to their cruelty to Lucy, one they claimed to love. It was a revelation to Riley, a sickening failing of the heart. It was the revelation of his impending apostasy. Unlike the temporary stall of other divorced men in Zion, Riley was in for a more precipitous fall.

At least now he understood what it meant when someone said "I know, I know" in testimony meeting, with knowledge that could only come through experience. Should he bear his testimony now, he would unequivocally describe what it meant to be crushed in the church's gears and the machinery not missing a single turn of the sprocket. He saw it happen to Lucy. When she died, no one from the Hartley family traveled out to pay her their last respects. Cade was returning from his mission. Dina and Riley were in the middle of a separation. Muriel, just north of Fresno, had a sick baby and could not drive the ninety minutes to Selma.

Riley found a small attic apartment in South Salt Lake that was situated across from a historical ward house and down the street from a large Catholic church. It was March, the separation had gone well enough, when much to his surprise Dina appeared at his door with a toaster for a house-warming gift. "You heard about Brother Derringer?" she asked, taking off her jacket and setting it over a chair. "Roland. You remember him, don't you? They're holding a court to excommunicate him. It's in the newspapers. It's controversial because he's at BYU."

She paused. "I always thought he was a little suspect." The color had drained from Riley's face. How quickly she had learned to talk like that. He turned away, alarmed. He had seen Roland six weeks earlier and hadn't heard anything about a church disciplinary court. Riley had sat in Roland's cluttered office and explained that his marriage had failed, while Roland had attempted, to no avail, to organize stacks of books that rose in towers virtually everywhere in the room. Then Roland told Riley about how once he had gotten so overwhelmed with the "Happy Valley Syndrome," he had flown to Los Angeles for the weekend, driven to West Hollywood, and taken a fourteen-year-old prostitute to dinner. He watched her eat to remind himself of what else was going on in the world. When Riley didn't leave, Roland stopped arranging the books and looked at him squarely. "Riley," he had said, "what are you going to do when the right thing to do isn't the Mormon thing?"

"I think we had a good marriage for a while," Dina said. "I got to be a part of your family, which was pretty cool." She paused, not sure how to proceed.

"You hated my family!" Riley said. "You called us Appalachian."

"Sometimes you were clannish, that's true," she snapped back. "And you were incredibly cold to me whenever you had talked to your dad on the phone. We never had a good conversation riding back from Provo. You all knew you were the poster family, even if none of you would admit it."

"I *admit* it," he said bitterly. For Riley, it seemed that nothing was what it claimed to be anymore, that today there would be an announcement that the earth was flat, after all. That she had married him to attain a Green Card. "Are they calling Roland an apostate?" Riley asked. "Like the others they've been tracking?"

"You'll have to read the article. Your dad always said Roland was a wolf in sheep's clothing, you know," said Dina.

"What an unconscionable gossip he is!"

"He's changed lives, Riley. How can you say that about him?" she said softly. "He'll probably be made a general authority."

"They deserve him," he shot back.

"I think you have the same goodness inside you, you're just too moody." Dina imagined she was offering an olive branch. "You and I, we didn't have what it takes for a marriage to work." She wanted to talk about their marriage, not about their former professor. She looked like she might cry.

Riley slumped down into a chair, and she touched his neck and began stroking it gently. He could smell her energy, her sex. "You know, Riley, we still have two days before the divorce goes through," she said with a smile. "I brought a condom with me," she said.

"What?" he said." He looked at her for a long time, her now short fine hair, her skewed front tooth, the way she looked in her tight turtleneck drawn over her delicious breasts. He heard himself saying to her, "Is it one of the lambskins we like?"

He never saw her again after that day. If Lucy's death was Riley's Abrahamic test, the reward was that he would never again feel guilty about having rejected celibacy. It would not even enter his mind as an issue, even though at April conference his father was called as one of the top Brethren of the church, allowing Gus to retire as the pitchman for day planners and assorted goods. Riley celebrated by buying his first six-pack of beer on the west side of town where he assumed no one would recognize him.

Back in his apartment, he was ambushed by memories of his father. How Gus at times would take in the stray Mormon, like Lucy. And the warmth he showed to his children. Before his mission, when Cade had suffered a devastating episode of cutting and burning, it was Gus who found his son in a snow drift out back and sat with him for the longest time to talk things through.

Even so, Riley knew he would be saying goodbye to his father now, and these memories only made it hurt all the more. Overnight Riley Hartley had transformed himself into Jack Mormon. He indulged in all of Jack's privileges—drinking, swearing, ten percent more in disposable cash, his Sundays off. At night he still slipped into the cotton comfort of his temple garments to sleep, not willing to risk bodily harm, either, in case something happened in the night.

Word must have gotten out that he was seeing a non-Mormon, because one-by-one his sisters began to arrive with casseroles, a potted plant, a Tabernacle Choir disk, and questions about Jenny. The first was Candace, who brought groceries, including a coconut, for "when you feel adventurous," she said. She was huffing up the exterior stairs to the attic apartment when he saw her arms bulging with the stuff, canned goods, even a ham. "It's fun cracking it open," she said of the coconut. "I want you to have fun."

They sat in the makeshift sitting room at the upper landing, Candace in the over-stuffed chair and Riley leaning against the door of a storage space under the eaves. His apartment was dark. They munched on chips and salsa she had brought, and she talked about her kids. When he asked about Sam, she went quiet.

"This salsa is hotter than I thought," she said and got up for a tissue. When she returned, she had transformed herself into the family emissary, her words sounding like their mother's. "I love you, Riley," she said. "We're all concerned for you and feel like we've let you down. I was an especially bad example when you were in high school," she said, "and I'm sorry for that."

"There's nothing to be sorry for," he responded.

"We miss Dina too."

"I know."

"Dad is concerned. He doesn't know what to do to help you, Rile. He thinks he's going to lose you."

"Lose me to what exactly?" he said. "Does he think I'll stop coming to the family Christmas pageant?"

"You know what I mean," she said. "He's afraid you'll leave the church." There it was, the priority they all held.

They talked some more, and Riley knew he was going to have to give his sister something to take back with her. The truth was, he *wanted* to give her some kind of hope, in case she really was worried about him. "I want you to know," he told her, "that every day when I was a missionary, I woke up and the first thing I thought about was how much I wished my sister Candace could have been with me. I wished you could have met the people I met. I know they would have delighted and amazed you, they were so different from here. I thought of you when I sat in class in college and heard about new things I knew you would have been amazed by. I always loved your recommendations for books and how you'd read something I suggested and we'd talk about it for weeks. Of all of my sisters, I identified with you the most."

The week following, Riley put on his temple garments and drove to Provo to visit his folks. It was supposed to be *his* olive branch, which he hoped would end the weekly trek of sisters to check up on him. It turned out it wasn't enough to satisfy their suspicions because the next week Jody arrived, having been thoroughly rehabilitated since her fall to polygamy. She had become her ward's Relief Society president. "I know what it means to disappoint Dad," she said. "Of course, we all know what it's like being Elder Nelson B. Hartley's child, but it must have been especially difficult for my brothers."

Riley held Jody's daughter, Amanda, in his lap while they talked. The five-year-old had climbed up into his arms as if she belonged there, revealing a luminous look in her eyes as she lay her head against his chest and fell asleep. Riley missed his nieces and nephews, the touch of their soft skin, their adoring looks, their responses to new experiences.

Jody and Muriel were similar in that they both thought of themselves as being different from run-of-the-mill church adherents. It made Riley wonder why they remained committed to people they wanted to distinguish themselves from. Still, he admired Jody for having been the bravest in following her heart. She had something more to say.

"I saw what Dad was writing in his journal," she said in a conspiratorial tone, looking at him pityingly.

"He thinks that journal will be canonized some day," Riley said dismissively.

"Why are you so unkind to him?" she asked.

"What did he write?" Now he felt perturbed and figured his sister would not have said anything if she had not intended to tell him everything.

"He wrote that if the devil doesn't get you, he'll get your kids," she said.

Riley didn't respond. The forever family! he thought—he was threatening to ruin their perfect record.

On the way out the door, Jody embraced him warmly. "Be careful, dear boy. Don't do anything out of spite. I know something about marriages that don't work out. I think you belong with your family, whatever else."

That Sunday, Riley put on his garments and ventured across the street to the local ward, his first time to attend church since he had moved there. The bishop was a man with a cheery face that Riley recognized from his ads for personal-injury lawsuits that adorned the sides of city buses. After listening blankly to the sacrament meeting vernacular, Riley made for the door.

"Hi there, I'm Bishop Warner," the man said, intercepting him and extending his hand. Riley took it reflexively. It seemed remarkable that the bishop, a few years older than him, had the identical face as the one in the ads, beaming in the flesh with the same bright sheen to the skin. "So glad you could join us today."

Riley released his hand and forced himself to step back. The scene was familiar, like walking across the BYU campus and hearing the carillon bell chiming. The just-vacated chapel had a recognizable dewy smell of a community awash in perspiration and lingering sighs. The children were giggling and clomping through the aisles into the foyer. The unadorned beechwood of the podium and lectern bespoke simplicity and a siren's call. This is what Riley had grown up with. The man before him was his double, the person Riley had been born to be.

"Are you a member?" asked the bishop, cocking his head slightly.

Riley had not rehearsed this part. "Yes."

"Wonderful! We'd love to get your records moved here. Do you have a family?" he asked.

"Divorced, no kids." Just enough to keep him off balance. "I live across the street in an apartment."

"The blue house?" asked the bishop. He looked around the chapel to orient himself, then pointed to the left.

"That's right," said Riley with a tight smile. "Maybe we can talk sometime," he said and ducked out the door. To his surprise, Muriel and Scott were across the street, in from California for a few weeks. They said they were "in the neighborhood." As the oldest,

Muriel could not have escaped being deputized as one of the proxies for their parents. She was pregnant with number four and had trouble moving up the stairs. Trailing her was Scott, balding and starting to show a paunch. Both of them were in Sunday attire.

"What are you going to do with your degree, Rile?" she asked, pushing against her knee on the last step to the landing. "Are you going to go to law school?"

He unlocked the door and invited them into the kitchen. They sat looking at empty Coors Light cans stacked in a pyramid on top of the refrigerator.

"I don't think I'm ready for graduate school," he said.

"Impressive sculpture," said Muriel, nodding at the cans. Scott sat ashen-faced. "Did you know I drank a lot of beer when I was a teenager?" she said.

"You?" Riley asked incredulously.

"Muriel!" Scott said under his breath.

"Oh sure, we used to go up on Squaw Peak road, you know, and Geniece's older brother would get a whole keg."

"I had no idea," Riley said, astonished.

"Apparently, you have to go to Wyoming now to get a keg," she said and laughed. There was a certain energy in how she recounted her former wickedness, sitting in her ready-to-pop pregnant state. "This one time I had to pee really bad and it was freezing out, so I sat on the bumper of Guy Sorenson's truck— remember Guy? Well, I ended up getting my bum frozen to the bumper. I couldn't move!"

"Oh my gosh," said Riley, a huge smile breaking out on his face. Muriel, like Lucy, could always make him laugh. "What did you do?"

"Well," she looked at her husband, who shook his head in disbelief. She brushed off his look with a grimace that said she had come to save her brother and would do whatever it took. "First I screamed a little. Then Guy offered to pee on the bumper to heat it up."

"Oh my!" said Riley, his mouth open.

As Muriel started laughing, her belly shook. "There wasn't anything else to do," she said between whoops of laughter. She bent over and spread her legs while she tried to catch her breath. Scott chuckled lightly at first and then broke out in full paroxysms.

"I think we've violated our covenant about loud laughter," Riley warned. Scott tried to hide his head in his arms while his sides heaved. Finally their laughter slowed, and Riley got up to fix toasted cheese sandwiches. When Scott excused himself to the bathroom, Muriel asked her brother if he was going to be okay.

"I don't know, Muriel," he said point blank. "I can't be like … you know … like Dad. I can't. I just need time. I miss Lucy. You know that, don't you?"

In her maternity shift, sleeveless over a white T-shirt—more often than not these days his sisters' common uniform—Muriel looked girlish. It was as if they had stepped back in time, back to Golan Drive, and were sharing the excitement of a new life spread out like a trackless field of snow in front of them. Like her sister Jody, Muriel brought out everything in her repertoire, in the end demonstrating that she too felt the invisible pull of the collective, which was what they were all most loyal to.

For the next seven months, his sisters, eight in all, continued to come bearing fruits and gifts. Winnie left in tears, but not before divulging that since his return from Mexico, Cade was getting crazy again at the gym and was still smoking. Chums accused Riley of being selfish, otherwise he would think of what he was doing to the family. When she threw her arms around him, she confided that she dumped her boyfriend because she was in love with a woman but couldn't act on it because she knew it was wrong.

He told her she was strong and beautiful and he didn't deserve such a good sister. When she left, he drank half a bottle of vodka.

Then came Agnes. She was a senior in high school and seemed to be in love with her seminary teacher. She giggled to hear how their father had used her as a medium to peer into the spirit world when she was two years old. She was in town visiting Gus in his new digs at the Church Administration Building, she said. "We've been fasting and praying for you," she added.

"For me?"

"On Sundays. Mom called a meeting and said you were struggling. Dina was there."

"Dina was at a family meeting?" Riley walked toward the window and saw a car parked out front with someone waiting inside. He folded his arms across his chest. He knew his little sister wasn't supposed to have told him that. "What did everyone say about me?" he asked.

"Maybe I wasn't supposed to ..." She trailed off, embarrassed. "We love you so much, we were worried, is all." She began to sputter, her lower lip trembling. He resisted going to her because he wanted more information.

"Who's in the car outside?"

"That's Dad's driver. Dad's busy with his new job, so he couldn't come himself. We got to meet the prophet, Riley. It was when Dad was set apart. We got to meet him!"

"What did Dad tell you?" he said coldly.

She looked profoundly unhappy about having decided to visit him.

"What did he tell Dina to do?"

"I don't know what you're doing that's so bad, but Winnie says you could get excommunicated!" she blurted out. "We're supposed to do whatever we can. Anything at all."

Riley had a vision of Dina in his head, two days before their divorce, suggesting they go to bed one last time. How far would she go? he wondered.

Agnes gave Riley a copy of the Book of Mormon. "I finally read this and it changed my life," she said. "I left a letter inside for you." He thanked her. "I miss you so much!" she added.

Her older sister Jessica showed up the following week with a recently returned missionary and a ring on her finger. The young man, Jake, was still in an obnoxious post-mission phase. "The church is being persecuted like when we were back in Missouri," he told Riley, "and that's because it's a sign of the times."

Susan, as skinny as Winnie but twice as confident, met Riley downtown when her high school acapella choir performed in a Christmas concert on Temple Square. They met in a crowded ice cream shop opposite the square, and everything she did took him back to the dream house, to that beautiful time when his closest allies were his siblings, when they believed everything their parents said was right, and even the steady accumulation of brothers-in-law felt like an encroachment to them.

Only Riley's brother Cade had failed to make an appearance

at Riley's apartment for his older brother's benefit. Susan brought him up in conversation. "Cade looks up to you," she said as she stood and buttoned her coat. Riley accompanied her across the street to the Tabernacle. "I think he needs you," she said. That was a new wrinkle, to employ one of the lost sheep to rescue another. The way he deciphered it, it meant his parents were running out of ideas.

There are days when I envy Verus. As we sit in the corner watching Riley and Susan eating ice cream, I feel impatient. All Verus has to do is materialize occasionally and get somebody to write his story, to everyone's amazement, whereas the Three Nephites have to putter around ministering to poor lost souls like Riley, whose greatest accomplishment seems to be eating ice cream at Snelgrove's bourgeois cafe. As soon as he settles into the pinewood pews across the street and hears his sister sing "Jesu, Joy of Man's Desiring," he'll be reintegrated into the fold. That's what I assumed, anyway, as Verus was finishing his banana split and telling jokes at the expense of the local population.

"They're leaving, Zed," he says, pointing at Riley and his sister with his spoon. "Better follow them. There's work to be done!" He laughs and dabs at the ice cream, his physical form only a few days away from molting back into a thirty-year-old. "I'll just finish up."

"You should join me, old man," I say. "It would give you a reason for living."

"I have a reason for living," he responds, "and that's to die." He leans into me and says confidentially, "Do you know what Mormon foreplay is?" He has a sparkle in his eyes.

"Stop it," I say, but then I want to know the answer. "Okay, Verus, what is it?"

His eyes widen, his mouth all pert. "Two hours at Snel-grove's!" He laughs while running his finger along the rim of the dish for the last few remaining drops of chocolate sauce.

"See you after the concert," I say.

"Will you?" he says. I help him with his coat. "This young man's a lot like us, if you think about it," he says thoughtfully, "because he's trapped, just like us." He shuffles toward the door, his cane dragging behind him as he buttons his coat. "Thanks for the foreplay!" he says, laughing louder this time.

The next day Riley found himself in a gym looking at blue weight-lifting equipment someone had planted in odd patterns like lawn sculptures. Except for Riley's brother, the gym was empty.

"I go around and say to people, Hey, do you want to see my insertions?" Cade explained. "They look at me like I'm asking them to look at my crotch," he said between puffs on a cigarette. "It's great, you should see it."

"What are insertions?"

"Right here, between my shoulder and my pecs," he said, poking a finger at stretch marks between a bulge in his upper chest and an equally large portion of his inner shoulder. "Pretty impressive, huh? You should see my Mom's inserts, is what I tell them," he said with a smile. He lifted the cigarette and took a deep drag. His chest, loosely slung in a tank top, rose up like a water balloon when he breathed in. The smoke seemed to go all the way to his toes before he exhaled.

"Where are you getting all this information?" Riley wanted to know.

"Bob Majors. He does marketing for the magazines. Drives an awesome Beamer too."

"Well, this is an amazing place," said Riley. He was trying to ignore the fact that his brother was smoking one cigarette after another. Riley didn't even know why he had stopped by. On a whim, he had knocked on the glass, at which his brother had ambled up like some kind of medieval knight lowering the drawbridge. Now Cade was sitting on a padded bench and Riley was trying to make out the tattoo on his brother's right shoulder.

"Two hundred pounds and springs of steel, right?" Riley said, bumping his brother on a shoulder that was so big it didn't seem to belong to him. Cade smiled a little brother smile, as if he had forgotten his new irreverent self.

"Yeah," said Cade, "to carry me down the track—like a leopard." He lifted the cigarette to his lips, his fingers trembling. "More like 220 pounds these days, though," he admitted. He turned his head and expertly blew a plume of smoke over his shoulder. "Remember that stupid article in the *Church News,*" he said, "with Dad in his rolled-up sleeves, wrestling that stupid defensive back from BYU?"

"Susan told me you arm-wrestled Dad and beat him."

"That's right, I beat him! Right there on the Postum table, cracked the glass top, too. Mom was furious, but I whooped him bad, Rile." He looked satisfied with himself. "He had his excuses. He said he had to earn a living and couldn't hang out at the European Health Spa all day. He still thinks I workout there. Nobody goes there anymore." He snuffed out his cigarette and began rummaging through his gym bag.

"After that, he wouldn't wrestle me," Cade said. "Too

chicken. I told him I was working out to get ready for the morning of the first resurrection."

"The Postum table?" Riley asked.

"Right there on the family altar," Cade said and turned around.

"Isn't it unusual to smoke while you lift?" Riley asked. He watched his brother fish for another cigarette in his bag. He found a pack. Tap. Tap. It was an alarming change for a son of Nelson and Joan Hartley.

"I only do it after hours. Jerry, our owner, says he doesn't want me upsetting our health nuts, let alone the Mormons who come here. Cade began singing:

Happy Valley to you
Happy Valley to you
Happy Valley of Mo-Mo's
Happy Valley to you.

Tap. Tap. He pulled off the pack's scarlet cellophane string and dropped it to the floor, a glitzy artifact he'd pick up later. Then he lit up, shifting from one leg to the other. From his neck to his flared back, from his wasp waist to his clean-shaven calves that bunched when he walked, Cade was vastly distorted to him but fundamentally familiar too. Only his freckled smooth face revealed the baby brother Riley remembered, who had sat next to him in Alvin Baines's house, the side kick hypnotized by the implosion of the adult world around him. The expectant younger brother, a mirror now to the menace Riley *thought* he himself had become.

What was the membership fee at an exclusive gym like this, Riley wondered. "Does Dad know about the tattoo?" he asked instead.

"Wish I'd had a camera when they saw it," Cade replied. "Let me see."

Cade twisted around so his brother could see his left shoulder. It was a shield that said CHOOSE THE RIGHT. "It's a little lame," Cade said, embarrassed. "I always liked my CTR ring, though, and kind of miss it. I did it on a dare. Steve, who works out with me, said he didn't think I'd get a tattoo, and it was the only thing I could think of."

"What are these?" Riley asked, pointing to some fresh scars between his brother's pectorals and shoulder.

"Oh my heck," he said looking at them as if he was seeing them for the first time, "the girlfriend's been gnawing at me again." He smiled. "No, it happens when you bulk up too fast. You ought to come to Vegas," he continued, changing the subject. "In *Ironman* they said I was expected to win the national invitation. I'll show you the article. Steve says there are movie agents looking for talent to take back to Babylon. How would that be?"

"You'd be the next Incredible Hulk, I guess?" Riley asked.

"It's not far-fetched," said Cade. "Bring on the green paint! *Whoo-whoo!*" How strange to hear the brother who liked church musicals talk like this. "If I had a set of guns like Lou baby, nobody would give me crap, not even Dad."

"He has something else in mind for you, that's for sure," Riley said.

"He wants me to get married."

"Are you going to get married?"

"Nah," Cade said. "Did you know the first Mr. Olympia was Mormon? Larry Scott, still lives in Salt Lake." He pointed his cigarette at Riley for emphasis, nodding and squinting as if this validated something vital to him. Riley gave him their mother's expressionless face, eyes cast down, the face that somehow means everything's not okay and you know it. Cade looked at him with a quiet resentment, then fell back down on the bench with a thud, his feet spread wide, and leaned forward with his elbows on his knees. After a while he tapped the ash off into the overflowing ashtray on the floor. He was quiet, like he had run out of gas.

Riley noticed more marks on his brother's arms below his elbow. Instinctively, he turned one of Cade's forearms over to get a better view. Cade stood up, and Riley dropped his arm. "What is that, Cade?" It looked like he had fresh scratches scattered across his arm in irregular, sometimes crisscrossing, lines.

"I'm expressing my artistic side," he said.

"Those aren't stretch marks."

"It's from the tanning salon. The uv light brings them out."

Changing the subject, Riley pointed to a contraption with black vinyl cushions. "What's that?" he asked.

"It's called the hack squat, after a wrestler named Hacken-schmidt who had huge legs. That's what Steve says. You know what, Steve will be here in a minute if you want to meet him."

"And this?" Riley asked, walking over to a vertical frame with a barbell on a sliding track.

"Smith machine."

"Not after Joseph, I hope," Riley said.

"You get more control for squats, and it's good for delts."

"I see," said Riley.

"Remember when Dad put in that chinning bar and I couldn't do a single chin-up? Now I can do as many as I want. I guess I should be grateful to Dad for that," he said. "Not just the chin-up bar, but the genetics too. They say I have what it takes."

Cade bent over and touched his toes, then grabbed the back of his ankles to stretch his lower back. Behind him was a mural of a Samson-styled figure in a headband, his sinewy arms upraised. A caption below it read, "I will praise thee, O Lord, For I am fearfully and wonderfully made." It was from Psalms.

"Sometimes, Riley, I look in the mirror and I can't believe it's me," Cade said. He looked at himself in the mirrors behind the rows of coal-black dumbbells. He pulled up his tank top to reveal beefy squares of muscle in high relief. He pulled his arms up at right angles in the traditional double-biceps pose. Riley could see his father's meaty legs and detect the long torso he inherited from their mother's side of the family. He saw his own narrow hips. There was something primal, sensual, and frightening about Cade, despite how much of him seemed familiar.

"But then I look again," Cade continued, "and it's like, whoa, cowboy! I'm not big enough at all. I'm not really sculpted. Then I work harder. Last week I couldn't get out of bed, I hurt so much." Cade let his confession hang in the air while he stared at Riley for a moment. There was a key at the front door.

"Sounds like Steve," Cade said.

Riley noticed his brother's heart rate jump. "You look great, Cade," he said simply and suggested he'd look for a way out through the back door in order not to interrupt their workout.

42 | EMPTY ARMOR

In the armory wing of the Metropolitan Museum of Art is the French king Henry II's "parade armor." The shield has small embossed images of helmets, shields, and gauntlets, a gilded portrayal of armor upon armor displayed behind glass and filtered light. Henry's costume is now a reminder of what happens to our defenses over time. The armory is an awful and awesome place where plaster horses with chanfroned heads forever ride through forgotten wars and empty armor comes to rest.

It wasn't until Riley Hartley returned here to New York City, years after his mission, that he realized what actually appeals to him about the city. There were the museums, of course. One thing he really loved, for some strange reason, was Babylon's garbage. There is no place to hide it in the Big Apple, no back-alley Dumpster. All the city's dark bowels are visible. All the refuse of the city's life is placed around your feet and in your face. He likes the intimacy of the subway too. People sit and stand and slump over in their respective personal shells. Everyone is there—children, the homeless, men in suits reading the *Wall Street Journal,* the Hasidic Jew sleeping over the pages of a frayed book—all rocking to the clackety rumble of the train, closed in and opened up to the sound of its doors when the conductor mutters, "Stand clear of the closing doors," followed by the ding-dong chime. "West 4th Street next. Stand clear … Broadway/Lafayette, stand clear …"

This afternoon, I, Zedekiah, am on the same F-train as my charge, beginning in Brooklyn where he lives with his new wife, Jenny. He's headed to mid-town, where he will meet her at the doctor's office for their test results. People of Riley's tribe know it's a short distance from sipping a contraband coffee in a café to facing mortality in the heart of the city. Even so it surprised him at how quickly he seemed to cross that distance. All he knew as he sped from there to here was that he was angry, and that his anger was somehow justified. Even Verus is astonished at Riley's maladaptation to the city. "Where do they find these people?" he asks me. "Oh yeah, in Utah!" He is back in his mid-thirties now— going on a hundred. As per usual, he brings out my defensiveness.

"I've never understood how, just because you're young again, with the body of a thirty-year-old, …"

"Thirty-three," he says, flexing his biceps for me. "Not bad for a Wandering Jew, eh? Everyone, you know, is going to a gym these days."

"… you can be so callous toward these souls who still look through a glass darkly and who will die. Just because you'll be vibrant and young again yourself."

"Oh, give me a break!" he says in the vernacular. "Your guy's categorically a mess. Don't try to deny it, Zed. I thought once he left his people he'd be fine. But look at him!"

Riley is sitting on the subway in his usual armor—hat, glasses, jacket, even fingerless gloves. A backpack. He's casing the joint through the visor of a heavy helmet. He is scoping out the imme- diate day, his day, as it will play out with him in it. He needs to know his place, to know his lines. The train is warm enough to take off his helmet and set it on the seat next to him. He runs his fingers through his hair.

"What he suspected about the outside world turned out to be true," I explain to Verus. "Anything seems to go here."

"Dangerous place for someone who's gone from collecting words to collecting tactile sensations."

"Not that different than you," I say, poking his bulging arm. "Really, all this careening through the latest iteration of humanity."

"Well," says Verus, looking around a bit forlornly, "where *is* he going, do you think?"

We watch him a few more minutes. The train picks up speed and Riley spreads his feet to keep himself stationary. We whisk past a Brooklyn station without stopping. "It's getting harder for him to keep the loose strings together. To perform convincingly," I say. "You're right. I don't know how much longer I can help him."

The doctor Riley is visiting is the same one Jenny saw when they first moved to New York and discovered they couldn't conceive children. Riley thought their childlessness would vindicate Gus—a sign that the Lord was holding back his spirit children from Riley and his Gentile wife. Wasn't it better to have a grandchild raised out of the covenant and carrying the family name than no grandchild at all? There was always Jenny's son, Matt, even though he didn't actually carry Riley's name.

"It's all going to end badly, isn't it" Verus says.

"He has to get it right, is all," I say. "He's not like us. And he's worth the investment."

At that, Verus springs to his feet and claps me on my shoulder. "This is where I get off. I've made friends with some Jamaicans," he says. "They call me Judah—Judah Mahn, like I'm one of them." He repeats JUDAH MAHN and mimics the accent.

"Enjoy the music," I say.

"My advice is to file your report and be done with it. You're too emotionally involved in this Riley kid. The world isn't going to change, you know. It's going to keep running, and we'll still be here." He gives me a fist bump and a half hug the way the Jamaicans do.

He was right about the world. One generation makes a few improvements over the previous one, but really it just exchanges old uncertainties for new ones, century after weary century. With every advance, there is a setback, an erosion in the human condition. It would take a messiah flying out of the sky to solve the problems that are life, and then it would probably be too late. I don't make a difference to the world, only to one boy. Verus has given me an idea, though. The Jamaican embrace reminds me of something.

I think about how Riley and Jenny met in Salt Lake City at the swimming pool ten years ago when she was a flight attendant, eight years older than Riley, raised Presbyterian in rural New York, divorced. She would come early and swim laps when the pool was empty. She wore a black Speedo, green goggles, and dutifully tucked her hair into a white cap. She smiled at him every day. One morning she brought her little boy and deposited him at the shallow end. He was ten. He wanted to blow Riley's whistle.

When Jenny and Riley moved in with each other, Riley

found the courage to take his temple garments off once and for all—or maybe it was just that one day he forgot to put them on. Finally, he cut the Masonic symbols out of the sacred underwear per protocol before handing them, now de-sacralized, over to Jenny to use as rags. Two years later they got married at the county court house, then moved to New York.

Now Jenny's Matt, is thirteen. What will this pubescent boy think if his mother is diagnosed with the virus that causes AIDS, an anniversary gift from Jack Mormon? For Riley, it's like this. Since Lucy's death, everything seems inevitable, like the moment you lose control of your car and every jag in its harried trajectory is the result of natural law, a fated conclusion. With Jenny at his side, Riley's departure from his family did not mean that he was rebelling, as Gus put it, but simply choosing differently. When his mother, in her campaign of letter writing to him, confessed she "trembled" for him at the thought of his broken covenants, Jenny sniffed, "Your relationship with a committed partner is the most healing thing you do. In fact, aren't you old enough to tell her that sex is the most healing thing you do?" But the former Miss Utah persisted. Those who swim in the sea of relativity "know the treachery of the undertow," she wrote, and it grieved her to think her son was too proud to reach for a life preserver, which THE GOSPEL would provide if he would use it properly and not as "a noose around your neck."

"So, swim for your life," Jenny advised.

Riley was surprised to find that after he returned east, he was the same man, regardless of who his wife was, and the universe had not bent for him and Jenny. His temper was apparent, there was no quick-change in his identity. He was happy at the same time he still felt trapped, just like he had at home. Maybe Gus was right and he was of a rebellious streak.

What seemed inevitable was that Riley would come to see his wife as a duty. He wanted to love her impulsively, not through some catastrophically programmed regimen. His anger was becoming his natural response to circumstances. He had traversed a seemingly varied but curious repeat terrain from his youth as a true believer to the uncertainties of his mission, from a progressive Latter-day Saint student and husband to a regressed and hairless image floating in the bathroom mirror, and from a happily independent married man pursuing graduate studies to a floundering apostate with an infected wife.

He could have gone elsewhere for his master's program but liked Brooklyn College. He thought he would like working summers as a lifeguard at the beach. At the same time, he was close enough to Manhattan to partake of its sour-smelling bars and clubs if he wanted to, even peek into the city's underbelly of massage parlors and sex shops. The lifeguard job didn't work out. It was *not* an easy transition from a swimming pool to the ocean. Jenny and he started fighting. That strong will of hers that had saved him was an equally potent threat when turned against him.

"It's like you're eleven," she said when she found herself with the STD. "You're all dressed up and nowhere to go, like a sports car with a rusty engine. Your parents think *I'm* the bad influence!"

"What attracted you to me?" he needed to know. "Did you think I had my act together? I didn't."

"You put on a damn fine performance, Riley Hartley," she said. "At least you'll survive the pangs of a guilty conscience because you think everything's alright as long as you're the one doing it. Do you know what? I'm not one of your ancestor's multiple wives! I'm in New York City, for god's sake, with a thirteen year-old son and my life in front of me—or maybe not, thanks to you!"

It was not a redeeming side of Riley's character that he still missed Dina. She was right to leave him, and now he had fallen as low as he could. He had walked through the veiled doors of the massage parlor on West 10th Street in the Village, the same as two fellow missionaries had done when Riley was in New York on a mission, and the two missionaries were sent home early. Emboldened by the smell of hedonism in the air, Riley had relished the utter sense of relief, the promise of ecstatic release in front of him. It made sense that he would behave like this, he told himself. It was not his fault. He was a victim of indoctrination. In the back of his mind, he wondered why he kept this secret from his wife and brought flowers home to distract her. It hadn't occurred to him that what he was taking home was actually herpes, or gonorrhea, or HIV.

It is two o'clock now. The subway rattles on. Riley has put pieces of his armor on the seat next to him. Swathed in the thick clothes of a homeless man with a torn beige corduroy jacket and knit watch cap, I sit opposite him. Riley can see my filthy left hand, the nails chipped, speckled like my patchy beard and moustache. I keep my other hand tucked away in my jacket where anyone might think I was clutching a wound, or perhaps hiding a weapon. The F train is the one Riley takes to work. It is as familiar to him now as I-15 used to be along the Wasatch Front. What he doesn't like about New York is that you rarely get up high enough to get your bearings. In New York his internal map is based on things he sees at street level. There are no wide-open spaces to prompt abstract thoughts, no mountain peaks from which to gaze out on the Promised Land. On most days Riley travels to his office cubicle in mid-town where he looks up facts for an investor journal. The narratives are of a type he hardly understands, much less cares about, but is supposed to make more accessible to the readership. Today, however, the end of the line is the doctor and an uncertain future with Jenny.

The train shoots out of the tunnel, up onto the Gowanus El, a mammoth yellow-brick bridge latticed with steel beams, rising above the industrial park next to the canal like a beached steamship. On top of the elevated platform, the tracks emerge into fresh air at Fourth Avenue.

"Where are you going today, Riley?" I ask through missing teeth. He looks at me, grabbing his helmet and hugging it. I raise my eyebrows.

He tries to make out what has just happened. "To the doctor's," he says, looking more puzzled for having responded. "To meet Jenny," he says, squinting at me. The car jolts violently—the helmet rubs against the backpack Riley is wearing as a breastplate—then stops at the platform.

"Smith and 9th Street next," says the conductor. "Stand clear of the closing doors." *Ching-chong*, the recording blasts, followed by the caesura that occurs when the doors close and people wait for the train to move. This time the break in the continuity stretches longer than usual.

"What if the test is positive?" I rasp. The train moves slowly. A baby in its mother's arms starts to cry and its pitch rises slowly to the level of the train's hum, then joins the rush of crunching metal and the sighing of humanity, everything moving purposefully forward to its destination. Riley wonders what happens to the children in heaven who were supposed to come to families like his in this life.

"It won't be positive," he says as he puts his helmet on the floor.

"Why bother going?"

"To be sure," he says. He seems calm.

"Still keeping your covenants, then?" I say.

"I left them behind."

"Everything? What about your new temple here, the Village Spa?" I say.

He looks puzzled again. "That's not for me, not anymore," he says.

"Why not?"

"There were unspeakable acts," he says. He is on guard, but he takes off the chain mail gloves.

"In the temple?"

"At the Village Spa," he says. "I saw things."

"Did you just watch, or did you do things?"

"I did things," he says and shifts uncomfortably.

"What exactly?" The man next to me folds his newspaper, stands and walks to the other end of the car to wait for the doors to open. The screeching wheels finally relent, followed by a rush of warm air. The doors roll shut again. Everyone's eyes are on me, but only Riley has figured out what I am. I clear my throat and lean back into my seat, my eyes closed, face hard. Outside is a never-ending row of tenements in light brown brick, seeming to sway in the sunlight. The KenTile Floors sign almost teeters on its rusted stilts. The harbor is scudded with white caps below the Verazzano Bridge. A rare view! The bridge floats like a giant blue fin. Riley unbuckles the leather straps on the sides of his breastplate. Better to breathe this way.

When I open my eyes, he is considering me. "What is it you wanted to see when you went there, Riley?" I ask. The speeding train loses its sound except for Riley's breathing.

"Does it matter?" he says. "After a while the bodies start to look the same. Triangles of flesh moving against each other." He leans forward and lifts the breastplate over his head, then deposits it on the floor.

"What did you see?" I repeat.

"I saw eyes rolling into people's heads, like Paris looking at me with that silly grimace."

"What else?"

"Dina."

"She was there?"

"For a minute or two. I pitied her, going home to Pap, his military haircut and his judgment."

"Did you leave?"

"It wasn't like I was even there, like I was someone looking at myself. I saw my mother there … crying."

"Smith and 9th Street. Bergen Street will be next." The doors open to the harbor's briny smell. There are buckles to unlatch on Riley's boots.

"Stand clear of the closing door, Riley," I say, grabbing hold of a pole and standing as the train moves off the bridge, back underground, and on its way. I hitch up my pants. "When did you request a male masseur?" I say. I shuffle across the aisle and grab the pole next to Riley.

"When I walked in there, people would look at me like they do when they watch my father preaching, like I was desirable. Like I was on stage somewhere with everyone adoring me." The lights in the train flicker on and off. His soccer jersey and boots join the rest of the armor roiling on the floor, as if caught in a tide pool.

"And there was someone behind a curtain who reached for you," I say.

"Yes."

"Like in the temple back home. And you thought that was it, that afterward you could step out onto West 10th Street into the bright sunshine and no one would know what you had been up to, any more than people do right now on this train."

Riley nods but feels puny, spent. He looks into my eyes. His voice sounds fainter as the tunnel lights flash by the car windows.

"Carroll Street. Stand clear of the closing doors." There is only one other person in the car. She looks at us. We are subterranean and headed under the riverbed. She prepares to get off at the next stop while we wait in silence. When she leaves, no one else gets on. What does Riley think about this? Does he think it's normal to be in a subway car alone, with one of three brethren who are walking the earth until the second coming of Jesus?

It's time for me to reveal my authority. If Verus were here, he would snort at this. I thrust out my hand, the one I've been hiding in my coat pocket. I grab Riley's hand. He recognizes the handshake.

"What is that?" I demand.

Riley is startled and shaking, but he answers by rote.

"Has it a name?" I return.

"It has," he whispers.

"Will you give it to me?"

It dawns on Riley that this is the handshake for the angel guarding the entrance to heaven, meaning his time has come. It had not occurred to him that this moment would come to pass under the East River. He looks at his hand, with its bent fourth finger—his sister Jody's hand. He remembers that the answer to the question is long but in its own way simple and almost quaint, achingly beautiful.

He follows the liturgy. He rises off his seat and leans forward to take me in a full-body embrace, just like he did many times at THE VEIL, with his sister Muriel's right foot by the side of mine, Candace's knee to my knee, Gus's breast to my breast, his mother's mouth to my ear, and Cade's hand to my back, every part of his physical self a corollary to another human being—flesh of his flesh, far from the fleshpots of Egypt. He will leave behind a distinctive forehead, the name of his grandfather, the little-girl giggles of Winnie and Chums, Jessica and Susan. Close in like this, he can smell the streets on me, every oily puddle he has tried to dodge on a rainy day. He also knows that somewhere, under all these layers, I am clothed in the garment of the holy priesthood. I am radiant in my filth, depositing the sweet acid of death on Riley's cheek. He opens his mouth, unclear what the answer is, what the name of the token is. Something comes out.

"As long as I hate them, I can say I'm not like them," he says in a new formula I haven't heard before. It is his answer. He is speaking more steadily, blind to heaven, but it sounds like fresh rain falling on dry earth. He continues. "And I don't have to acknowledge that I'm capable of the same cruelty, that I am flesh of their flesh. That I can destroy a marriage, preach fear, beat caged birds, … endanger the life of my wife, … orphan the only child I will probably ever have, while at the same time believing I am above it all."

"Riley," I moan, and my grip loosens.

It is Riley this time hanging on tightly, insistent while his accessories roll at our feet. "Is there no other way?" he asks. "What do I do now that I've become the thing I fled? Now that I've become the thing I loathe? Now that I know who I am? What more is there?"

"That is correct," I say.

There is a pause while Riley reaches for a pole to steady himself. The lights in the car flash off and on again.

"What is wanted?" I finally ask, returning to the liturgy.

Riley is shaking. "Having conversed with the Lord through THE VEIL, Riley Hartley desires to enter into his presence."

"Let him enter," I say in a whisper.

"David Pace's novel is a wonder to behold. He takes the soul of a true believer from the "perfect Mormon family" in the Provo foothills (where David also grew up) and exposes him to the outside world, seen and unseen, including an encounter with one of the three immortal Nephites. As Riley struggles to hold onto his beliefs, it may seem like little enough for some readers, but for some of us it is hugely sufficient and satisfactory. This is a dazzling contribution to Mormon literature." —**Phyllis Barber,** author of *How I Got Cultured: A Nevada Memoir* and *To the Mountain: One Mormon Woman's Search for Spirit*

"Who better to tell the story of the coming of age of a bright and confused Riley Hartley—son of an LDS Church icon—than the 'old jaded Nephite' Zed (short for Zedekiah), one of the three ancients allowed to wander the earth forever? Zed proves the perfect guardian and storyteller, a cynical wise man whose 'eternal, ineffectual musings' draw us into unexpected places—a heart of darkness. Chekhov said that an author needs to correctly identify a problem and solve it, but that only the first task is obligatory. Pace has met this obligation. In the grip of an Abrahamic moment, Riley can find no solace or consolation. The metaphysics of the novel may be religious, but the answer cannot be found in any catechism." —**Darrell Spencer,** author of *A Woman Packing a Pistol*, *Our Secret's Out*, and *Bring Your Legs with You*